NIGHT
WATCHMAN

With much love
to Ellen, Matt &
the girls

for Rolf

By

Rolf Richardson

CONTENTS

1

MARCH 9th.

Captain McGregor felt he was somehow responsible for the Leaning Tower. This was nonsense, but his was perhaps the butterfly effect that triggered it off. Chaos theory suggests that the future is beyond predicting, because the flapping of a butterfly in the Caribbean may eventually lead to a typhoon in China. Tiny initial cause, massive final effect.

McGregor's trip to San Francisco was routine, no suggestion of any flapping butterfly. Routine peck on the cheek for wife Jane, before setting off in his BMW. Routine drive from his home in Maidenhead to Heathrow, on this occasion rather better than normal, because the M4 was not the usual parking lot.

The first hint that 'routine' might not be the appropriate word came at flight briefing. It seemed innocent enough at the time, just a note from Captain Melville, the airline's head of training, that co-pilot Alan Hardaker had only recently converted onto the 747: his landings still tended to be 'arrivals', and needed some polishing up.

As an old hand on the Jumbo, McGregor was familiar with the problem. Ever since Wilbur and Orville invented the flying machine, pilots had relied on the Mark One Human Eyeball to get themselves safely back onto terra firma.

Until the 747 came along. The first clue that something

different might be needed came early on, when a Boeing test pilot undershot the runway, badly damaging his company's new toy. This monster was not only twice the size of anything that had gone before, but the cockpit was located on the upper deck and the landing attitude was nose up; this meant the main wheels of a 747 were so far behind and below the pilots they hit the ground when the Human Eyeball thought there was still a long way to go.

Years of visual experience had to be discarded. You were *not* about to land in that field beyond the end of the runway, it just looked that way. The drill became to trust your instruments, or the special visual approach slope indicators Boeing had been forced to install at every major airport, and just fly the slope until the radio altimeter registered fifty feet. Then you started to think about putting her down. At the thirty feet call you got serious. For new boys this last bit might be something of a controlled crash, but it was safe. And once your Mark One Eyeball got the hang of the new conditions, you'd be touching down without upsetting the customers. First Officer Hardaker only needed a bit more experience and he'd be greasing in the Jumbo with the best of them.

McGregor mentally filed the training captain's note and studied the pre-flight information. A time of ten hours forty one minutes, on the great circle route across Greenland and Arctic Canada, approaching San Francisco from the north. On a Mercator map it looked an odd way of getting there, but it was actually the shortest and avoided some nasty headwinds further south.

The Met forecast warned of moderate Clear Air Turbulence (CAT) north of Scotland. After that, a nice smooth ride. In spite of many years and umpteen millions spent trying to crack the problem, CAT forecasting remained little more than guesswork. These bumpy bits were usually just irritating, very occasionally scary. In either case there was little you could do except strap them in and take your punishment.

Their destination was going in for a light westerly wind, with the chance of sea fog. You hardly needed to be an expert to make such a forecast. Every picture of the Golden Gate Bridge has downtown 'Frisco swathed in a white mist, murky and cool, while across the bay in Oakland it's sizzling.

Although the airport lies on the lee side facing the bay, fog is unpredictable stuff. McGregor remembered watching one display, the fog rolling in over the hill, threatening to blanket the airport, but the air warming just enough in its downward path to melt the fog just before it reached ground level.

Yes, fog was unpredictable, which meant the trip's script wrote itself. The usual formula was for pilots to share the flying, so McGregor, as captain and the more experienced, would take the more challenging first sector into San Francisco. Alan Hardaker, new to the 747, would fly the return into Heathrow. Good old familiar Heathrow. Home territory. Just the place for a tyro first officer to polish up his landings.

No one realised it at the time, but a butterfly had flapped its wings.

2

Rather to his surprise, Damian White MP had come to enjoy his surgeries. Like many a budding politician he had started off with grandiose notions of changing the world. The Mother of Parliaments beckoned in all its glory. He would help make Britain a place fit for heroes. Etcetera.

He soon discovered that the Mother of Parliaments was a decrepit rabbit warren that would have been condemned as unfit for human habitation by most local councils. Worse still, the rabbits - members of parliament - that scurried around its corridors, were a fractious lot, agreement on any subject as rare as virgins in a brothel.

We're not talking here about ideological differences between parties. Winston Churchill put it in a nutshell, when showing the Commons chamber to a new colleague, who commented: 'So *we* sit here, facing the enemy?' 'No, no,' replied Winston. 'Facing us is His Majesty's Opposition. You'll find the enemies on *our* side'.

All political parties are uneasy alliances of big egos, with little in common bar a thirst for power. Warfare is constantly simmering below the surface, often to erupt into open conflict.

But party members *have to* agree for parliament to function. The alternative is anarchy. You can think what you like, but party bullies - the Whips - are on hand to make sure you toe the line for the serious stuff: the voting. Then you do as you're told.

On this basic principle Damian all too often found

himself at loggerheads with the party he represented. The Tory member for Mid Oxon not only thought for himself - that was bad enough - he also voted according to his beliefs. The French have a word for such behaviour: 'insupportable'.

Damian White was 'insupportable'. Every party has a sprinkling of such characters, who are usually tolerated as examples of what a broad church that party is. The press loves to snipe at the usual voting by party edict, so anything that softens this image is seen as good PR. However, if the government has a slender majority, just a few mavericks may bring the whole house of cards tumbling down. Then they become truly insupportable.

Damian, like the others of his ilk, soon realised that taking the maverick path was to abandon all hope of political preferment. No front bench for him. So he joined the ranks of parliamentary plodders, many sitting there unrecognised by the world at large for thirty, even forty years. They were the essential cannon fodder for when the division bell rang. Their lack of ambition was tacitly appreciated by the party bosses, who always had more than enough predators fighting for the top jobs.

Backbenchers did little harm. Except when the government had a slender majority and they became mavericks.

With no ministerial career in prospect, Damian White MP, was in his constituency office plying the other political trade open to him, his 'surgery'; a combination of agony aunt and general listening dogsbody. It was a mystery why the country's legislators - the people who ran the whole shebang - also had to concern themselves with what amounted to minor domestic matters. But Damian had come to accept and then rather enjoy these meetings.

The man sitting opposite him, a Mr. Morgan, was thickset, almost bald, early fifties, and had a dustbin problem.

"Never bloody empty 'em properly," he complained, adding: "Well, they empty 'em sure enough, but not all of it in the lorry. Rest of it goes all over the road. Bloody mess. And do they bother to clear it up? Do they hell!"

A common complaint. Damian poised his pen over a sheet of paper and asked: "May I ask where you live, sir?"

The man winked. "Your old stomping ground. Know what I mean?"

Damian could guess. "Blackbird Leys?"

"Got it in one."

It was well known - in fact, it helped get him the job - that Damian White was a local lad, born and raised in Blackbird Leys, a dormitory estate on the eastern edge of Oxford. Its reputation was.... let's just say that if a felony had been committed in the city, the blue flashing lights of Thames Valley police could often be seen heading towards Blackbird Leys.

Damian wrote down Mr. Morgan's address and promised to do what he could about his bin problem. Without much conviction. It was a County Council matter and the best he could hope for was to rattle a few cages. As the local MP, his words might carry a bit more weight than the fellow sitting in front of him, but that wasn't saying much.

Business done, Mr. Morgan should have got up and left. Instead, Damian heard him say: "Saw you play for West Ham. Never forget that goal you scored against Chelsea: edge of the box, two defenders left for dead. Bang! Into the right hand corner of the net. Fantastic!"

Damian smiled. "Yea, those were the days." He suspected that some people came to his surgeries not to discuss rubbish collection, but to chat about old times. To chat with a celeb. Because, that's what he'd been: a star of the back pages. The striker England had been looking for. Another factor that had helped him to his present job.

"A shame they was cut short," continued Morgan. "Your playing days."

Damian shrugged. "Water under the bridge." He always tried to make light of it. Pointless having regrets. But he'd never forgive that brutal defender from Ivory Coast, who'd hit him with a two-footed tackle. The only punishment had been a red card and one week suspension, while Damian ended up with a broken leg. Mended okay, but he was never quite the same again. In his prime, Damian White had been light and lean, with an explosive acceleration off the blocks. Some said he'd been faster over twenty yards than the legendary king of speed, Usain Bolt. A nightmare for defenders. But a promise never fulfilled, thanks to that bastard from Ivory Coast.

"Followed you later on Strictly," continued Morgan, who seemed disinclined to leave.

Damian didn't mind. As a subject for discussion, his career was better than dustbins.

"Yea, lot of fun, that. My leg might have had it for scoring goals, but it was no problem for dancing. Mind you, I had a good partner."

Another wink from Morgan. "But not popular with the missus."

This was scarcely news. It had filled the gossip columns for weeks. How ex footballer Damian White had partnered the lovely Lucille in Strictly Come Dancing, won the event, but lost his wife.

"No gain without pain," he said. "Wouldn't be sitting here now, if it hadn't been for Strictly."

"Running the country, eh?"

Damian grinned. Morgan did a nice line in humour. He

replied in similar vein: "Nothing more important than fixing your dustbins."

Morgan finally got to his feet. Held out his hand. Said: "Thanks for the natter, Damian - may I call you Damian?"

"I believe you just have."

"Best MP we ever had. Might even *vote* for you next time."

"That would be nice."

"The Whisky man, they call you. Black and White. No offence, I hope."

"Of course not." Damian had lost count of the number of times he'd heard this.... well, it had become a term of affection. Endearment. Black and White. Because his name was White, while his skin was Black. Actually, more the colour of milk chocolate than the dark bitter stuff. Even so, unusual for a Conservative member of parliament in the shires.

3

As the door closed behind Morgan, Damian sat back and relaxed. No hurry. Nowhere particular to go. Since the Lucille affair, Mandy and their two kids had taken over the family home, leaving Damian with an apartment in Wheatley for constituency work and a flat in Pimlico for when Parliament was sitting.

The Lucille 'affair'. Only it wasn't. That's what made it so damned annoying! Lucille had been ready and willing, that had been plain. Dancing is a close contact sport and the whole country had seen them at it. Week after week.

The press had stoked it up. Damian had always been the sports editors' darling, the cheeky chappy about to transform the miserable record of team England. When that promise had been cruelly cut short by Ivory Coast, their adulation had transferred to the dance floor. Athletic, good looking, charismatic, Damian had been the bookies' favourite from day one. He had not disappointed.

Everyone had assumed that his vertical embraces in front of the judges had led on to horizontal ones in the bedroom. Everyone, including his wife, Mandy. In spite of constant denials - that he had done the decent thing, resisted, been a gentleman - no one had believed him. Least of all Mandy. Might as well have indulged Lucille, after all, he thought, bitterly. That would have made his marriage break-up almost worthwhile.

Life was shit!

Damian sat up straight. Pull yourself together man!

You have a job many people would kill for. 'Water under the bridge' was what he'd said to Morgan. Time for positive thinking.

For the thousandth time he marvelled at how a little 'whisky' boy - black skin, white name - had come to represent the people of Mid Oxfordshire in parliament.

Going back to pre-history, how had he come to acquire the surname White? Caribbean names have nothing in common with those in West Africa, even though that's where most of them came from. Slaves transported to the Americas lost not only their liberty, but also their identities. Life before transportation didn't exist. Today a roll call of Caribbean names is almost exclusively European: like cricketers, Richards, Sobers, Lara, Lloyd, Walcott, Weekes and Worrell. Nothing remotely African. Had Damien's distant ancestor been sold to a Mr. White? Or had the slave master merely had a warped sense of humour? Named a black slave White? He'd never know.

What Damian *did* know, because his father never tired of telling him, was that granddad had been a 'Windrush' man. For a black man in Britain this was an accolade similar to an Aussie being able to trace an ancestor back to the First Fleet of convicts that arrived in New South Wales in 1788.

The MV 'Empire Windrush' had left Jamaica in 1948 with just 492 passengers, among them Joshua White. Most had no idea what they would do when reaching the other end, so they drifted up to the big city, which apparently needed cheap labour. It was the start of what turned out to be a flood of humanity from the dying empire to the mother country.

Joshua found himself a job on the 'tube' - the London Underground - and settled in Brixton. Married a girl newly arrived from Barbados and had three children, the middle one being Errol.

By the time Errol reached adulthood, the black community in south London was well established and the younger lads were looking for pastures new. So when White junior saw an ad for job vacancies at the Cowley motor works, he was off.

Unlike areas of south London, which soon became almost all-black ghettoes, Oxford was more racially mixed. So it came as no surprise when Errol fell for a girl from the other end of the old empire, India. Like him, Rosie had been born in England, but her parents came from Bombay.

When *their* first born came along, they named him Damian, for no particular reason except it sounded nice. The lad grew up with an interesting mix of genes, Errol being large and solid, although not overly tall, and Rosie barely topping five foot. It was due to Rosie that he stopped growing after reaching a modest five foot eight inches; thanks to Errol that he inherited his superb African physique.

Damian was the ideal recipe for a West Ham striker: strong, supple, not overburdened with weight, he could turn on a sixpence and be off before the defence could gather its wits. On the dance floor he had the balance of a ballet star.

Unfortunately, top level sport can be a brutal mistress and fate, in the shape of a lunging tackle from Ivory Coast, had cut him off in his prime. Ball skill and his subsequent battle against injury had made him a minor celebrity. This had led to Strictly Come Dancing and more public acclaim. But being a TV personality wasn't a career. Damian needed a purpose in life. He found it in a most unlikely quarter: politics.

Maybe he'd been infected by the nearby dreaming spires of academia, because by the time he reached the West Ham youth squad, he was turning to the latest Westminster scandals before the sports pages. A cause of much ribbing

11

in the boot room. Damian didn't care. He found the personalities and mechanics of politics fascinating. So when he came to be laid up after that attack from Ivory Coast, he started asking himself where his allegiance lay. With Tory? Labour? Lib Dem, UKIP, Greens?

He quickly eliminated the smaller parties, not on account of their policies, which might have been admirable, but because they had no prospect of putting their ideas into practice. Nigel Farage may have been able to engineer Brexit from outside the Westminster village, but that had been an aberration, unlikely to be repeated. Usually first-past-the-post elections kept fringe parties, like UKIP, firmly in their place.

Damian's view was practical: you went into politics to get things done. Which whittled the choices down to two: Labour or Conservative.

On this point the dreaming spires of academia did not speak to him. The intellectual hotbed up the road was overwhelmingly left wing. It dealt in ideas, often abstruse ones, rarely related to the real world. Damian was a pragmatist. If the current fad or 'ism' worked, you did it; if not, you tried something else. That made him a Tory. Not that he agreed with all their views, even most of their views. But there was no alternative.

Damian was not stupid, so when he presented himself at Conservative central office to begin the process of getting his name on the candidates list, he exhibited no doubts. He supported every syllable of their manifesto, heart and soul. The powers-that-be were impressed. Not with his words; every interviewee told similar fibs. But they liked what they saw: a man that was popular, presentable and black. Every political party had the same image problem: too white, too male. People outside these parameters were especially welcome.

That he was also well known was a bonus. Anyone not

a recluse would at least have heard of him. Millions would have seen him on the box. Familiarity could be counted on to translate into at least some votes.

Damian White was duly registered on the Conservative list of candidates allowed to contest general elections. He got himself onto the local District Council, which kept him moderately busy. But it revealed a disconcerting fact about himself; although in love with politics as a game, he found the practice of it tedious: endless committee meetings with people over fond of their own voices, wittering on unchecked. Strong chairmen were conspicuous by their absence.

Whenever a parliamentary by-election came up, Damian had a go. With little hope of being selected. But it made a change. So when the sitting member for a famously nationalistic Glasgow constituency died, Damian headed north. At one time the Conservatives had been almost wiped out north of the border. Then the 2015 election had seen previously all-powerful Labour hammered and the Lib Dems decimated, leaving the Scottish Nats reigning supreme, everyone else mere stage extras. Although 2017 had redressed the balance, Tories remained little loved in Scotland's biggest city.

It was a surprise to find that the local Conservative party even had an organisation. At the last general election their candidate had managed a derisory 8% of the poll, about average for a Tory in urban Scotland. All of six local party members had turned out to select their candidate for the coming massacre.

The location was a dreary hall somewhere in the sprawl of suburban Glasgow. Damian had arrived in a taxi, but if asked to find it again, would not have had a clue. However, the atmosphere was surprisingly up-beat, even festive. All five victims were offered a slug of the 'peaty stuff' to calm their nerves, before being invited to say their piece.

Last on the list, Damian listened attentively to his rivals; attentively, but without the faintest notion what they were talking about; accents and subject matter were impenetrable. All were local, all were earnest. They could have been discussing the Siberian grain harvest: in Russian.

So when it came to his turn, he had nothing to lose. As a Sassenach - a *black* Sassenach, his chances had to be below zero. The peaty concoction from Islay no doubt assisted his recklessness.

"I have no local knowledge," he began. "But don't write me off as just another import from the auld enemy. Because, as you can see, my folks came from the auld *empire*. And Glasgow was the second city of that empire. Which was largely created by *Glaswegians*. We all know that whoever you choose today doesn't have a snowball's chance in hell of winning this seat. What we *do have* - because it's a by-election with the whole country watching - is an opportunity to show off. Wave the blue rosettes. Put Glasgow back on the map for a day. If you choose me, I'll do that. Have some fun."

The five candidates spent an eternity sitting in a bleak anteroom, while the six local Tories mulled over their choice. When finally called back, the chairman apologised for the delay and continued:

"As you'll have gathered, it's been difficult coming to a decision. Some of us felt that loyal service should be rewarded. Come the next *general* election, we expect to do just that. But a slim majority has been swayed by the words of Mr. White, who pointed out that in a *by-election*, with media attention from around the country, we should consider which candidate would most benefit the Conservative party as a whole. With his background as a football and TV star, there's no doubt who will be best placed to provide that, so it is with pleasure that we have selected Mr. White as the Conservative candidate."

With the promise that one of the locals would get the nod next time around, the other hopefuls were magnanimous in defeat and Damian set about the business of 'having fun'. West Ham footballers and TV dancers are no more than entertainers, so he was on familiar ground. With no pressure to win, no Ivory Coast to break his leg, no partner to wreck his marriage, he had a ball; knocked on a million doors and spoke at packed meetings. Always with a ready repartee and smile on his face. Up here football was either Rangers or Celtic, but most people had at least heard of West Ham. And, like south of the border, *everyone* had been hooked on Strictly.

When the votes had been counted, the Returning Officer announced that the Scottish National Party had, as expected, won by a handsome margin, with Labour a poor second. The Conservatives, in the shape of Damian White, had managed a creditable third, with 16% of the vote. A triumph!

He returned from Glasgow on a high, hoping for a winnable seat at the next general election.

4

Such naivety!

Under Britain's archaic electoral system at least half the constituencies were considered 'safe' for one of the major parties. You could tie a rosette, red or blue as the case might be, to a donkey and that animal would be duly elected. In these cases the fight to enter the hallowed halls of Westminster took place not during an election campaign, but long before, when the dominant party selected its Prospective Parliamentary Candidate - its PPC.

Although there were a large number of these safe seats, most had sitting members, political leeches, who would do anything to hang onto their cosy jobs for life. However, a few were always up for grabs. Of these, some would see established stars parachuted in; in 2015 London's mayor, Boris Johnson, offered himself to the Tories of Uxbridge, who duly obliged.

For the rest, the competition to be selected a PPC was ferocious. Even a minor star, like Damian, found that his 'success' in Glasgow - if one can call coming third a success - counted for little in the scramble for winnable seats. There were an awful lot of rivals, most with better CVs than his. A friend in central office hinted that his Glasgow campaign had not won universal approval. Yes, it had been fine for a by-election in a no-hope constituency, but it carried warnings about his suitability for mainstream politics. He was seen as being a mite too frivolous: not 'sound' enough.

During the next three years Damian toured Britain from north to south, east to west, seeking the holy grail of selection as PPC for anywhere with the remotest chance of success. When a sitting member died or indicated that he/she would not stand again, the local party was always keen to get a new candidate in place as quickly as possible. Time and again he had to listen to someone else being congratulated. All most depressing.

With nominations for the next general election closing in a few days, he had given up all hope of finding a constituency. He would spend the campaign helping Len Jenkins retain Mid Oxon for the Conservatives. A busy and exciting time. He was in the flat he had bought in Wheatley after Mandy had left him, when the phone rang.

It was Alec Warbeck, the Tory election agent. He came straight to the point:

"Bad news, I'm afraid, Damian. Len's just died."

"What! How?"

"Looks like a heart attack. We'll know after the post mortem. No time to grieve, though. Len wouldn't have wanted that. Point is, we have to get our skates on to find another candidate."

"Of course. So when.....?"

"Right now I'm sending emails and letters to all party members advising of hustings in two days time. That'll give the successful candidate twenty four hours to get his papers in. A tight schedule, but it should be possible. I'm ringing you with advance notice, because I know you'll be interested."

As a local lad and District Councillor, Damian knew everyone there was to know in the Mid Oxon party, including Alec Warbeck, their election agent.

"Kind of you, Alec. Don't know what to say..." Damian was in shock.

"Don't say anything, just start thinking about that hustings speech," said Alec. "And remember Tony Blair."

"Blair was Labour." Damian didn't know what Alec was driving at.

"Clever boy. What's less well known is that Blair was the last person selected for any party when he first stood for Sedgefield in eighty three. There'd been boundary changes and it was a new constituency. There was confusion: a bit like here, if for a different reason." Alec's knowledge of elections was encyclopaedic.

"So....?"

"So nothing. Except whoever gets in here will probably also be the last one to be selected. With Blair, it turned out that 'The last shall be first', as the Good Book says. Maybe that'll be an omen for whoever makes it in Mid Oxon."

"I'll be happy to just win in two days time. Never mind the top job."

There was a pause at the other end. Damian thought he'd been cut off. Then he heard: "You'd make an interesting prime minister."

"Yea, yea...."

"And you'll get in here."

"You reckon?"

"I've made soundings, as they say. Just don't go overboard with the funny stuff. Be a little serious, if you can manage that."

"No repeat of Glasgow?"

"Exactly."

Alec's advice was spot on. At the hustings Damian started by describing his early days in Blackbird Leys; a local lad, but one from the wrong side of the tracks. On to West Ham, sporting success always good for a few votes.

Then came his broken leg; end of career, sob, sob. Sympathy votes in the bag. Strictly Come Dancing had been watched by just about everyone in the kingdom, so mentioning that did no harm either. As a coda, he took Alec's advice and became serious. Reminded his audience how he had doubled their vote in that harshest of Tory environments, Scotland. The party faithful took barely twenty minutes to make up their minds. They selected Damian White as their candidate at the next election.

Mid Oxon being one of the safest seats in the country, all they then had to do was tie a blue rosette on their donkey - correction, Damian - and he'd be off to Westminster.

5

Japan planned its attack on Pearl Harbour for a Sunday morning in the expectation that the Americans would be half asleep. Which they were. It's rare for the day of the week to make any difference, but had the coming events occurred on a different day and time, the outcome, as at Pearl, might have been different. We should therefore record where the major players were and what they were doing during the preceding hours.

Starting on Tuesday, when McGregor and his crew began their return flight to London.

The captain had not done the landing into San Francisco, after all. They had arrived to find the Pacific sea fog in fine form, the Runway Visual Range down to 100 metres. In the bad old days this would have meant a diversion to Oakland, but nowadays just about every aircraft has autoland, which can get you down in zero/zero conditions. With one proviso: a human pilot is not allowed to touch the controls. So they had sat and watched, fingers poised over the disconnect, while the autopilot did its usual faultless job: much more reliable than its human counterpart.

It had been MacGregor's sector, so nothing had changed for the return leg. First Officer Hardaker would still be taking the 747 back to London.

The flight plan said ten hours twelve minutes, again over Canada and Greenland, but on a more southerly track than outbound to take advantage of a helpful jetstream. No CAT, so hopefully smooth all the way. With a depression in the Irish sea, Heathrow was forecasting an eight hundred foot cloud base, with a blustery south-westerly. Reasonable conditions for First Officer Hardaker to earn his spurs.

Still Tuesday, but in Africa, Captain Benjamin Osajefo was preparing to take an Airbus 330 of AfroAir to Heathrow. Osajefo - the name meant 'Redeemer' - was the first son of a local chief and head pilot of AfroAir. He was usually to be found flying a desk, but as this was their inaugural service to London, someone of stature needed to be in charge.

For the occasion, the passengers included the country's president, Lionel Zumweski, and a host of lesser dignitaries. The hand-picked crew were nervous. Those in the cabin because their politicians were a notoriously volatile bunch; the two first officers because Captain Osajefo was a domineering personality, who did not suffer fools. At all.

Osajefo was six foot five in his socks and big boned. He sported a straggly beard, which was jet black, like his skin. His four-times-great grandfather was said to have eaten one of the first missionaries to have brought Christ to the dark continent. However, the missionary's spirit had had the last laugh, because Osajefo's tribe was now fervently Christian, so much so that they enjoyed going off on unofficial crusades against those not of their persuasion.

First Officer Nkrane, thankful to be only the relief pilot, was merely nervous: he aimed to keep well out of the way until called upon for his stint, when the boss went off to sleep. First Officer Johnson, the copilot, was rather more than nervous. Although a mature man in his thirties, with over five thousand flying hours to his credit, he had flown with Osajefo before and had not enjoyed the experience. The problem was not just the captain's abrasive personality, he was also a poor pilot. Flying an Airbus was more demanding than operating a desk.

All might have been well had not one of President Zumweski's mistresses discovered she was pregnant. This was a common enough situation, where ritual demanded a sort of post-courtship dance. The mother-to-be yelled and screamed, insisting on an absurd pension to bring up the president's bastard. On his side, the father-to-be stomped around in a fury, telling his beloved she was a whore, the amount she was demanding out of the question. Then, aflame with lust, he hurled himself on his lady, whose howls now became those of pleasure not protest. They made love twice more before reluctantly parting, having made another assignation.

All this took time. AfroAir's scheduled departure had been for 2100, but it was nearly midnight before President Zumweski appeared, invigorated by his recent battle and smiling broadly. By now Captain Osajefo, who came from a rival tribe, was in a foul mood. And everyone was tired. Not the best start for a long flight. Another butterfly had flapped its wings.

Over now to London, again Tuesday, but earlier in the day. Damian White, into his fourth year as Conservative member for Mid Oxon, was enjoying a rare day pleading a case in the Mother of Parliaments.

Affairs of state passed him by. He voted for his party when he felt their cause was just. When not, he didn't. At first this had infuriated Bessie Robotham, the Tory Chief Whip, but she had eventually given up in disgust. Bessie was a big Rochdale girl, who had migrated to the bluer fields of Cheshire when discovering that her home town was not the best place for right wing views.

On this Tuesday Bessie couldn't have cared less. That little twerp White could sound off as much as he liked. It wouldn't make the slightest difference. The debate was about how much Britain should give in foreign aid, a subject that usually scaled the heights of apathy. Back in 1970, the United Nations had suggested that developed countries should give 0.7% of their GDP to those less fortunate. Conscientious Scandinavians were actually exceeding this target, but the big beasts had put up the proverbial two fingers, the USA with less than 0.2%, Russia less than 0.1%. David Cameron had pledged the UK to the full 0.7%, a figure his successors had been reluctant to change. It remained a bone of contention.

A bone of contention maybe, but by now everyone was bored silly by it. How this current debate had ever got onto the parliamentary agenda was unclear; probably the 'seen to be doing something' syndrome. Most people were in favour of foreign aid, but nit picking about the level of that aid was not something to stir the loins. A mere fifteen souls - a Rugby team - from across the political spectrum had gathered on those green benches to do battle.

The debate droned on and on, in mind-numbing lethargy, until Speaker Jeremy Cauldwell, almost asleep himself, gave the nod to the member for Mid Oxon. That should liven things up. Cauldwell was old and traditional, White young and irreverent, poles apart, but the Speaker had a soft spot for the former West Ham striker, partly because he usually spoke without notes. This had once been the *only* way to address the house, but nowadays members were more like those shambolic TV detectives, who couldn't solve a case without consulting dog-eared scraps of paper. Damian was also concise, an almost extinct virtue in a profession where verbal diarrhoea was the norm.

Anyway, the member for Mid Oxon had the floor:

"Mr. Speaker, we've just heard from both sides of the house about what should be the level of foreign aid.

However, my constituents are asking a different question...."

"Hear, hear!" ....From the opposition benches.

The interruption, completely out of context, may actually have been a startled ejaculation from someone abruptly woken from a snooze.

Damian took advantage of the interruption to repeat: "My constituents, Mr. Speaker, are not so much interested in the level of foreign aid. They are asking why we give *any* aid at all."

There was a feeble murmur of "shame".

"My constituents say," continued Damian, for the third time, "that taxes should benefit *only* the society that pays them: the citizens of this country. Charity is a fine and worthy thing, but should be voluntary: Oxfam, Red Cross, Cancer Research, whatever your tipple. My constituents want to know why their government subsidises wannabe pop stars from the Congo and, through the back door, tinpot African dictators?"

Damian was unaware that an AfroAir flight would shortly be taking off for London with one such tinpot dictator, whose pay-off to his mistress would in part be funded by the generous taxpayers of Britain.

The chamber of the House of Commons erupted: surprising how much noise a mere rugby squad size could make. Speaker Cauldwell shouted "Order! Order!" and smiled to himself. This was more like it; glad he had let young White off the leash.

"Y' mean *zero* foreign aid?" Came a shout from the solitary Lib Dem.

"Order!" Repeated the Speaker, in an attempt to quell further interruptions.

"In cash, yes," replied Damian. "Zero. Zilch. But

there's one gift in kind we *should* give. You can see where my folks came from, so *I* can say this. The continent of Africa produces almost nothing.... well, there's gold, copper, lots of metals... perhaps I should say it creates very little *wealth* to improve the lot of its people. Africa produces only one thing in serious quantities and that's babies. Babies who grow up with no jobs and no prospects; babies who, all too often, starve. By far the best and most cost effective aid we can give Africa is.... Condoms."

The rugby sized crowd in the chamber dissolved into a verbal scrum. As he vainly shouted "Order!", Speaker Cauldwell was well satisfied. That had been a proper debate.

Damian White was also satisfied. He'd not made any new friends, but reckoned much of Mid Oxon would be behind him. Said things that needed saying. Wouldn't make any difference, of course. In that respect Bessie Robotham had been right.

The member for Mid Oxon's speech set no butterfly wings a-trembling. But it *had* been noticed in certain quarters, which would have a bearing on later events.

6

Wednesday dawned wet and windy, one of those days when the season of spring had taken a couple of steps back into winter. Damian White MP was in no hurry to get up, partly because he was still savouring the rumpus he'd created the previous day. Telling what he considered to be home truths about foreign aid had been fun. But the main reason for his lack of haste was that this was PMQ day.

At twelve noon the house would gather for its weekly ritual of Prime Minister's Questions. Parliamentary sketch writers and TV cameras would be out in force to capture the best production of Circus Westminster. Most Commons debates were depressingly dreary, so PMQs made a welcome change and attracted full houses.

Damian had quickly tired of this charade, which he reckoned was the Mother of Parliaments at its worst; intemperate and childish with ya-boo exchanges. Surely it was time they abandoned the adversarial system and began conducting their affairs in a more adult fashion.

So nowadays he gave PMQs a miss. After a leisurely breakfast, he would amble over to Portcullis House, where he had an office, and get down to reducing the size of his In-Tray.

Bessie Robotham would also be an absentee at PMQs, but for a different reason. She thoroughly enjoyed her job of Conservative Chief Whip, but it was demanding, stressful, and had to be focussed on one simple target: to get everyone - or as near everyone as she could manage - into the correct lobby when the division bell rang. PMQs were theatre, with no vote at stake. A diversion. Therefore eminently missable.

7

Still Wednesday. In the skies above London the usual flock of metal birds were homing in on Heathrow. Tim Adamson, Approach Director in Terminal Control, had a feeling it was going to be one of those days.

He envied his colleagues at Departure Control, who only had to get flights *away* more or less on time. At the start of the jet era this had been a free-for-all, but queues waiting for take off had grown to such an extent that some aircraft burned all their reserves waiting on the ground and had been forced to return to top up. So nowadays departure delays were absorbed at the gate, engines only started when cleared. Nice and easy.

It was far from easy for Tim Adamson, a slim and gangly veteran of the radar screen. Politicians had consistently funked decisions on London's major airport, with the result that Heathrow staggered along, working at 100% capacity, no slack in the system. Unlike departures, arrivals couldn't be parked in limbo until a slot became available. Because it costs fuel to carry fuel, which is an expensive item, no one tanked up with more than the legal minimum. If arrival delays became serious, everyone would start screaming that they *must* land a.s.a.p.

Like traffic on the ground, Heathrow has predictable rush hours. It's the *un*predictable rush hours that cause the problem. These may occur because airline schedules are merely an average taken over a complete season, summer or winter. As with any average, there will be variations on either side. The Atlantic jet stream might have moved, causing flights from North America to arrive up to an hour late. The same effect could see flights from Asia turning up *early*. Either or both of these could impact on already busy rush hours. The permutations were endless.

Tim glanced at his watch: 11.25. His job was to gather the arrivals and feed them into the funnel of the Instrument Landing System (ILS), after which they would become the responsibility of Heathrow tower and he could forget about them. With a wind just to the west of south, the Runway in use today was 27 Left, so Tim was sequencing his arrivals to a point roughly over Brixton, South London, from where they would lock onto the ILS for their final approach.

At one time he could simply have peeled them off the London stacks, Bovingdon to the north and Ockham to the south; easy once you got the hang of it. But those days were gone. Not before time, because having large aircraft flying tight racetrack patterns on top of one another, separated by only 1,000ft, was a primitive business. 'Altitude busts' - flights descending beyond their assigned levels - had been known to occur and he marvelled there had never been a major disaster.

Now Tim Adamson was in charge of a more complex, but safer, computer aided system, known as Linear Holding, which varied speeds and headings, so that each flight arrived at 'long finals' over Brixton at exactly the correct time and speed.

He wriggled in his seat in front of the screen. An arrivals surge was on the way.

Concentrate.

29

8

AfroAir's London bound flight was no longer heading towards its intended destination, although Captain Osajefo was unaware of the fact. First Officer Johnson would normally have been trembling in his nice black uniform shoes, dreading what his boss would say when he found out, but he was by now almost past caring, anaesthetised by lack of sleep.

To prevent just such a situation, airlines are required to abide by Flight Time Limitations, a book almost as thick as a Bible and needing a PhD to interpret. Variables included: time of day the flight started: length of duty day: amount of time off *before* the flight: number of crew members: type of rest onboard. And that was merely to work out the allowable *schedule*. Once a duty day started, another set of rules laid down how long you could carry on in the event of delays, remembering that you can't clock-off at 35,000ft.

Despite his European sounding name, Johnson was as African as his captain and lived in a nice suburban house with a wife and five children. He always tried to get some sleep before a long night flight and always failed. A posse of young kids running around outside his bedroom didn't help. So when he reported for duty at 8pm he was scarcely daisy-fresh.

That should not have mattered, because the aforesaid Flight Time Limitations decreed that his coming schedule was long enough and nasty enough to warrant an extra crew member. Take a bow First Officer Nkrane. The Airbus had two bunks in a little nest under the flight deck and the normal regime would have been for Captain Osajefo and First Officer Johnson to operate the first couple of hours, after which one of them, the captain say, would take himself off to the bunk, to be replaced by relief pilot Nkrane. Halfway through the night the captain would return and it would be Johnson's turn to sleep. Shortly before their arrival, Johnson would come back to rejoin the captain for the approach and landing.

Captain Osajefo did not operate 'normal regimes'. Perhaps it was just that his usual workhorse, a desk, did not require rest periods, like those pesky pilots. Whatever the reason, Captain Osajefo absented himself early in the flight, giving no indication when he might return. Nkrane lowered himself into the left hand seat and the two first officers proceeded to guide the Airbus in the direction of London.

All long night flights are tedious, but this one was also frustrating. The Inter Tropical Convergence Zone, alias the tropical rain belt, was being particularly obnoxious and with the Airbus still too heavy with fuel to climb clear of the storms, the pilots spent forty minutes glued to the weather radar to avoid the worst of the bumps.

Then, when clear of the weather and now light enough to climb, they found a higher level blocked by a Nigerian flight. They could see its red anti-collision light blinking away just ahead. This was annoying because jet engines operate most efficiently at high altitude, flights plans being based on the assumption that you climb in stages, when light enough to do so. If these higher levels are denied, you use more fuel. A jet stream over the coast of North Africa that was stronger and more northerly than forecast plundered their reserves even further.

By the time they reached France, First Officer Johnson was not only whacked, he was also angry. It was now full daylight, the captain had stolen his rest period, but *still* showed no signs of appearing. As two pilots had to be at the controls at all times, he had been unable to leave the cockpit, so had asked a steward to go back and remind the captain of his commitment up front. The steward had returned, shame faced, to report that Captain Osajefo was in deep discussion with President Zumweski. You didn't disturb the president if you valued your job - not in Africa, you didn't.

Osajefo and Zumweski were from different tribes and normally loathed each other, but strange things happened in African politics. Was a new alignment in the offing?

Johnson was too tired to care. His job was to fly the Airbus and this he would continue to do. With or without his captain.

When Johnson heard the news from Heathrow, he said to himself: "That prick Osajefo is still in the back playing politics, refusing to speak, so it's up to me. It's decision time. My decision."

Heathrow's latest weather report gave a 700 foot cloud base with rain; wind from 200° at 35 knots, gusting to 45knots. There's not much in the way of weather that can stop the relentless march of aviation, but wind is one of them. Especially too much wind from the wrong direction.

Early airfields were just patches of grassland with a windsock; a simple matter to launch your frail craft into wind. When they started building runways, the usual pattern was a triangle; one of the three bits of concrete would be near enough into wind. But with the advent of big jets and mass travel, wind became less important than coping with high traffic volumes. Any airport that needed another runway would now build it in the same direction as the other one: or two; or three. This meant that crosswind operations became commonplace. This was no problem up to a point, which was usually set at a maximum of 25 knot crosswind component for landing.

First Officer Johnson considered the evidence. Heathrow's two runways are aligned exactly east-west, so a near southerly wind at 35 knots would be over their crosswind limit, never mind if they caught a 45 knot gust. Their fuel reserves had taken a beating on the way up, so if they had a go at Heathrow, with delays already at twenty minutes, and found on their arrival that the wind still too strong, they would be seriously short of funkholes; really just Gatwick, with similar weather and runway direction.

However, as long as they didn't waste time trying for Heathrow, they had plenty of gas for Birmingham or Manchester.

Yes, Manchester, with its lovely southwest pointing runway, almost into wind. And no delays. It was no contest. Johnson asked ATC for a diversion to Manchester. Fifteen minutes later, having crossed the English coast, he started a slow descent.

AfroAir had just passed through 20,000ft. when Captain Osajefo finally made an appearance; a big, dark, menacing figure, smelling strongly of aftershave. The captain looked to have spent a restful night, unlike his co-pilot, who was beginning to feel slightly sick. A failed dalliance with a fried breakfast, extreme fatigue and now that whiff of aftershave... Ugh! Johnson made a big effort to appear normal and professional.

Meanwhile, relief pilot Nkrane hurriedly vacated the left hand seat and disappeared in the direction of the bunk. He might manage a brief kip, but the main thing was he would be well clear of the action when the shit hit the fan. As he knew it would.

Captain Osajefo lowered himself into the Commander's seat, looked across at his co-pilot and asked: "All in order, Mr. Johnson?"

"Yessir."

"And our ETA?"

"Eleven thirty seven, sir."

"In my absence we seem to have lost some time." He made it sound as though they would still have been on schedule had he been present.

Co-pilot Johnson gulped. He could delay the dreadful news no longer. "That's our ETA for Manchester, sir."

Osajefo just sat there. He found that long silences unnerved people. At last he uttered a single word: "Manchester?"

"Yessir. Heathrow crosswind is above our limits. Also long delays and we're none too healthy on fuel. Manchester is our only safe option."

"Nonsense. Are you aware that crosswind limits are purely advisory?"

Johnson remained dumb. He knew they were mandatory, but was not about to argue with his chief pilot.

"What's more, President Zumweski is expected at Heathrow, not Manchester," continued the captain. "Red carpet welcome, British Foreign Secretary there to meet him. It's no secret that I've not always seen eye to eye with Zumweski, but I've just had a long chat with him and am delighted to tell you we've reached an accommodation. A new chapter in relations between our communities. I've no intention of delivering the president to the provincial backwater of Manchester. Tell ATC we're returning to London."

"But sir....." began Johnson, then realised arguing was hopeless. If delays were restricted to twenty minutes they should be okay. Just about. If things became really fraught there was always the last ditch option of declaring an

34

emergency.

Two minutes later AfroAir was heading back towards Heathrow.

9

London weather was also making life difficult for Captain McGregor. Although his First Officer was very experienced with many years on other types, the jumbo was different. And the training captain had pointed out he could do with more practice. So should Hardaker continue flying the sector, as planned and promised? Or should McGregor plead bad weather and do the job himself?

He hated taking landings off first officers. Showed a lack of confidence in them. Which of course was precisely the case. Being new to the 747, Hardaker would understand. Even so...

A pity Heathrow no longer had Runway 23, which would have been ideal under these conditions. It had been a short runway, but that was no problem when landing into a gale, the only occasions it had been used. Actually, not quite the only occasion..... Back in 1968, aviation's Jurassic age, that short stretch of concrete had been a life saver for a BOAC 707, which had suffered an engine fire on take-off, but managed to scramble back to safety on Runway 05, the opposite direction to 23. All but four people had escaped from the subsequent inferno, whereas if the 707 had been forced to return to the standard runway it's doubtful whether anyone would have survived.

No good wishing. Runway 23/05 was long gone, a victim of Heathrow's expansion, the area now covered in aircraft parking stands.

McGregor made up his mind. Hardaker *would* do the

landing. He, the captain, could always take over if the first officer seemed to be having difficulties.

When McGregor's flight appeared on Tim Adamson's radar screen, the arrivals surge was already well under way. There were the usual four blips on finals, the rest scattered above greater London. No longer in stacks, but on seemingly haphazard routes, waiting to be vectored towards the mouth of that finals funnel over Brixton.

What about AfroAir? Well, captain Osajefo was now heading back south, after First Officer Johnson's misguided idea of diverting to Manchester. They would be appearing on Adamson's screen shortly.

Delays were holding at about twenty minutes. A normal day at Heathrow. Perhaps not quite normal. The weather was not always this filthy. But it was certainly not *unusual*. Tim wriggled in his seat again. Concentrated on the radar screen.

The clock showed 1142 when Adamson slotted McGregor's flight into the back of the finals queue over Brixton and handed him over to Heathrow tower; promptly forgot about him and turned his attention to the next ones.

Arrival delays after long night flights were irritating, but an all too common fact of life. Unlike Osajefo, McGregor had used his relief pilot in the proper manner, so everyone had managed a few hours in the bunk. No one could be described as bright-eyed, but they were in far better shape than Johnson in AfroAir.

Hardaker followed the Instrument Landing System towards Heathrow, something both of them had done a million times before. The latest wind had been from 220° at 38 knots, a slight improvement, but that meant little. Wind readouts are merely snapshots of a swirling, turbulent fluid: seconds later or yards away, it might be a totally different story. Now, close to the ground, the gale was giving them a rough ride.

They broke through the overcast at 600 feet. The crosswind was generating a lot of drift, but Hardaker was holding the centreline nicely. McGregor smiled to himself. Home by early afternoon, a couple of hours in the sack to recover, then he should be fresh enough for that Parents and Teachers meeting at his son's school.

Traffic ahead cleared the runway via the high speed turnoff and tower gave them landing clearance.

It was then it started to go wrong.

A backing and strengthening gust of wind? A moment's inattention from Hardaker? Maybe a combination of the two. The reason didn't matter. At 200 feet on the radio altimeter the 747 suddenly found itself over the right hand edge of the runway. Correcting from an upwind position if the wind slackens is easy; recovering the line from a *downwind* position if it strengthens is much more difficult. Hardaker did his best, but in heading yet further into wind he opened up a huge angle with the runway. They seemed to be flying almost sideways along it.

McGregor gave it a couple of seconds more. At 100 feet on the radio altimeter they were still so far adrift that the rear wheels would be over the grass. From this position no one could guarantee a safe landing. Saying "I have control", in one swift movement he pushed the thrust levers forward and eased back on the control column.

"I see you're overshooting," came the voice from tower. "What are your intentions?"

McGregor paused to tell Hardaker: "Gear up: after take-off check". Then pressed the transmit: "Sorry about that. We'd like another approach."

Go-arounds are not popular when traffic is backed-up, but McGregor's airline was well regarded, so the tower paused for only a moment before saying: "When able turn left onto a heading of one zero five and climb to three thousand feet. Call Director on One Two Zero decimal Four."

For the second time that day McGregor became a customer of Tim Adamson. Who was not amused. Delay surges are intensive at the best of times, but follow a well defined pattern. A go-around disrupts this pattern. A rogue aircraft, McGregor's, had to be recovered from an unusual position - just after take-off - and slotted into the flow again.

There was no question of returning this flight to the back of the queue, if only because the last one to join, number thirteen in line, was still at ten thousand feet over the outer reaches of Essex. Of more importance, go-arounds use a lot of fuel, so McGregor could not be kept waiting too long.

Short of a dire emergency, Adamson did not want to disrupt the four flights already on finals. A quick calculation told him he could get three more in after them before McGregor was in position over Brixton. Adamson gave instructions to get him there at the appropriate time, then turned to his main problem: reconfiguring the other arrivals to cope with the extra delay created by the go-around. It was a headache, but Tim Adamson was an old hand and managed the trick without anyone noticing. He thought.

McGregor's flight, now piloted by the captain, had no problem with its second attempt. In a fierce crosswind the technique was to crab in, then straighten up with a dab of right rudder just before touchdown. Fast and firm. Not pretty, but safe.

As he finished docking the 747 McGregor relaxed. Turned to his first officer:

"Tough one, Alan. Don't get a gust like that every day of the week. Sorry I had to take over."

"Back to training for me, I suppose?" Hardaker looked crestfallen.

Confidence is everything, so McGregor replied: "No, no. I'll just tell Melville conditions were against giving you the landing. Put this one down to experience. Next one is bound to be better."

"Thanks." His first office still looked glum.

"Get the baby sitter in. Take the wife out for a slap-up dinner," suggested McGregor, who had already established that Hardaker was married with two young children. "Now, I'm off to mum. And a Parents and Teachers meeting. Tomorrow is another day."

10

The day might have been all wrapped up for McGregor and Hardaker, but not for Tim Adamson and his airborne charges, who now had to cope with the effects of the missed approach.

With delays all too common and their lengths uncertain, the awaiting mob continued gyrating in the heavens above London, patiently awaiting instructions from Adamson. A couple recalculated their fuel reserves; one decided he'd had enough and made straight for Manchester.

A new recruit to the line of hopefuls was AfroAir. First Officer Johnson twice pointed out that their fuel reserves were now critical, but Captain Osajefo replied that delay forecasts were always pessimistic: "Ten minutes at the most, just you see".

How could a man who normally flew a desk possibly know, thought Johnson, in despair. But the co-pilot was so stupefied by lack of sleep - and terrified of his commander - that he didn't press the point.

Osajefo's predicted ten minutes came and went. AfroAir was meandering at seven thousand feet over north London, Adamson juggling his motley fleet into some sort of order for their final approach, when Johnson could contain himself no longer:

"Sir.... I think we should declare an emergency."

"What!"

The co-pilot resisted that corny phrase 'flying on fumes', but that was almost the reality. Instead, he said: "We can no longer make either Stansted or Gatwick. Could still manage City Airport....that's if the runway's long enough for us. I don't know...."

"Find out how much longer," ordered Osajefo, finally appearing to wake up.

Johnson did just that.

Adamson came back: "Should have you on the ground in fifteen minutes."

"Fifteen minutes!" Johnson almost shrieked the words. Only Osajefo heard him, as he had not pressed the transmit.

Unaware of McGregor's missed approach, Johnson had been working on the original estimate. It was now a lot more. Impossibly more!

Captain Osajefo, sweating and beginning to grasp their predicament, *did* transmit: "We need an immediate landing. I repeat *immediate*."

"Understand you are declaring an emergency?" enquired Adamson, calmly.

"Of course it's a fucking emergency!" All thoughts of a red carpet for President Zumweski had been banished by the spectre of another sort of red: red blood for all on board if they didn't get down at once.

With barely a pause, Adamson said: "AfroAir One, take up a heading of one four five, descend to three thousand feet on altimeter niner niner eight. Speed one eight zero."

He couldn't recall ever having heard the word 'fucking' used in the London Control Zone, so things were obviously serious.

Captain Osajefo re-directed the autopilot onto this new heading, started to descend and scratched his large bony head. Something was puzzling him.

Turning to Johnson, he said: "They're taking us *away from* Heathrow."

"Landing on the westerlies, sir. Expect they're positioning us somewhere over central London for finals," replied Johnson.

When flying in cloud under radar steers one's exact position doesn't matter. Normally. But today was not 'normal'. When Osajefo finally pressed the panic button they had been almost due north of Heathrow. With solid cloud now down to six hundred feet, a visual approach was out of the question, even if Heathrow had allowed it. The co-pilot was right. However desperate their plight, they *had to* lock onto the Instrument Landing System to get in.

Although they were now on their way down and flying the prescribed heading of 145°, Osajefo had so far *not* followed Adamson's other instructions. He appeared to have gone straight from denial mode to panic and was muttering to himself.

Johnson reminded the captain to re-set his altimeter to the local 998 millibars: a nasty low sitting out there to the west.   After a pause, the captain still seemingly stuck in a frozen state, Johnson reminded him: "And they want our speed back to one eighty."

The world of aviation lives on precision: people can die without it. Precise altitudes, exact headings, speeds on the button. Their high altitude speed had been a fuel-efficient 200 knots, but now, as they were fed into the final landing sequence, Adamson had asked for a speed reduction to bring them into line with the rest of the traffic. Osajefo was ignoring this: they were still thundering down at 200 knots. Johnson didn't have to be a mind reader to realise the reason. A slower speed would not only take them longer to kiss the blissful tarmac of Heathrow's runway. It also demanded more flap, extra pieces of wing that allowed them to fly these slower speed without stalling: more flap creates more drag, thus requiring more power. A double whammy for their parlous fuel state.

Airbus designers don't really trust pilots, which is not as daft as it sounds. Automatics are always more accurate. As part of this philosophy, they made traditional power levers redundant, instead installing 'auto-thrust', which continually adjusts engine power to a selected speed. As the captain had not actioned the request for a speed reduction, Johnson started doing it for him.

And received a smart slap on the wrist.

"But sir....." he began, before realising the futility of objecting.

"This is an emergency," snapped Osajefo, now fully alive to the mess he had landed them in. "We have priority."

Johnson nodded dumbly.

Down on mother earth, Adamson had already started the full emergency procedure: fire crews deployed at Heathrow, back-up help in the control room. His boss, a gnarled old-timer called Harry Fuller, was already scanning the screen with him.

Flights in the London Control Zone must have secondary radar, a device that transmits vital details back to the ground. The radar was showing AfroAir descending through 4,000 ft., doing 200 knots.

"Still maintaining two hundred knots," observed Harry.

Adamson nodded. "Looks like he's in real trouble. I'll let him have what he wants."

"He'll soon be too close to Virgin ahead of him," observed Harry. "I'll dog-leg Virgin, let AfroAir in ahead. You concentrate on our problem child."

The controllers continued their juggling act and soon

AfroAir's altitude lock levelled them at the instructed 3,000ft.

When suddenly the cockpit erupted in a cacophony of sound. And a light display worthy of Guy Fawkes. The starboard engine roared up, making the aircraft yaw to the left. In-flight failures are designed to wake you up, but multiple failures trigger warning overkill.

"Number one engine failure," yelled Johnson, now also close to panic.

"Do the drill," ordered Osajefo, who was trying to cope with a tripped autopilot and other failures. He was now using his sidestick, flying as manually as Airbus ever allowed. Leaving 3,000ft and starting a right hand turn, he told London:

"I have engine failure. Must land immediately. I repeat immediately."

"Jesus!" whispered Harry Fuller, who never swore. "I'll clear all traffic ahead of him. And alert the west London fire services."

"Head one niner zero," said Adamson. When able, lock onto the localiser for two seven left. You are cleared to land. And good luck."

They say you make your own luck. If so, Captain Osajefo had long since squandered theirs. He had just settled onto that 190° heading when their remaining engine gave up the ghost. They were now flying a glider. With President Zumweski, the crew and 322 passengers on board. Airliners are streamlined and therefore make good gliders, but gravity can't be denied forever. It was clear they hadn't a hope of making Heathrow.

But Johnson had read the book. And seen the film. Sully. With Tom Hanks playing the hero. How Captain Sullenberger had suffered a double engine failure on take-off, but managed to save everyone on board by ditching his Airbus in the river Hudson. Could the River Thames be their Hudson?

First Officer Johnson pressed the transmit: "Other engine now failed. Unable Heathrow. Request vectors for a Sully on the Thames."

Adamson had been trying to shut his mind to the awful possibility of an airliner crashing in the heart of London. This suggestion offered a chance of salvation. Maybe only a slim one, but it was their only hope. The AfroAir blip on his screen was now down to 1,600ft, heading 190° and still doing 200 knots. The Airbus would be flying blind in cloud, but Adamson could see that almost dead ahead lay a fairly straight stretch of the Thames; bridges in the way, certainly, but beggars can't be choosers. With cloud down to 600ft., AfroAir's crew would have only seconds of visual to put her down.

A closer look showed the stricken airliner to be slightly to the right of the river, so Adamson issued an amendment:

"AfroAir turn left heading one six zero. When you break cloud the river should be at your two o'clock."

Tim Adamson and Harry Fuller could do no more. Tim had the ungracious thought that if AfroAir made a mess of it, the best place was on London's waterway. Rather than Mayfair, or - God forbid - Buck House.

In AfroAir's cockpit panic had given way to resignation. Osajefo told the passengers to take up the brace position, in the slender hope they might make it in one piece.

The captain ordered full flap, brought the speed back as far as he dared - below 150 knots. Inevitably, they continued on down.

At 500 ft. they broke cloud. River in sight, but blocking their way was a monster out of Grimm's fairy tales. Dead ahead a Gothic tower.

400ft. The Gothic tower's clock face appeared to be almost at eye level. The giant hands registered 1223. The captain's sidestick did not seem to be working properly, perhaps due to the fact that the Airbus system did not allow pilots to control the elevators and ailerons directly; instead, the two sidesticks sent messages to a bank of computers, which made the ultimate decisions.

300ft. Osajefo saw the reason for his control problem: First Officer Johnson was also thrashing away with his sidestick, sending the Airbus computers hopelessly confusing signals. Not that it mattered. Nothing the two pilots could do mattered any longer.

200ft. In a desperate attempt to avoid the tower, Osajegfo slammed his sidestick over to the right. Because Johnson belatedly had the same idea, this *did* work – sort of; the Airbus started an agonisingly slow turn to starboard. They were now faced with only the monster's main structure. Lower, maybe, but still a huge gingerbread barrier.

100ft. The barrier was racing up to meet them. Captain Osajefo yanked his sidestick back as far as it would go. Instinctively, Johnson did the same. In vain. With empty tanks and zero power, AfroAir was in thrall to gravity and could only continue its descent.

It landed just to the right of the monster's tower. The shockwave was felt over the whole of London.

Etched on Captain Osajefo's mind during those last few seconds of life was the time shown on the giant clock:

Twelve twenty three.

11

The Palace of Westminster is not large enough for every elected member to have an office there, so Damian White MP had been allocated one across the road in Portcullis House. He should have been tackling the stack of papers in his In Tray, but chance had handed him a welcome diversion in the shape of Chloe Pettigrew, a reporter from the Oxford Herald.

Damian had been careful to cultivate the local press as a source of free publicity. Mid Oxon might be considered a safe Tory seat, but boundary changes could turn it into a marginal or an ambitious rival from his own party might try and unseat him. A record of visibility in the media was sensible insurance.

It worked both ways, because Bert Forrester, editor of the Herald, was always in need of good copy. Contrary to what the TV series Morse might suggest, Oxford was chronically short of murders. Morse could expect a weekly diet of one decapitation, a corpse in the Thames and a couple of serious assaults, whereas Forrester usually had to make do with something like a fracas in Carfax and an arson in Kidlington. A local MP making waves in Westminster might not be earth-shattering news, but all those column inches had to be filled with *something*.

So Forrester kept an eye on what Damian was up to and when he heard about their MP's part in the Commons Foreign Aid brawl, he felt it was worth bringing to the attention of his readers in the provinces.

He chose Chloe Pettigrew for the job because she was a mature lady with long auburn hair, usually bunched up on top, and a prominent nose that made her striking rather than beautiful, a combination Damian was guaranteed to appreciate.

She was also the daughter of Brian Pettigrew, one of Forrester's drinking companions, who ran a string of superior car dealerships in the area. Brian called her his 'problem child', hardly an accurate description, because Chloe was knocking on thirty. However, she was certainly a problem, having tried marriage – twice. And twice spurned it. The second attempt had barely survived the honeymoon, after which she had renounced long term relationships and reverted to her maiden name. She had tried various outlets for her energy: barmaid, sculpturing, market research. For her latest effort she had enlisted the help of her father, who had persuaded his old drinking buddy Bert Forrester to give her a go at the Oxford Herald.

Bert had agreed largely to help an old mate, but his initial misgivings had so far proved groundless. Chloe had only been with the Herald a couple of months, but she was proving a better journalist than he'd expected. Why not give her a proper test? See what she was made of by sending her to the big city. Sexism and nepotism rolled into one were excellent reasons to choose Ms. Pettigrew.

So the Oxford Herald reporter was now closeted with the Member for Mid Oxfordshire in Portcullis House, built at the turn of the millenium to house the overflow from the antique palace across the way.

From the outside Portcullis House was an attempt at revivalist Gothic, a rectangular block with a series of gaunt towers mimicking Pugin's from a century and a half earlier.

Inside it had a bright atrium, open to daylight, with a row of trees and some cafeteria tables. The second floor housed the MP's cell-like offices, where elected members could follow the monastic rituals of their order. The decor was modern rather than mediaeval, well-lit with plenty of veneer. Facing the inner courtyard just above the atrium were French windows, currently closed due to the weather, which was spraying rain against them.

Damian White MP was sitting at an L-shaped desk, also made of light wood; to his left an angle-poise lamp, in front of him a laptop; on the right a photo of Mandy and their two children, Rory aged nine and seven-year-old Sophie.

His attention had wandered off the picture of his estranged wife but that understandable, because in front of him sat the representative of the Oxford Herald, dapper in tartan skirt and knee-length leather boots. Introductions complete, Chloe was about to start the interview when she remembered something, got up again and placed the latest electronic gizmo on the desk.

"Hope you don't mind?" Her smile must have made a substantial impact on global warming.

"'Course not. Good of you to ask." What with public CCTV and all manner of personal recording devices, it was accepted by everyone that even one's thoughts were no longer private.

Chloe liked to start her interviews with some ice-breaker personal questions. Where they lived, perhaps. Or some family history. In this case, perhaps not. She glanced at the picture of Mandy and the children. The national media had already covered Damian's marital problems in exhaustive detail, so no need to rub salt into the wound.

Knowing how easily lady interviewers could be led astray by Damian, Forrester had instructed her to concentrate on politics. A pity, she thought. This was the first time she had seen the Victor of Strictly in the flesh and he looked interesting: certainly more interesting than either of her husbands. Maybe a little frayed around the edges, but he must be well into his thirties and Westminster was a hard taskmaster. Or so they always told you.

Chloe was forcing her mind back to politics and how to phrase that opening question, when there was an almighty crash. Portcullis House, a modern and well constructed building, shook as though threatening to collapse. They leapt to their feet. Looked around. Nothing was obviously amiss, the rain still hammering at the windows.

They flung open the door, rushed out, joined everyone else in the corridors with the same thought: what the hell had happened? Gradually the mob gravitated to windows facing south, which offered views of the Palace of Westminster. Big Ben was still there....although there was something odd about it. But everything behind and to the right was obscured by a pall of smoke and dust. Traffic in Parliament Square was gridlocked. A lone policeman in high-vis jacket was waving his hands, as though he felt he had to do something, but had no idea what.

"A terrorist bomb!" shrilled a young girl, whom Damian recognised as working for the Home Secretary.

"There's always a second bomb", she added. "Let's get outta here."

This led to a stampede for the exits. Chloe was about to follow when she felt Damian's restraining hand. He shook his head, said: "No point in panicking."

It wasn't only that he was sceptical about the second bomb theory, more that he didn't reckon anyone would get very far. Government centres are infested with security people trained for rapid reaction. He doubted whether they would let anyone out of Portcullis House. If evacuation were deemed necessary, it would be on their orders. All they could now do was sit tight and wait.

"It's the middle of PMQs" said a female voice behind them.

They turned round. It was the chief Whip, Bessie Robotham, large, wide-eyed and out of breath.

"I tried to get through the tunnel," she gasped. "But they wouldn't let me." She was referring to the underground passageway that connects Portcullis House with Parliament. Having failed there, she must have climbed two floors to try and see what was going on, rather puff-making for a large unathletic lady.

"Looks like another Airey Neave," she added, between bosomy heaves.

"Airey who?" asked Damian.

"Before your time," she replied. "Nineteen seventy nine so before my time as well, but I've read about it. A chap called Airey Neave, war hero and shadow Northern Ireland Secretary, was blown up in the Parliament car park by an IRA bomb."

"That was then," said Damian. "Before we had proper security. Couldn't happen now."

"Well, *something* has happened,"

They watched as a helicopter arrived, hovering to one side of the dust cloud, which was starting to subside. And yes, there *was* something odd about Big Ben. It wasn't quite straight. Down below, traffic remained stationary. The inhabitants of Portcullis House, now confirmed as being confined to barracks, continued gazing out at the mayhem, uncomprehending.

"We'll get to know what's happened soon enough," said Damian. "How about going down for a coffee while we wait?"

12

For a short while the two events existed in their own separate capsules: one event around Parliament Square, the other on a radar screen.

Tim Adamson and Harry Fuller had watched, mesmerised, as the altitude read-out on the AfroAir blip slid inexorably towards zero. At 100ft. altitude the speed figures had tumbled to under 100 knots. Then nothing. The AfroAir return had vanished.

Harry picked up the direct phone line to Heathrow. Said that AfroAir was down somewhere in the West End of London. Could have made it to the River Thames. Nothing more he could tell them.

There followed a communications frenzy as first Britain, then the world, tried to work out what had happened. One of the first to make the connection was Foreign Secretary Adam Tichbold, who was in Terminal 5's Aspire Lounge, awaiting the arrival of President Zumweski.

AfroAir would normally have been allocated Terminal 3, but the president had let it be known he would like a wash and brush-up on arrival, so his flight had been transferred to British Airways' T5. Adam had even managed to secure the adjacent A18 arrival gate. It cost nothing to butter up psychopath dictators and the Aspire Lounge could offer showers, a spa, champagne, everything the weary traveller could desire. Well, almost everything. A man from the embassy had indicated that the president would also appreciate an 'escort' service. A request politely declined. His Britannic Majesty's Foreign Office was not in the business of supplying willing ladies to visiting dignitaries.

By now Adam Tichbold was thoroughly fed up. The Aspire lounge, with its floor-to-ceiling windows and spectacular views over the airport was nice enough, but he had been wasting valuable time, hanging around far too long. First he'd been told the flight was diverting to Manchester. Good riddance. By rights Zumweski should be serving time in prison, not being welcomed as a head of state. Some hapless fellow up north could now have that pleasure. Tichbold was about to get into his limousine when another message came through that the president would, after all, be landing at Heathrow. So it was about turn to the Aspire, where the luxurious facilities did little to improve his temper.

It was lunchtime, blood-sugar levels in need of a top up, and although he did not normally start drinking until the evening, he was seriously contemplating breaking this habit.

As he was standing there, feeling sorry for himself and wondering what to do, a British Airways uniform hurried up, led Adam by the arm to a quiet corner and whispered: "Bad, news, I'm afraid, Minister. Looks like we may have lost AfroAir."

"What do you mean 'lost'?" snapped the Foreign Secretary.

The uniform squirmed. "It's still down on the board as 'delayed', but....well, we think it may be delayed indefinitely. Permanently."

"Good God! You mean crashed?"

"Shh!" Uniform hopped around as though standing barefoot on hot coals. The Minister had responded far too loudly. 'Crash' was not a word one uttered at an airport.

"How? Why? Where?"

"Radar lost contact with it over central London. That's all we know."

"Good God!" Normally a man of many words, the Foreign Secretary was now lost for them.

"I'll let you know soon as we have anything definite. And please..." Uniform put a silencing finger to his lips and scuttled off.

Adam Tichbold collapsed into one of the lounge's deep chairs. Tried to get his brain into gear, a difficult exercise as it had virtually nothing to work on. He was without his usual retinue. Protocol had to be observed, but President Zumweski was not someone His Majesty's Government wished to encourage. The bare minimum would suffice, so the Foreign Secretary was on his own.

With nothing he could usefully do, Adam called up a waiter, ordered a Caesar Salad and yes, under the circumstances he *would* break that habit, also a glass of Chardonnay. He should really be back in Whitehall, but that could wait for two items: food and more clarity in the situation.

Both arrived within fifteen minutes, more clarity in the shape of the nervous British Airways uniform, with the information that there had also been an incident at the Palace of Westminster. Pressed to elaborate on the word 'incident', he replied "Some sort of explosion. Terrorist related."

"Bollocks!" said the Foreign Secretary.

"Sir?"

"I'm no Einstein, but it's bloody obvious. You never have *two* incidents within minutes of each other. We're talking about *one* event. Forget the terrorist angle. Whatever has happened at Westminster must be something to do with our friend Zumweski. Perhaps he

55

wanted to see how democracy worked and got too close."

Adam gave a guffaw at his own joke, then realised it might not be in the best of taste, so added hastily: "Now that Zumweski won't be appearing, I'd better get back to work. But I'm going to finish lunch first, so let me know if anything new comes up in the next few minutes."

The BA uniform confirmed that he would do so and departed, leaving Foreign Secretary Adam Tichbold thoughtful.

Although information was still sketchy - in truth almost non-existent, it was clear something dramatic had occurred. Such events often offered opportunities for the fleet of foot and unscrupulous. Adam prided himself on being both of these, but so far the Everest of politics had eluded him. Would events now unfolding finally enable him to grasp the top of that greasy pole?

Ever since being selected for the safe Tory seat of Surrey West while still in his twenties, Adam had been the party's glamour boy. Nature had been generous in building him a frame of six foot four inches, with dark hair and a profile that might have been chiselled out for Hollywood. He had continued the good work on his own account with a Savile Row tailor and shoes from John Lobb. His trademark was the triangular tip of a handkerchief, peeking out of his left breast pocket: always a Conservative blue hankie. Even the fact that he had been educated at Eton did not appear to be a handicap.

Adam Tichbold was a good speaker, worked hard and *always* voted the party line. He had often been tipped as a future PM, but this remained a promise unfulfilled. Admittedly he had indulged in some youthful scrapes, some skeletons rattling away in his cupboard, but no more than was usual at Westminster. His frustrations were probably due to no more than the unpredictability of politics.

The Foreign Secretary finished lunch, pulled out a mobile and told his driver to meet him outside in five minutes.

Into battle! Details of the Westminster 'incident' were obscure, but opportunities for advancement must surely exist. If so, he was determined to find them.

13

Shortly before 3 pm it was confirmed that the two 'incidents' were in fact one. AfroAir had failed to reached the Thames and struck the Palace of Westminster.

With the possibility of terrorism eliminated, the curfew on Portcullis House had been lifted. Damian White, Bessie Robotham, Chloe Pettigrew and everyone who had been imprisoned there the past couple of hours were free to go.

But go where? And do what?

A massive rescue operation was underway, necessitating the closure of Parliament Square and causing traffic standstill over much of central London. You could walk down Whitehall or onto the Embankment. And catch the tube from Westminster station situated underneath Portcullis House, as long as you didn't want to use the Circle and District lines going west, because these ran so close to the surface that safety checks had to be carried out on the section alongside Parliament: eastbound trains and the deep north-south Jubilee line were operating normally.

This limited mobility was of little use to the inhabitants of Portcullis House, whose overriding aim was to discover what was happening across the road. Normally there's a surfeit of information: annunciator screens with all the latest news; laptops similarly force-fed; clanging division bells should there be a sudden vote. Now nothing. There had clearly been a major disaster: a plane crash, someone said. No hope, of course, for anyone on the plane, but what about casualties on the ground? It didn't look good there either, but no details were forthcoming.

It was all intensely frustrating. Bessie was wandering around, like a lost soul, muttering "PMQs... Everyone there... PMQs". Chloe Pettigrew, by chance on hand for the biggest scoop she was ever likely to get, was continually thwarted by police, impervious to her press card. Damian White, with no special agenda, simply wandered around watching history in the making.

Foreign Secretary Adam Tichbold's blood pressure problem was caused by the traffic, which brought him to a complete halt just short of Hyde Park Corner. They had already spent ninety minutes on the journey from Heathrow and enough was enough. Adam told his driver he would walk the rest of the way, slammed the door shut, and set off.

Although it was still blowing hard, the rain had eased, low cloud racing across, a hint of brightness in the west. Adam negotiated the rabbit warren of Hyde Park Corner underpasses and took the exit down Constitution Hill. Passing Buckingham Palace he heard the 'thump-thump' of a helicopter, which hovered briefly before disappearing from view. Probably the king. Not many people had the privilege of direct access to the palace.

Adam skirted the Victoria memorial and took the scenic route through St.James's park. The king.... Now, there was a thought. The British monarch had been left with precious few powers, but still had *some*. In theory it was his job to send for the person he thought best suited to be Prime Minister. Not that many years ago he would still have had some choice in the matter. Nowadays he had to accept Parliament's decision, but what if the 'incident' Adam was approaching had cut off so many of Parliament's limbs that it was temporarily unable to govern? What if Parliament was *hors-de-combat*?

The Foreign Secretary quickened his pace, exhilarated;

he really should get more exercise. Leapt up the steps into King Charles Street, past the watchful eye of Clive of India - there was a man after his own heart! Then into Whitehall. Parliament Square was blocked off, but no matter. He had established that Portcullis House remained operational and reaching it was no problem.

Time to resolve the chaos.

14

It was inevitable that on this Wednesday afternoon Bessie Robotham and Adam Tichbold should meet. As Chief Whip and Foreign Secretary, they appeared to be the two most senior members of the government still at large. Bessie had been around Portcullis House all day, Adam had just arrived. Both were acutely aware that events could no longer be allowed to drift. Someone had to get a grip on things and they seemed to be the only ones capable of it.

This was ironic, because of all the personality clashes that entertained the Westminster village none was so well established as that between Bessie and Adam. It was not only that Adam, suave and handsome, came from what was perceived to be the ruling elite, while Bessie, rough-hewn and without personal charm, had clawed herself up from humble origins. It ran deeper than that. Those claiming to be in the know hinted at some 'event' during undergraduate days at Oxford. Adam had been at Balliol a year ahead of Bessie at Somerville, both studying Philosophy, Politics and Economics, which was probably what had brought them together. The participants remained tight-lipped about any youthful fallings-out, so the scandal-mongers had mostly lost interest, but one thing was certain: the Chief Whip and Foreign Secretary did not get on.

With no information yet available about survivors from the wreckage across the road, Bessie Robotham had set about doing *something*. She had consulted her 'Little Black Book', actually an iPad which contained megabytes of material about every Conservative Member of Parliament: Male or female? Straight or gay? Faithful to partner or not? Miserly or spendthrift? Alcoholic or TT? She included any fact that might one day assist her to persuade, cajole or blackmail that member into the correct division lobby. The Black Book also contained much mundane data, such as the location of everyone's parliamentary office. She had trawled through the Portcullis House register to obtain a partial roll call and told those she could find not to leave the building.

She had been helped in this work by Damian White, whom chance had thrust in her path at the start of the crisis. Her opinion of him was beginning to soften. He might be far too independent when it came to following the party line, but today his behaviour couldn't be faulted; perhaps not the 'little twerp' she had always thought, but a rather helpful little man. Bessie still thought of him as 'little', because her seniority over the member for Mid Oxon remained at about three inches in height, thirty kilos in weight and twenty five years in age. To say nothing of sixteen years more in the Commons.

When Bessie reckoned all her flock in Portcullis house had been accounted for, she suggested some refreshment in the atrium cafeteria. The party included the third member of their involuntary troika, Chloe Pettigrew.

Chloe had started the day with the abortive Damian White interview, after which no one had objected when she stayed. During the curfew there had been no choice and now she was part of the scenery. With historic events taking place under her nose, Chloe vowed they would only be able to remove her yelling and screaming. She would stay the night; if necessary the next one as well; however long it took. Where didn't matter. If necessary, sleeping on the floor. She might have had no success so far in getting any closer to the action across the road, but access to the Chief Whip and what appeared to be the tattered remnants of any government was a prize worth hanging on to.

The three of them had just sat down to enjoy a cup of builder's tea and some fattening buns when a shadow appeared over their table. It was a bedraggled Foreign Secretary; black hair, which he always wore long, was in disarray; shoes had fought a losing battle with too many puddles; and his normally jaunty breast pocket blue hankie was drooping.

"May I join you?"

Bessie paused just long enough to hint she'd rather not before replying: "Of course, Adam. Fancy a cuppa something?"

He shook his head. Said: "Had a bite at the airport." Sat down and continued: "Can anyone tell me what's going on?"

"Thought *you* might enlighten us," replied Bessie.

Another shake of the head. "Apparently that old tyrant Zumweski decided to take a header into the Mother of Parliaments. Looks like he made a mess of it. Any news of the Prime Minister?"

Bessie shook her head. "Presumably under the rubble with the rest of them. It was Prime Minister's Questions, remember, so it would have been a full house."

"Who's running things? Whose finger on the pulse?"

"Good question. Just had a call from Jacob Wells asking the same question."

"Wells the spook?"

"You know he hates people calling him that. Says the James Bond boys are the ones across the river in Six. But yes, it was Wells, Director General of MI Five. He sounded concerned. Said he no longer had anyone to report to. Insisted we fix it a.s.a.p."

"I see what he means," said Adam. "With the finger on

our nuclear button under six feet of rubble, the Russkies could zapp us with no fear of reprisal."

"Don't be frivolous, Adam. No one is going to nuke us just because our PM is out of the loop."

"Exactly the point I've been making all these years," said Damian, suddenly coming to life. "Do Spain, Germany, Italy, Sweden, all the rest lose any sleep because they can't obliterate the world? Trident is dangerous and expensive. Get rid of it."

"You silly little unilateralist....." Bessie's newfound admiration for Damian went into reverse.

"Shut up, you two," snapped Adam. "This is not the time to revisit *that* argument. My fault, I suppose, for bringing it up. We have work to do, so let's not squabble."

"Agreed," said Damian. "Did Jacob Wells say anything else, Bessie? Like the latest from across the road? If anyone knows, it should be Homeland Security, or whatever they call themselves."

"Jacob said he would be holding a news conference at five thirty: that's in just over an hour. He added that the media mob would then descend on us, so we'd better have some answers ready."

"Then we can't afford to waste time," said the Foreign Secretary. "I'll commandeer the Attlee suite, which can seat about a hundred people. Meet me there in five minutes."

"May I suggest we let Ms. Pettigrew sit in on our discussions," said Damian. "She's a journalist from Oxford."

Chloe shot Damian a grateful glance and explained: "My interview with Mr. White seems to have been overtaken by events, but you're always talking about open government, so...."

The Foreign Secretary *hated* open government. On the other hand he found it hard to resist a pretty face. There was also his place in history to be considered. Every politician is obsessed about his place in history. Today was **HISTORY** in bold capitals and he was determined that one Adam Tichbold should have the starring role. Having a scribbler present to get *his* version of History straight might be a good idea.

15

The Attlee suite on the first floor of Portcullis House is a light and airy room with five rows of grey-green seats. Facing the audience is a long oak-coloured desk with half a dozen chairs for those running the show.

A room of this size was needed because Bessie had told the Portcullis information machine to summon all Conservative MPs to the Attlee as soon as possible. She had no idea how many would turn up, because most members would have been lured to the weekly excitement of PMQs, therefore still trapped. Maybe dead.

Adam Tichbold opened up the room and sat himself down in the central position. He appeared to be the senior government minister to have escaped the carnage, therefore the obvious one to chair the meeting. So he told himself. No one was prepared to argue with him. Bessie Robotham sat down on the Foreign Secretary's right, with Damian White on his left.

Damian wondered whether either of the two big beasts of the political jungle would object to him, a mere backbencher, grabbing a place at the top table, but you didn't get on in politics by being a shrinking violet. In the event they said nothing.

Chloe Pettigrew selected a prime spot in the front row of the main section, took out an iPad, crossed her lovely booted legs, and smiled. The two men smirked back. With a figure-hugging fawn top over that tartan skirt and strands of auburn hair starting to stray from the bunch on her head, she was a great improvement on the human scenery one saw at most political meetings.

After ten minutes only about twenty people had made it to the Attlee. Stragglers would no doubt continue to roll in, but Adam could wait no longer. He banged on the table. The hubbub died down. He began:

"Ladies and gentlemen, thank you for turning up at such short notice. By now we would normally have been briefed by the Home Secretary, but he is.... unavailable. In his absence I have been promised a preliminary report from Jacob Wells of our security services in forty minutes from now, at five thirty. I won't try and pre-empt Jacob's findings, but the salient facts are already clear. Horribly clear. As the party of government we shall shortly have to make some difficult decisions, and I've called you here so that we can do just that. Meanwhile, this is what we know so far....."

The Foreign Secretary and Chief Whip shared what information they had with the rest of their MPs, who continued to trickle in. And waited for the clock to reach five thirty.

16

As the BBC News logo appeared on the TV screens, a hush descended on the Attlee suite. Adam Tichbold had been preparing his followers for the scenario that they, the rump of the Conservative party, would have to assume the reins of power. At least until a general election could be held. Now he stopped talking.

After a brief introduction, the newscaster transferred them to a BBC reporter in the MI5 building on Millbank. Opposite him sat Director General Jacob Wells, a spare and ascetic man in his fifties, who looked more like an Oxford don than head of the country's security. Normally Jacob kept well out of the limelight, leaving all that to the Home Secretary, but with his political master unavoidably detained he had to face the music on his own.

Jacob started with a resumé of how AfroAir had run out of fuel, then moved on to what everyone was waiting to hear: the latest from the scene.

"In its attempt to avoid the Elizabeth Tower - Big Ben - The Airbus crashed directly onto the House of Commons Chamber," he began. "The rest of the Palace of Westminster - the corridors, Committee rooms, bars, House of Lords, were unaffected and quickly evacuated. But the Commons Chamber is a major disaster area. How bad we have yet to establish, but we fear the worst."

"Prime Minister's Questions is the most public event of the parliamentary week, so there's good TV coverage of the moments leading to impact. We don't have an overview of the whole chamber, but there's enough coverage to suggest that it was, as usual, pretty near full. As the House of Commons can seat four hundred and thirty seven members, that will probably be roughly the number still buried beneath the rubble."

"Rescuing survivors is of course our most immediate concern, but we face severe obstacles. An Airbus Three Thirty with full payload but empty tanks weighs in the region of two hundred tonnes. It's last recorded forward speed was just under one hundred miles per hour, which is a stalled condition, so its vertical speed would have been rapidly *increasing*. Imagine that hunk of metal striking a fragile old structure with this sort of violence and you'll have some idea what our rescue services are up against."

"Earthquakes involve a similar type of damage, so we have a good idea what to expect; highly unstable wreckage that can collapse further if you so much as sneeze. The biggest hazard is the Elizabeth tower - Big Ben - which is leaning at such an angle it may at any moment capsize onto the rescue site. Rushing things may cause further deaths, not only amongst those still buried, but also the rescuers. Patience is therefore our only option. We'll let you know as soon as there's anything more to report."

The BBC reporter thanked the Director General, then signed off with the comment: "For the political implications of this extraordinary day, over now to my colleague at Portcullis House, where Foreign Secretary Adam Tichbold has been meeting surviving members of the ruling Conservative party."

The Attlee suite TV screens went dead, allowing the waiting BBC team to swing into action. Cameras in place, the reporter welcomed Adam and invited his comments. The Foreign Secretary had contemplated a quick repair job in the men's room, but decided instead that wild hair, a crumpled suit and further disarray of his trademark blue hankie might give the impression he had been heroically

69

scrabbling around in the wreckage. He had of course only been taking a windy walk in St.James's Park.

The Foreign Secretary remained silent for a moment. He may not have been trained at RADA, but like any good actor he knew the value of the pregnant pause.

Finally he began: "Ladies and gentlemen, all our thoughts and prayers are with our colleagues trapped in the wreckage."

He stopped, wiping a phoney tear from his cheek. The "thoughts and prayers" mantra was obligatory at such events. Even card-carrying atheists like Adam couldn't avoid calling up the deity. In fact, his thoughts and prayers were *very much* on the fate of his colleagues, but not in the manner most would have assumed. His most fervent prayer was that the whole lot should remain immured for all eternity, allowing him a free run. It's not every day that fate eliminates all one's major rivals in one go.

When he judged that a suitable degree of emotion had been exhibited, Adam continued: "However, those of us that have been spared have a job to do. The Conservative party has a clear mandate to govern so we, the survivors, will not shrink from carrying out the wishes of the people. We now have to decide who shall lead us in that endeavour."

"May I propose the Foreign Secretary, Adam Tichbold."

All eyes turned to the back row and the bald, rotund figure of Jasper Maitland, Secretary of State for Culture, Media and Sport. Jasper was embarrassingly camp and known as the "Luvvies' Minister". Unlike Adam, he *had been* trained at RADA, but had failed to hack it on the stage or TV. So he had turned to politics, where his talent for toadying had propelled him nicely upwards. Jasper was not only a well-known stooge for the Foreign Secretary, he was also the only Cabinet Minister other than Bessie and Adam so far known to have escaped the carnage.

"I'm deeply touched by the words of my cabinet colleague, but am I worthy of that honour?" asked Adam, with a heartrending display of humility. He had, in fact, promised the Luvvies' Minister all sorts of goodies for popping the question, but tradition dictated that some hesitation be shown before grabbing the prize. The best example of this was the election of House of Commons Speaker, who always had to be seen protesting loudly before being installed in his chair, even though he would have been stabbing rivals in the back to get there.

"I'm sure there'll be plenty of seconders," replied Jasper, beaming.

A dozen hands went up. Bessie Robotham pointed to a middle-aged woman in a pleated skirt sitting in the front row. Said: "Thank you, Amanda."

There was nothing the Chief Whip wanted *less* than to see Adam as leader, but the Foreign Secretary clearly had the wind in his sails so she was helpless. For the moment. Adam could hardly be seen to be engineering his own elevation, so, as the next most senior person present, Bessie announced:

"Let the record show that the motion was proposed by Jasper Maitland and seconded by Amanda Smith: That Adam Tichbold be elected our provisional leader. All in favour?"

Just about every hand in the Attlee suite went up, including that of Chloe Pettigrew, who found herself so swept up by the fervour of the occasion that she promoted herself to a Tory Member of Parliament. Fortunately no one seemed to notice.

Next day the image was all over the front pages: Bessie Robotham manufacturing a smile as she shook the hand of the new Conservative leader. Also the *country's* new leader.

17

Adam Tichbold thanked the assembly for its support, then declared a recess until nine thirty the following morning. There was little more they could do now. The situation should become clearer overnight and everyone could do with a good night's sleep. The surviving Conservatives filed out of the Attlee suite in a daze.

The Foreign Secretary rushed off on some unannounced errand, leaving the troika of Bessie, Damian and Chloe to shut up shop. As the Chief Whip closed the door of the Attlee suite, Chloe asked: "What now?"

No one had an answer.

Parliament is like a school, with short intensive sessions (terms) relieved by lengthy recesses (holidays). MPs only spend about 150 days a year in Westminster. When Parliament is in session the days follow a well planned schedule - like school lessons. But now? Now MPs suddenly found themselves without a purpose in life. The mass of legislation that had so occupied them until a few hours ago, was either postponed indefinitely or dead in the water.

Damian looked at his watch and announced: "Sun over the yardarm. I need a refresher. Any takers?"

Bessie looked doubtful. And, unusually for her, helpless.

"As Adam said, there's nothing more we can do," prompted Damian. "Or were you planning something?"

Bessie shook her head. Asked: "What do you suggest?"

"My pad for when I'm in Westminster is an apartment in Pimlico. Plenty of pubs and eateries around. I usually walk from here. Clears the head after a day of hot air. Takes about twenty minutes. I suppose we could try for a cab, but under the circumstances...."

"No, we'll walk."

As Bessie started galumping off, Chloe asked: "Mind if I join you?"

The Chief Whip stopped in mid-galump and asked: "Shouldn't you be getting back to Oxford?"

The reporter grinned. "Mr. White still owes me an interview."

"So I do." Damian rubbed his chin. He was beginning to enjoy having Chloe around, so said: "An interview in a pub? Why not. When we've finished I'll point you in the direction of Paddington, make sure you don't miss the last train home."

Damian wondered whether it was wise to take on two women - two very different specimens at that - but hey, life was a challenge! So off they went, Bessie at a rapid waddle, initially skirting Parliament square, still closed to vehicles, but now open to pedestrians. With half of London up to see the latest home disaster, everyone was kept moving by the police; nevertheless, snatched views of the rescue proceedings were possible. The scene was lit by a gaggle of floodlights - it was now nearly dark - and dominated by the face of Big Ben, a one-eyed yellow monster miraculously still lit up. It appeared to be about to topple onto the ants below. The Leaning Tower of London.

They pressed on, initially down Victoria Street, then south towards Damian's *pied-à-terre* and sustenance. Little was said, everyone preoccupied with their own thoughts. Finally they arrived at the promised land, a traditional pub with much dark wood and an impressive row of beer handles. The sign outside said 'Dog and Bacon'.

They found a table and ordered up, while Chloe busied herself texting a piece back to the Oxford Herald. Although TV had already broadcast the salient facts, the reporter felt she had plenty of interesting background to add. Few members of the media could have been closer when AfroAir crashed and this piece of luck had enabled her to build up a rapport with the Foreign Secretary, Chief Whip and member for Mid Oxon. All destined to be crucial players in the days ahead.

A familiar face is a reporter's greatest asset and Chloe intended to work this to her advantage, her ambitions now reaching beyond provincial Oxford. If she could come up with the right stuff, her editor, Bert Forrester, would send this on to the national dailies - from where the sky was the limit. Bob Woodward and Carl Bernstein would be forever linked with Watergate. Could Chloe Pettigrew manage something similar with the Leaning Tower of London? She had already hinted to Bert Forrester that this headline was her patent, but it was difficult - nigh impossible - to claim originality for the written word and her rivals were a ruthless bunch. But she could try. And dream.

Eventually the food had been ordered, drinks were on the table and Chloe had finished tapping out her piece to Forrester. They could relax.

"Don't get many days like this," said Damian, his upper lip newly moustached with foam from a pint of Guinness.

"Thank God," said Bessie, starting on her Chardonnay.

"What happens now?" asked Chloe, aware that she was in danger of repeating herself.

Two pairs of eyes turned towards the Chief Whip, the oldest and most senior of them. But Bessie just sat there, ruminating. She was perfectly happy in a structured environment, updating her database of MP's facts and foibles, then whipping any backsliders into the correct voting lobby; but she didn't like uncharted waters. So she replied, rather lamely: "I expect Adam will come up with something at tomorrow's meeting."

"I'm *sure* the Foreign Secretary - correction, our provisional leader - will come up with something," said Damian, who *loved* uncharted waters. "But the rest of us need to make sure he doesn't overstep the mark."

"You can say that again!" Muttered Bessie.

Like everyone at Westminster, Damian had heard the rumours that Bessie and Adam had 'history'. But he decided to tread carefully, so just asked: "How many of you in the cabinet?"

"Twenty three."

"Of which we've so far only seen three survivors: you, Adam and Jasper. Culture, Media and Sport is a lightweight portfolio, so we can discount pretty-boy Jasper, which leaves you, Bessie, as the only political heavyweight able to stand up to Adam."

"Sounds like you don't trust Tichbold," said Chloe.

"In Westminster *nobody* trusts *anyone*," said Damian. "I jest of course. Bessie's favourite word for me is 'frivolous'. To be serious for once - and this is off the record, okay....?"

Chloe nodded.

"....You can use as background my opinion that Adam Tichbold is clever, well-connected, and a hard worker. But as slippery a customer as you'll ever find. Would you agree Bessie?"

"You're being far too generous. Also off the record."

"What are you afraid of?" asked Chloe. "What can your new leader actually *do*?"

"Difficult to say," replied Damian. "That's the problem. There are people who can rattle off whole chunks of Erskine May...."

"Erskine who?" from Chloe.

"Bible of parliamentary procedure," explained Bessie. First came out in the eighteen forties, with later updates. Gives chapter and verse for what we can and can't do."

"I don't suppose Erskine May covers the current situation, so it's impossible to forecast *what* Adam might do," said Damian. "Our constitution works largely by precedent and we've never lost most of the government overnight before. It's like being in a boxing ring and discovering the Queensbury Rules no longer apply. Your opponent may suddenly be able to hit below the belt, kick or bite. Until we get things sorted, we need to make sure no one tries anything underhand."

"Surely Tichbold can't be *that* bad," said Chloe.

"No, no, I'm not suggesting that for a moment...." began Damian.

Bessie interrupted: "Why not? I wouldn't put anything past Adam."

There was an awkward pause. Damian had underestimated the strength of animus between the two.

Chloe broke the silence: "How long until things are back to normal?"

Damian shrugged. "First priority is a full house again. A normal quota of six hundred MPs. Not much point in having hundreds of by-elections, so that'll probably mean a general election; which takes a fair amount of organising. Then there's the little matter of *where* we can meet. A replacement for the House of Commons chamber should ideally be somewhere near home base in Parliament Square. May not be easy to find."

At that point the food arrived: fish and chips for the ladies, lamb shank for Damian. They continued to dissect their new situation, with Chloe noting down interesting snippets. Just after nine Bessie announced she was knackered and would be calling it a day. She rang for a cab, her lodgings being up in West Kensington, too far to walk.

When Bessie had gone, Damian turned to Chloe: "Better get you off as well. Pimlico tube station is just around the corner: Victoria line to Oxford Circus, then onto the Bakerloo for Paddington. Twenty five minutes, with luck."

For a moment the reporter said nothing. Then: "Think I'll stay in town. Need to be here for that nine thirty meeting, so there's no point in going home to Oxford only to have to come all the way back again first thing."

Damian smiled to himself. Had seen this coming. Playing along he asked: "Where had you thought of staying?"

Chloe shrugged. Tried acting the waif - and failed: wasn't the waif type. Finally replied: "I'll find somewhere. If necessary sleep on the floor."

"That *won't* be necessary." Damian got up. "Can't have the Oxford Herald telling its readers that their MP is in the habit of throwing ladies out onto the street."

"Are you sure?"

"Come on." He took her arm. "A five minute walk. I've got a nice sofa, so no one need sleep on the floor."

18

Damian had omitted to say that although his apartment was about five minutes away on the flat, there was then a four storey climb to what had originally been an attic for servants, but today housed the likes of city high rollers and MPs. Fortunately they were both fit, Damian careful not to have lost all of his body tone from West Ham days, while Chloe was young enough not to have to think of such things.

Only slightly out of breath, Damian opened the door to reveal a modern interior with off white walls and hidden lighting. In a corner stood a glass-topped dinner table; along one wall a phoney-coal gas fire; in the middle a large low-backed sofa, most acceptable as a bed should it be needed: and on the walls four paintings with lots of colours and patterns - and no discernable relevance to the real world.

"Nice," said Chloe, looking around.

"It's what I call home when I'm in town." Damian drew the curtain. "Fancy a nightcap?"

"What have you got?"

"Take a look." He indicated a drinks cabinet. "Pour yourself something. While you're at it, do one for me. Should be some Laphroaig left. One thumb, no ice. Got a taste for it during that Glasgow by-election."

Chloe announced she was going to try a Drambuie and found a couple of glasses. With London's streets still soggy after the storm, she had taken off her boots and was sitting on the sofa with her feet up. Her hair, a halfway colour between brown and red, was starting to come adrift from its perch on top of her head; when fully collapsed it would be below shoulder length. He had been given to understand she was a cub reporter, new to the game, but she didn't appear to be new to life: late twenties, perhaps.

Damian moved his personal viewing chair from opposite the big TV screen to a more companionable position closer to her, said "Cheers!" and let Scotland's finest suffuse his system.

Now he could really relax, something that had not been possible with Bessie around. It wasn't only the generation gap - she was old enough to be his mother - it was more that he always felt guilty when defying her voting orders. She was a nice old bird, honest to a fault, which was almost unique at Westminster. And strangely pathetic. She had never married - married to politics was the usual phrase - and apart from that one hint at a youthful indiscretion, appeared to have no private life. Although Damian liked and respected the Chief Whip, there was always some tension between them.

Now that Bessie had departed, leaving just Chloe, Damian was not only more at ease, he was also curious. Looking at the reporter lying there, glass in hand, she reminded him of that old rhyme that girls are 'sugar and spice and all things nice'. He reckoned this particular example was more hot spice than sugar. Sweet things did not choose a career in journalism and she had already shown herself to be single-minded in pursuit of her trade. Chloe had not latched onto him because of his good looks - maybe a bit of that as well, he had always got on well with the ladies. No, her main aim was a good story, for which he was the conduit.

That suited him fine. He still missed Mandy and the kids and since their departure female company had been at best fleeting. So if Chloe wanted to use him, why not? He was a sucker for being used by attractive ladies.

"Reckon you got a good story?" he asked. "Saw your fingers dancing away texting."

"If I haven't filed a good one after today's events, I deserve the sack," she replied, taking a sip of Drambuie. "It's what happens next that interests me now."

Damian smiled. "What do *you* think will happen next?"

She twirled her glass around, considering a reply. Although that square jaw and Roman nose could hardly be described as beautiful, her full figure and poise promised a seductive political discussion.

"First thing is to find out how many of the government are still alive," she said at last. "If the PM really is dead, as seems likely, your new provisional leader will then be able to decide what to do."

"I think you've got it the wrong way round."

"What do you mean?"

"My guess is that Adam will decide what to do *before* we know the fate of the rest of them. You may have noticed he didn't hang around after the meeting. Rushed off to.... God knows where. He won't have been sitting at home twiddling his thumbs. We'll find out what he's been up to in the morning."

"You don't much like Tichbold, do you?"

"Whether I like him on a personal level doesn't matter. In fact, I hardly know him. He's Foreign Secretary, remember, and I'm a new and lowly backbencher. But Tichbold gets things done, which in my book is a plus. The downside is he's often headstrong, which can get him into trouble."

"Miss Robotham certainly doesn't like him."

Damian nodded. "Goes back to student days, although

no one seems to know what happened."

Chloe nodded, thought for a moment, said: "Getting into that meeting today was a bit of luck: I just happened to be around. Tomorrow will be more difficult. Think you could swing it for me?"

Damian smiled. "Can certainly try. As one of the few Tory MPs still alive and kicking, I have to be there of course. I'll say you're my Personal Assistant."

He levered himself out of the chair: "We need to get there in good time to make sure of a place. By nine at the latest. So time call it a day."

Chloe also rose, came towards him, put her arms around his waist. More hair had given up the struggle against gravity and was cascading over her shoulders. She murmured; "Personal Assistant. I like it."

He looked into her eyes, which were a walnut brown: artificial light distorts colours, so he would have to check again in daylight. Doing his best not to be hypnotised, he said: "If we're to be up at the crack of sparrows, I'd better assist you to your boudoir. I'll take the settee."

Tightening the armlock around his waist, she said: "I *hate* sleeping alone."

Damian nodded solemnly. "In that case perhaps I should give you my mattress test drive. Good Personal Assistants are hard to find and I need to know whether you're up to scratch."

Chloe grinned, took his hand and led him bed-wards. "Vroom vroom! Be warned, I'm a Ferrari."

"Then go easy. Tomorrow is an important day and we need an early start."

19

MARCH 14th.

The alarm woke them at seven. Chloe had managed her nocturnal Personal Assistant test without coming off the road, although there had been the equivalent of much burnt rubber and squealing tyres. She must have passed because they had both slept well and were ready to go.

While Damian shaved, Chloe turned on Breakfast News for the latest from the Leaning Tower.

"The first six bodies have been brought out," she shouted towards Damian in the bathroom. "No names, except they were all MPs. No sign of life under the rubble, so hopes for survivors are fading. But structural engineers have given the Leaning Tower a cautious bill of health; said the one in Pisa has lasted a few centuries, so London's should be able to manage a few more days."

Damian's breakfast was always continental so Chloe was stuck with the same: mug of coffee, banana and/or tangerine, yoghourt, toast. They watched the box as they ate, but there was little more to add. They were keen to get going, so set off shortly after 8.15, the weather sunny after yesterday's storm, albeit still windy.

Damian had wondered whether getting Chloe into Portcullis House would be a problem, but her press pass plus his personal guarantee earned her an easy entry. They went straight up to the Attlee suite, where Bessie Robotham was already fussing around. Good old dependable Bessie. She greeted them absentmindedly, her attention on the TV team, who were setting up their equipment. Damian suggested to Chloe that she take a back seat - literally. The Attlee was not a big room and today it would play host not only to the surviving Tory MPs, but also the world's press. If places became tight, someone might try and eject Chloe should she be too obvious.

Damian aimed to be *very* obvious. Yesterday, by chance and cheekiness, he had managed a seat at the top table beside Bessie and Adam. Familiarity breeds acceptance, so could he manage this trick again? At the worst they could only demote him to a place amongst the plebs.

So he sat down in the same seat as yesterday. Removed some papers from his briefcase, tried to look important. Shuffled papers around, intense and busy. Someone *Not To Be Disturbed*. Bessie took no notice. No one took any notice.

At 9.20 Adam Tichbold breezed in, his usual dapper self. Yesterday the storm-ravaged look had been appropriate but today he wanted to give the impression of calm. A man in control. He always wore his hair long, so it was generally assumed he rarely visited a barber. In fact, a personal coiffeuse attended him once a week to make sure those fulsome black locks were *exactly* the right length and any hint of grey had been airbrushed out. Many men of his age were bald, or at least thinning on top, so Tichbold was proud of his full mane. His trademark blue hankie, peeping out of his breast pocket, was again immaculate

The Tory Provisional Leader gave Damian no more than a passing nod before sitting down next to him in the centre chair. They were soon joined by the Chief Whip, making the same triumvirate as the previous day. On the dot of 9.30 Adam Tichbold brought the meeting to order. Every chair was taken, many of the press corps having to stand.

"Ladies and gentlemen, welcome: if that's the right word in these tragic circumstances." Adam did 'tragic' as well as any Shakespearean actor. "Fourteen bodies have now been recovered from the wreckage, including that of our beloved Home Secretary, Freddy Bosanquet. May I ask for a minutes silence to remember Freddy and all those who have given their lives in the cause of democracy."

Damian always found such silences embarrassing; difficult not to fidget. But it was soon over - only one minute, after all - after which Tichbold turned business-like:

"We must now put our grieving on hold, because those of us that are left have a job to do. Yesterday I was honoured to be elected as your new leader..."

Damian heard Bessie give a sharp intake of breath. Adam had been elected their *provisional* leader, an adjective he was now omitting.

".....and I realised there was no time to lose. The country can't afford to be rudderless any longer, so I requested an audience with His Majesty the King. As you may know, His Majesty was at his West Country estate when the incident occurred, but as soon as it had been established that no terrorism was involved, he was airlifted to Buckingham Palace. It was there that he received me last night. I kissed hands and he delivered to me the Seals of Office."

Bessie Robotham held up her hand: "What happens if *the* Prime Minster is in fact still alive?"

"Then we revert to the *status quo ante*," replied Adam smoothly. "However, my information is that this is most unlikely. No survivors have so far been found and the possibility that there may still be anyone left alive seems remote."

Bessie made some grumpy grunts, but could find no

rational objections.

Adam continued: "We now have to govern this country until a general election can take place and a new Parliament installed. You will remember that a previous administration reduced the number of members of Parliament from six hundred and fifty to six hundred - a figure some people still consider too high. As of yesterday morning we, the Conservatives, had three hundred and eighteen members, with Labour on two hundred and twenty three; the balance made up of Lib Dems, Greens, Scottish Nats, Northern Irish. Our small majority was more comfortable than it might seem because of the divided opposition."

"By yesterday evening this had all changed. Every party has spent the past few hours in a frantic roll call to try and establish who has *not* been buried in that necropolis across the way. We have so far only been able to confirm seventy six Conservative MPs as being alive and well."

As Adam paused for this to sink in, the Reuter's man, whose maths was faster than others, shouted: "Does that mean two hundred and forty two Conservatives are unaccounted for?"

Adam nodded grimly. "When the dust settles I doubt whether we'll manage more than eighty living MPs. My Labour opposite number tells me they've only been able to locate fifty three of theirs. The fringe parties, especially the SNP, appear to have suffered less, but as yet I have no figures for them."

The Reuter's calculating machine had another question: "So you're left with about one hundred and thirty people from the two major parties and maybe forty from the others; say one hundred and seventy in all, is that correct?"

Adam agreed that seemed about right.

"How do you propose to govern with that number?"

"Much as we did with the full six hundred," replied the new, if provisional, Prime Minister, irritably. "I don't anticipate any major legislation, more a holding operation until we're back to full strength again."

"Where will all this take place?" Persisted Reuter. "Where will you hold your debates?"

"I'm glad you asked that," replied Adam, immediately in a better mood. "This room would be far too small, so His Majesty and I discussed other options, the most obvious one being that we take over the House of Lords. However a couple of phone calls put the kibosh on that: first problem was that the whole area is still a disaster zone and likely to remain so for a while: secondly, we've been talking for years about moving *all of us* out of the Palace of Westminster, the place being in need of a complete overhaul; no point in moving into somewhere that was unfit for purpose even *before* this latest event."

"We're therefore left with taking over other premises, the main contenders being County Hall across the river, then on this side either the Queen Elizabeth Conference Centre or Central Hall Westminster. County Hall is now more of a hotel than a meeting place. And the Queen Elizabeth turned us down flat; said they were booked solid and if they threw out a series of big clients it would wreck London as a business centre."

"Wouldn't even do it for the Mother of Parliaments?" asked Reuter."

"Implied *especially* not for the Mother of Parliaments," replied Adam. "They were very brusque. Said the country could only survive by creating wealth for which London was essential. This left us with the Central Hall Westminster and even here I had to do some arm twisting. In the end, they let us have their Lecture Hall on a short let. Capacity four hundred and fifty, which should be enough in our depleted state."

"When will you be holding your first meeting there?" asked Reuter.

"They'll have to prepare the venue," replied Adam. "And we'll need a reliable census of surviving MPs. Today is Thursday, so I'm suggesting next Monday as the earliest practical date."

"During which time you will be the country's chief executive?"

Tichbold nodded gravely. "Unless, of course, our beloved former leader is rescued alive and well." All Adam's colleagues were 'beloved' as long as they remained satisfactorily dead.

"Will there be press facilities at this new location?" asked Reuter.

"I will ensure that there are," replied Adam. "Now, if you'll excuse us, there's work to do. I hope to see you all in our new location at the beginning of next week."

20

Damian picked up Chloe from the back of the room and filed out with the rest of them.

"Three days to kick our heels," he commented. "Normally I'd have had a full workload up here, then three pm Friday back to Wheatley for my surgeries. Now..." he shrugged. "Don't know what to suggest."

"I also need to get back," said Chloe. "Change of undies.... change of boyfriend..."

"There's a boyfriend? You never said."

"You never asked. Anyway, it's become pretty on-off. I seem to get through men rather fast."

"Is that a warning?"

"I've already managed to lose two husbands. That should answer your question?"

"Suits me. We keep it strictly business."

She seemed relieved. Said: "I've been speaking to my editor, who's keen for me to develop my contacts up here...."

"Contacts like me?"

"And Chief Whip Bessie Robotham. And our new Prime Minister. *Must* be back first thing Monday, so would it be possible....?"

Damian grinned: "To book a place at White's B and B?"

"I would of course pay the going rate."

Damian considered this, said: "I could do with a good housekeeper. Who up here can demand quite ridiculous rates. So let's call it quits."

Chloe grinned. "Personal Assistant and now also Housekeeper. Onerous duties. I'll need a job description."

"Easy. Sharing the chores; writing a reasonably truthful account of events as they unfold; keeping the master happy. Starting Sunday evening, if that's agreeable?"

"An offer I can hardly refuse."

"Worth celebrating with a cup of coffee." They had reached the Portcullis House atrium with its cafeteria and he could think of nothing else to occupy them.

If they'd been counting on a cosy *tête-à-tête* they were to be disappointed. Bessie appeared and asked to join them. She seemed ill at ease and edgy.

Unburdening herself, she said: "Should now have been busy with the First Reading of the Armed Forces Bill. A tight vote in prospect, lots for me to do. But now...?" She spread her hands.

"Have to wait until Monday; see what Adam has in store for us," said Damian.

"Yes, Adam....." Bessie scowled. "Pretty damned impertinent of him. Going off to His Maj like that. Behind our backs. Unconstitutional, I'd say."

"Someone has to run the country," Damian pointed out. "And we *did* vote him in as our leader."

"*Provisional* leader. Never thought he'd go off kissing hands with His Maj, pretending to be a *real* Prime Minister."

"It's early days," said Damian. "Things will sort themselves out. It's been a horrible twenty four hours, everyone's upset. We need a break, so why don't you come round to my place this evening...." he made the offer on the spur of the moment. "...I've just engaged a new housekeeper, who might be persuaded to postpone her trip to the country to do us a feast. How about it Chloe?"

"Great idea. Clean undies and P Forty Five for old boyfriend can wait until tomorrow. It'll be good to unwind. What time do you suggest?"

"Seven-ish?"

Bessie nodded slowly. "You're right. I *have* been getting a bit uptight. About seven, then."

21

Damian and Chloe spent the afternoon getting some exercise and fresh air, the day still sunny, the wind abating. Their walk took them past the ghouls swarming around Parliament Square, where the police were still doing their best to keep pedestrian traffic moving. The rescuers must have given up hope of finding any survivors because there was now a large crane on site, hauling wreckage clear with little finesse, much noise and rising dust as the remains subsided. Elizabeth Tower - Big Ben - was still standing. And still leaning.

In late afternoon they returned to Pimlico, after a diversion to Damian's local minimarket to restock his larder and wine cellar. At 6pm they settled down with a drink to watch the early evening news on TV.

Which reported that one hundred and twenty bodies had now been recovered, including that of the Prime Minister, his corpse crushed on top of the despatch box. A noble way to go.

"No way Bessie can now claim Adam is not the *real* Prime Minister", was Chloe's comment.

Another news item, little noted at the time, but which would later become crucial, was that Gerry Farthing, Labour's shadow foreign secretary, had flown in from Teheran, where he had been on a fact-finding mission. Gerry was in his seventies, a remnant of the Labour old guard, now superseded by the Young Turks, who made up almost all the shadow cabinet. But most of these Young

Turks, like their opposite numbers in government, had been in the Commons Chamber when disaster struck. The future belonged to the rag-tag band of survivors. People like Adam Tichbold, Bessie Robotham and Damian White. The opposition could now register theirs with Gerry Farthing.

The bell announcing the arrival of Bessie Robotham rang at 7.10. Damian leapt down the stairs two at a time to help her up. The only way he had been able to afford a flat in Pimlico, even a top floor one, was the lack of a lift. For him it was an advantage, helping him keep fit, but it was not so good for visitors, especially if they were elderly or infirm: or, in this case, large and out of condition.

They eventually made it to his attic, Bessie clutching a bag, which she opened to reveal a full bottle of gin and some tonics.

"Need a stiff one," she gasped, sitting down on the settee next to Chloe. "With ice and lemon if you have it."

Damian set off to do her bidding, reflecting that Bessie was not one of Westminster's usual dypso brigade. The hard drinkers were well known, but the Chief Whip had no form in that direction. Perhaps it was just that her world had collapsed and she needed some solace.

The three of them settled down to discuss the latest news, especially the fact that the prime minister was now known to be dead.

"No stopping that bloody man now," was Bessie's comment. No need to specify who that 'bloody man' was.

Damian pointed out that Adam - indeed the Conservative party - might not have it all their own way, when what was left of Parliament reconvened on Monday. The government had not enjoyed a large majority and who knew what that majority might be when they totted up the survivors.

Bessie insisted that the Tories continued to have the right to govern by virtue of the last election result. Damian wasn't so sure. They threw this back and forth for a while until a 'ping' from the kitchen announced dinner was ready. Chloe had done a free range chicken, roast spuds and veg, which they proceeded to demolish. Wine - red or white according to taste - replaced gin or aperitifs and the conversation continued to flow.

Bessie latched on to the item about the return of Gerry Farthing, who had now been confirmed as Labour's provisional leader. The opposition's answer to Adam Tichbold.

"Never made it to the top because he's too honest for his own good," was her comment.

"An odd coincidence that *both* the top jobs are now occupied by people who were in foreign affairs," said Damian.

"Probably because everyone else was busy here at home," suggested Bessie. "Can only get away when there's a recess. Only Foreign Secretaries, real or shadow, can swan off in the middle of a sitting, when the rest of us may be needed for important votes. Anyway, Gerry's a bit like you, Damian: something of a free spirit. Goes his own way."

Dessert - chocolate mousse - came and went. Drink continued to flow and Bessie became increasingly maudlin. Sensing that alcohol was starting to erode her defences, Damian chanced a remark:

"Lots of rumours about you and Adam, Bessie. From the old days."

"Ah yes. The good old days. *Good* my eye!"

"Undergraduate life... wild parties. I missed all that," said Damian "*Sounds* a bit of all right."

"Trouble with Oxbridge is that you do it at the wrong

time" said Bessie.. "Should happen a bit later, in your thirties, say, when you're more responsible. More mature. Less open to temptation."

"But you've done okay. Chief Whip, famous in your chosen profession. A success by any standards."

"Hmm. Know what they say about me? Married to politics. That's because I've had no choice. Thanks to that bastard Tichbold!"

"Something that happened at Oxford?

"Just the usual. Young girl from the provinces is smitten by that handsome upper-class cad. Finds herself in the family way…"

Chloe put her hand to her mouth: "Couldn't you...?

"We're talking about forty years ago. Only two choices then: keep the child or get rid of it. Of course I wanted to keep it. But Adam would have none of it. Said it would ruin our lives. Some such nonsense. I hinted at marriage, but that made it even worse. I knew what he was thinking: marry that scrubber from Rochdale? No way! Five years later Tatler was full of the 'Wedding of the Year': Old Etonian Adam Tichbold to the Honourable Hermione, daughter of Lord something-or-other. That was what he was after."

"You could still have kept the child," said Chloe. "Even without marriage."

"I could have. And should have. But Adam talked me out of it. Something I'll regret to my dying day. So I went to some nasty clinic - which botched the job. Made sure I could never have more children."

There was moment's silence, no one knowing what to say.

Then Bessie announced: "End of story! We'll now talk about *anything* else. And I shall get absolutely paralytic!"

She was as good as her word. They discussed films, TV,

music, anything inconsequential, Bessie becoming increasingly incoherent. At around eleven Chloe went off to clear up in the kitchen, while Damian needed a pee. When he came back, Bessie was slumped on the settee, snoring. They covered her with a blanket, tidied up and then went off to bed themselves.

22

That long weekend, from Friday to Sunday evening, was hectic for those working the rescue site. With survivors no longer a possibility, their priority was to clear the wreckage and recover *all* the bodies, so Britain could start the next week knowing exactly where it stood.

For those *not* involved in the rescue it was limbo time, little they could do except wait.

Once Adam had signed up the Central Hall Lecture Room as the temporary House of Commons Chamber, the rest could be left to his officials, who would have the ticklish job of informing those who had booked the place that they would have to find somewhere else to meet. This left the Provisional Prime Minister free to depart to his Berkshire estate and comfort his wife Hermione, whose favourite horse had just been put down.

Bessie was packed off in a cab to her flat in West Kensington, where she had several days to recover from her hangover.

The new Labour Leader, Gerry Farthing, had to change his mindset from dealing with the devious mullahs of Iran to the equally daunting one of trying to chart the path ahead for the remnants of his party.

Damian White and Chloe Pettigrew took the tube to Paddington, then a train to Oxford, Damian to sit in his constituency office to answer any surgery posers, Chloe for a laundry blitz and to terminate her past relationship.

For everyone it was the lull before the storm.

23

Central Hall Westminster is a 1912 End-of-Empire building, not that distant in time from MP's previous home in Barry and Pugin's 1860s pile. But the two buildings could not have been more different. Augustus Pugin, the Gothic impetus behind the Palace of Westminster, was eventually committed to Bedlam's asylum for the insane, so his creation is rather wacky. Central Hall Westminster, on the other hand, conveys a message of calm, with high ceilings, cream-coloured walls, classical columns and large vertical windows. The political refugees could well find their new home rather more soothing than their old recently demolished one.

Even with seating limited to 450 and the media out in force, the place was not full, a testimony to the carnage caused by Osajefo's unplanned landing on the palace of Westminster.

For this first meeting of the Provisional Parliament a central aisle separated two blocks of blue chairs - no political bias intended, they just happened to be that colour. On a waist-high stage at the end of the room stood a small table and two chairs. The right-hand one was occupied - appropriately - by the Conservative leader and Provisional Prime Minister, Adam Tichbold; the left hand chair by the new Labour leader Gerry Farthing.

Surviving MPs had drifted in to form little tribal

cliques: the Tories opposite their new boss; Labour camped below Gerry Farthing; the Scots Nats somewhat further back; two Lib Dems looking rather forlorn at the sides. The solitary Green from Brighton was nowhere to be seen, the entire party wiped out by AfroAir.

Today there was no way Damian could sneak in to the top table, but he had managed to find a front row seat close to Bessie Robotham, who was back to her old self, efficient, in control, no sign of that weekend drunken lapse.

TV cameras and the press had been allocated space at the back in an area demarcated from that of the MPs. All rather *ad hoc* and amateurish, but this was the first time out and the system would no doubt be refined with experience.

Chloe Pettigrew sat with the rest of the press corps, who were now beginning to accept her as a familiar face, although still unsure where she fitted in. A Daily Mail lady columnist greeted her with a friendly "Hi there!", while the Sun man awarded her a leer.

As ten o'clock struck, Adam Tichbold banged on the table. The hubbub quickly died.

"As I said when addressing party members immediately after this catastrophe, I can hardly use the word 'welcome'." He spread his hands. "But what else can I say? So welcome to the task of rebuilding Britain's democracy. This, I need hardly say, encompasses everyone: Conservatives, Labour, Liberal Democrats, Scottish Nationalists, whichever party you've pledged your allegiance to. And to every nation within our United Kingdom: English, Scots, Welsh, Irish...." he smiled "....and to anyone else I've omitted to name."

"There will no doubt be arguments in the days ahead, but before that I want to place before you some figures:

human figures. The rescue services have been heroic and tell me that all the victims of the disaster have now been recovered. The death toll has been heavy, not only amongst our own, but also in the public and press galleries. I will confine myself to the list that just concerns us: the Members of Parliament."

Adam smoothed out a sheet of paper on the desk in front of him:

"The dead recovered from the ruins of the House of Commons chamber are as follows: Two Hundred and Thirty Nine from my party, the Conservatives...."

He paused to allow the collective gasp of horror to subside.

He continued: "One Hundred and Sixty Eight from Farthing's Labour party. Also Ten Lib Dems, Eleven SNP, Six Irish and one Green. Making a total of Four Hundred and Thirty Five."

There was silence as the room tried to take in the scale of the tragedy.

Then a voice from the back, the Reuter man again: "Does that mean everyone is accounted for? That you can now tell us how many people are left to make up this Provisional Parliament?"

"Indeed I can. Thanks to our esteemed Chief Whip, Bessie Robotham, who keeps tabs on such things, I'm happy to say that Seventy Nine Conservative MPs have survived and are now with us. Figures from the other parties are Fifty Five Labour, Thirty Three SNP, Two Lib Dems and Four from Ulster."

As people scribbled down these numbers, Reuter asked: "I make that a Parliament of One hundred and Seventy Three. Is that correct?"

"I believe so."

"In that case, your Conservative party no longer has a working majority," observed Reuter. "Only seventy nine members in a Parliament of over One Hundred and Seventy."

"Our job will be merely administrative," said Adam, irritably. "Arranging for a general election. And hopefuly selecting a larger venue for a permanent parliament. We do not anticipate any legislation during this period, so the usual party politics won't apply."

"No party politics!" said Reuter, *sotto voce*. "I'll believe *that* when I see it." There was an appreciative titter from his colleagues.

"However, there's *one* Parliamentary function we *must* attend to," continued Adam. "It would be quite improper for me as Prime Minister to chair these meetings. We must elect a new speaker. Jeremy Cauldwell is of course no longer with us and will be a hard act to follow. We need to find someone like him, able to stand above the hurly-burly of debate. Be impartial. Do I have any nominations?"

A moment for thought, then Bessie Robotham got to her feet: "If you want someone truly impartial, you can do no better than the member for Mid Oxfordshire, Damian White."

The hint of a snigger from the Tory ranks was quickly suppressed. Damian was considered impartial to the point of mutiny. Under normal circumstances this had placed him close to treason. For a Speaker it was ideal. Chloe started to clap, a most un-parliamentary thing to do, but this was hardly a normal parliament. It triggered a general burst of applause.

Damian was stunned. Got to his feet so that everyone could see him. Flapped his hands feebly. Until recently his relationship with the Chief Whip had been fraught, mostly confined to telling her why this or that Bill was rubbish and he would be voting against it: or at best abstaining. But chance had brought them together and, with the cause of friction now removed, they had got on rather well. If you collapse in a drunken stupor on someone's settee, it must mean something."

Damian's moment of glory did not last long. As the applause died, Gerry Farthing was heard from the top table:

"Thank you, Bessie. A most interesting nomination. I would now like to propose one from our side of the House. Although Speaker Cauldwell has been tragically lost to us, we're fortunate in still having one of our *Deputy* speakers. I'm referring of course to Angela Harding. Angela has won our respect for her handling of affairs on those days Jeremy was absent. I therefore commend her to you as the Speaker for this Provisional Parliament."

Once more Damian found himself on the wrong side of a vote. Angela Harding knew the ropes, was the obvious choice. He was secretly relieved; didn't think he was really Speaker material. Bessie had been quite wrong to describe him as 'impartial'. On the contrary, he had been far too *partial* for party discipline. Although he could never subscribe to Labour's vision of a Big State, there were also occasions when *his* party embarked on something idiotic. If that happened he saw no reason to support them.

So Ms. Harding was duly elected Speaker and took her place on the stage, while Adam and Gerry, the two party leaders, descended to the floor. The new Speaker was a prematurely greying lady in her fifties, dressed in comfortable tweeds and sensible flat shoes. She quickly established that the only agenda for what she called 'This Interim Parliament' was to arrange for a general election at the earliest possible date.   Adam Tichbold moved that there was nothing to discuss. The mechanism for general elections was well established. All they had to do was set the process in motion.

Gerry Farthing demurred, saying this should not be rushed and requesting forty eight hours for his party to consider the matter.

Tichbold was annoyed, but could hardly object to such a short delay. It was therefore agreed that the Interim Parliament should re-convene two days hence, at 10 am on Wednesday. They would then rubber-stamp the calling of a general election.

As Damian and Chloe walked off to find somewhere for lunch, she patted him consolingly on the back: "Never mind. You had your moment in the sun."

"Becoming a habit," he said. "Just brief moments: score a goal for West Ham and I'd get a couple of minutes of yelling; in Strictly Come Dancing it lasted a little longer. This time....well, I never really wanted the job."

"Brief moments add up," commented Chloe. "People get to know you... get to like you. Can't do any harm."

Ms. Pettigrew would turn out to be absolutely right.

24

The Labour party had always consisted of two contrasting streams: the 'coal face' and the 'classroom'. 1945 Prime Minister Clement Attlee had been a middle-class lawyer, a 'classroom' type; his Foreign Secretary Ernest Bevin a tough Trade Unionist from the 'coal face', who never knew his father. Later mismatches included university educated Tony Blair and former cabin steward John Prescott.

Of the Labour remnant now gathered in Central Hall Westminster, their new leader Gerry Farthing was from the 'classroom' branch. He had grown up in Winchester, where both his parents had been doctors, and had gone on to study medicine at Cambridge. An infection of socialism had brought out his humanitarian instincts, so after graduation he'd joined Médecins Sans Frontières, sparking a lifelong interest in matters beyond the confines of the British Isles. A politically minded wife had then brought him back to England and eventually a safe Labour seat in Birmingham.

While not as rebellious as the Tory member for Mid Oxon, Farthing was nevertheless something of a nonconformist. He had *ideas*, often strange and uncomfortable ones; fatal for advancement at Westminster. His thirty years in the Commons would not trouble historians when they came to write up the epics of our era.

Now into late middle age, a well-built and kindly soul, Gerry had taken refuge in his 'interests', which included, as we have seen, foreign affairs.

While Captain Osajefo was busy driving his Airbus into the Palace of Westminster, Farthing had been in Iran, a country that had attracted his special attention. No one could fathom why. After all, this was little more than a troublesome slab of colour on a map somewhere east of Suez.

But to Gerry Farthing it was ancient Persia, which had boasted a flourishing civilisation when Britons were still wandering around painted in woad. True, it had fallen on hard times, but the Shah was having some success bringing it into the 20th. century, when the roof fell in. And the country retreated to the Middle Ages.

Or so it appeared. But that wasn't the full story, because the flourishing middle class didn't disappear when the religious fanatics took over - well, some did, they emigrated - but most just kept their heads down. The tug-of-war between extremists and moderates had continued ever since, a complex drama, which Gerry did his best to keep abreast of. Hence his latest expedition. Iran's population greatly exceeded that of its southern neighbours, so it had *clout*. Forget history, what happened in Iran *today* mattered.

Gerry Farthing shook his head. Had to clear it of Iran clutter. Could come back to that later. Now another of his interests held centre stage. Totally unexpectedly. He was just off for a conclave with a few of his closest allies for some detailed plotting. To try and take advantage of a situation that might not occur again.

25

The second meeting of what Speaker Harding had named the *Interim* Parliament promised to be more low key than the first. Not only had the novelty worn off, but the only item on the agenda was the simple matter of dissolving the current Parliament and calling a general election. Boring stuff. Probably over in ten minutes.

One TV camera was there for the record. Also a handful of the press, those with little better to do. Amongst them was Chloe Pettigrew, who had her editor's blessing to continue working her contacts: Damian White, Adam Tichbold and Bessie Robotham. Even though excitement in that direction seemed to be over, Forrester was allowing her a few more days. Never could tell. Besides, there didn't seem to be any headlines worth pursuing around Oxford.

Chloe herself was becoming more interested in one particular contact rather than any news he might generate. *Much* nicer than her previous lovers. Worth hanging on to.

Speaker Harding opened the proceedings and invited the Prime Minister to address the House. Adam Tichbold got up and turned round to face his audience. It felt very strange having the whole house - or rather its surviving remnant - sitting there *in front of* him. He was used to having the weight of support, with encouraging 'hear hears', *behind* him. And the opposition benches - hopefully cowering under his onslaught - *in front of* him. Never mind, this weird situation would not last long. He would see to that. In a few words, the Prime Minister moved that he be given the authority to go to the king and request a dissolution of Parliament, so that fresh elections could be held. He sat down, well satisfied.

Speaker Harding then called the leader of the opposition.

Gerry Farthing was somewhat older than his opposite number, also broader in the beam and not nearly so well endowed in the hair department. Whereas Tichbold was like a greyhound, keen to leap out of the trap and race off, Farthing was more contemplative and professorial.

He now contemplated his audience for a good ten seconds before any words emerged. When he finally spoke it was to agree with the Prime Minister that a general election should be held at the earliest opportunity. It was a useful ploy to agree with your opponent before launching an attack.

Gerry Farthing then launched that attack with a single word: "However."

Another lengthy pause, then: "During the past two days I have been taking soundings. And it has become plain there is a mood for change. Elections in this country have altered little since the days of Gladstone and Disraeli. The same black tin boxes for votes, the same skewed results at the end. The MPs who troop into Westminster after an election never represent the true will of the people. One party may poll millions of votes and not get a single seat, another may win by a landslide on less than forty percent support. It's an absurd situation which cannot be allowed to continue."

"We have a crisis, man!" shouted Adam. "This is not the time for crazy experiments."

The speaker called for 'Order' and Adam simmered down, smoothing down his mane.

106

Farthing allowed the hubbub to subside, waited until he had their full attention again, before continuing:

"If the Prime Minister had bothered to venture beyond the Straits of Dover he would know that what he calls 'crazy experiments' are now commonplace. *We* are the political dinosaurs - and everyone knows what happened to the dinosaurs."

Before Farthing could say any more, Speaker Harding banged on the table and announced: "I think we have what might be called a spanner in the works. Most of us assumed this session would be speedily concluded with a simple motion to prorogue Parliament and call an election. That no longer seems to be the case. Both of you have expressed a desire for an election at the earliest opportunity and I shall hold you to that. On the other hand, we clearly need a short period for consultation. 'Short' being the operative word, I suggest we meet up again at ten tomorrow morning. Before we go, perhaps the Labour leader would give us some indication of what he has in mind to replace our present electoral system."

"Of course, Madame Speaker. Without boring everyone with detail, there are three main options. First a Party list system, as practised in much of Europe. Secondly Mixed Member Proportional, a combination of Party List and First-past-the-Post, this used since the war in Germany and more recently in New Zealand. And thirdly the Single Transferable Vote, or STV, Ireland's choice for the past hundred years. Far from being, in the Prime Minister's words, 'crazy experiments', these have been around for donkeys years and all ensure that the number of seats won is roughly proportional to votes cast. Our choice would be for STV, but I'm open to argument. The only thing that is not negotiable is that we carry on as before."

There was a brief hiatus, as everyone tried to absorb what they'd just heard. Then the Speaker said:

"Until tomorrow at ten, then. We need to do our homework. Class dismissed."

Not very parliamentary, but Madame Speaker had a sense of humour.

26

The formal part of the meeting might be over, but hardly anyone left the room. Party leaders and whips had asked their members to stay on so they could assess the mood, something that was more easily done while everyone was gathered in one place. Electoral reform had been background noise at Westminster for decades, but there had been little action: just a half-hearted attempt back in Cameron-Clegg coalition days to see if the Alternative Vote might appeal. As AV had nothing to do with proportionality it was a red herring and had duly sunk without trace.

Chloe spent the next few minutes sending a report back to her editor Forrester in Oxford, with the suggestion that he might try and sell it on to the any of the absent dailies; under her by-line, of course.

Damian registered his opinion with Chief Whip Bessie Robotham, more as a courtesy than anything else, as this was one of the many subjects on which they had previously clashed. The Tory establishment was against any change in the voting system; Damian and a sizeable minority of his colleagues thought it couldn't come soon enough.

Her piece to Forrester finished, Chloe was about to suggest that she and Damian went off for lunch, when she noticed Bessie plying her trade with a Tory MP. Poor old Bessie, a one-track existence with little visible home life. Could this be turned to the Pettigrew advantage?

Chloe touched Damian on the sleeve and said: "When Bessie has finished totting up the numbers, she'll need some R and R. Why don't you invite her round to your place again for dinner? I'll fix the food."

"Think she'll sign up for another hangover?"

Chloe shook her head. "Bessie's a big girl now. Will have learnt her lesson. But I think she needs to unwind. Not alone in some dingy West Ken cell, but with friends."

Damian grinned. "Friends without any ulterior motive?"

"I'm as ulterior as they come. So are you. But what's wrong with that? A good evening should be had by all."

"You're a conniving witch! And absolutely right."

So Damian popped the question, Bessie was delighted to accept and they agreed an earlier time of 6 pm. There would be much to talk about.

27

Damian's doorbell rang just as the BBC was getting into its stride with the latest political news. Again he ran down to help Bessie up the stairs, this time his task a little easier as he had forbidden any alcoholic baggage. Climbing the Pimlico mountain still left the Chief Whip out of breath, but she refused any spirited restorative; just an orange juice.

Bessie collapsed into a chair with a wheeze, like a balloon losing some air. Normally a sturdy woman, she seemed a tad diminished. The past few days had been draining for all of them, but especially so for those well on the wrong side of their half century.

"A rough day?" ventured Damian.

Bessie sipped her fruit juice, grimaced and replied: "I've had better. Adam's been impossible."

"Not as much support for the status quo as he'd hoped?"

"That's putting it mildly. Whenever the subject's come up in the past, we've never had any trouble keeping the troops in order. But now....."

"It's always been the establishment that was most scared of change," said Damian. "Now that most of our officers have been wiped out, we're seeing what the other ranks think."

"*Our* other ranks seem to be in a state of mutiny," said Bessie grimly. "I've spoken to all but two of them and if this was the army I'd have been ordering up firing squads. I suspect it's the same in the Labour camp. Apart from Gerry and a few of his mates, they've always supported us."

"So you think the motion to change to a proportional system will be passed?" asked Damian.

"Looks like it. Even if we and Labour manage fifty-fifty, which is doubtful, the other parties will likely decide the issue."

"Over thirty of the Haggis brigade are still alive and they've been using PR in the Edinburgh assembly for years," agreed Damian. "No fear of the unknown for them."

"You said Adam has been impossible. In what way?" asked Chloe.

"The Prime Minister insists that this Interim Assembly has no competence in the matter. That the Parliament elected at the last election would never have passed a Bill like the one proposed by Farthing. Adam says that if we want to change our electoral system that's fine, but it can only be done by a new parliament. And that must be one elected under current legislation."

"He has a point," said Damian.

"Maybe," replied Bessie. "But our former majority is now lined up in coffins. It's the living that make the rules."

"There must be lawyers who know those rules," said Chloe.

Bessie gave a hollow laugh. "*Of course* there are. In Westminster every second person wears a wig. They've spent the past few hours drowning me in legal argument, all of it contradictory."

"No precedent for losing three quarters of our lawmakers," observed Damian.

Bessie nodded. "You know the saying: to the victor the spoils. We may not have been at war, but the principle's the same: it'll be the victors - the survivors - who decide what we do next."

"So the last election no longer matters?" asked Chloe.

"The dead have lost the right to vote," replied Damian. "Adam may not like the idea, but that's the fact."

"So you and Gerry can do what you like?"

Damian smiled. Chloe had put into words a notion that had been germinating in his mind for a while. He replied: "Until another parliament has been elected those of us who are left represent the will of the people. What we decide becomes the law. Or so it seems to me."

They went around in circles with this argument a while longer until Chloe called a halt. Time for dinner. Salmon steak, peas, parsley, new potatoes. Bessie agreed to partake of some South African Sauvignon Blanc, asking them to make sure she didn't overdo it.

Chloe then announced that politics and food didn't mix and banned further discussion until they'd finished. Conversation turned instead to Damian's old club West Ham, which had been enjoying its usual rocky ride. Although many years since the move from Upton park, they had never really settled into their new Olympic stadium. Their most recent disaster had been a three nil home defeat by Leeds, of all sides. After years in the lower leagues, Leeds had acquired a charismatic new manager from Argentina, who had managed to drag them back into the Premiership. This latest result had left West Ham just three points clear of the drop zone, a cause of much concern to Damian, who expounded at length on the reasons for their plight and his suggestions for rectifying the situation.

Chloe was clearing the plates, Damian wondering which single malt to select, when the phone rang.

"Gerry?.... Ah, yes. *That* Gerry. What can I do for you?"

Damian signalled for some hush and sat down. The new leader of the opposition was known to him only by name and reputation. He had often seen him in the Chamber and the corridors of Westminster, but their paths had never crossed verbally. Gerry Farthing was from a different party, a different generation. They appeared to have now found electoral common ground, but...?

"Hope I'm not disturbing you?" said the voice from the other end.

"No, no, just finished dinner. I'm all yours."

"Just been crunching the numbers, expect you've been doing the same," began Farthing in his donnish voice.

"Yea, looks a close call."

"In our camps, maybe. But if you add the Picts and Paddies it'll be no contest. We have them by the short and curlies."

"You may be right. Bessie's of the same opinion."

"Is Madame Robotham with you?

"She is. Sitting opposite, in her full glory."

"That's convenient. You see, I have a problem...."

"Very well, I can take a hint. Where are you phoning from?"

"I reckon about ten minutes away."

"Okay, come on over...."

"Confidences guaranteed? My lot would do terrible things to me were they to hear I'd been consorting with the Robotham."

"Our lips will be sealed. Promise. Unless you give us the nod."

"Does that include your new and lovely personal assistant from the Dreaming Spires?"

"You know about her?" Damian was shaken.

"My dear fellow, Westminster may be a model of inefficiency, but its rumour mill is world class."

"Yes, that includes Ms. Pettigrew...." He glanced across at Chloe, who had given the thumbs up. "She says Scout's honour - maybe that should be Brownie's honour."

"Excellent. See you in a jiffy." The line went dead.

28

Judging by his ascent of the Pimlico alps Gerry Farthing was in better shape than the Tory Chief Whip. But there wasn't much in it. By the time Damian ushered him in, the Labour leader's brow was distinctly moist, his breathing as laboured as the party he represented. Compared with the sartorial splendour of the Interim Prime Minister who always wore an impeccable suite and waistcoat, Farthing was a mess. To say that he had *selected* a pullover to wear under his jacket would be inaccurate. Gerry didn't so much select his clothing as simply grab what had been discarded the night before. This tended to be comfortable rather than snappy. And none too clean.

The leader of the opposition accepted a large Glenfiddich, then slumped into a chair with a sigh.

"What can we help you with?" asked Damian.

"It's your boss, the PM."

"Yes...? And...?"

"Foolish of him to rush off to Buck House like that, get himself anointed by His Maj before he knew the numbers."

"You mean the makeup of the surviving Parliament?"

Farthing nodded. "When we had a full house you had a majority - just. Not always easy, but you managed to push through most of the Bills you really wanted. You may still be the largest party, but now that overall majority is gone. Might not have mattered had Tichbold seen sense with the only item on our agenda, electoral reform, but he's decided to be bloody minded. Thwart the will of the majority. It really won't do."

"You can always demand a vote of no confidence," said Damian. "If you win, off he goes."

Farthing squirmed. "Yes, as a last resort. But it would be much....cleaner if you could settle the whole thing internally."

"Good God! You want us to stage a palace revolution?"

Gerry smirked. "Why not? It's something the Tories are rather good at. The name Thatcher springs to mind."

"By the end Thatcher had leaked a lot of goodwill," said Damian. "But everyone was *very* enthusiastic when we elected Tichbold. No way we could get rid of him even if we wanted to."

"It's not often that I agree with the leader of the opposition," said Bessie, entering the fray. "But I think this is an avenue worth exploring."

Anything that might scupper Tichbold was worth a try, so she continued: "It's true that a lot of hands went up when Adam was elected, but if he is seen as a stumbling block - a barrier to the will of the people, that could change. Nowadays it can be from hero to zero overnight."

"Who would replace Tichbold?" asked Damian, beginning to get annoyed. "He stands head and shoulders above anyone else." Another thought struck him: "You're surely not angling for the job yourself, Gerry?"

"Good grief, no! I'd hate it. Not PM material. Even if I were, the country's leader *must* come from within the largest party. Not that this always happens under PR, but we're not yet ready for such a big leap."

"If not Tichbold, whom *do you* want?"

"You would do nicely."

"Me?" Damian was stunned. "Don't be ridiculous! I'm a simple backbencher and likely to stay that way. Never been near a red box."

"It may have escaped your notice but almost all the red boxes have been eliminated. I believe only three are left on your side of the House: the one we're trying to jettison, Tichbold: Bessie, who I suspect is as un-keen as me....?

Madly signalling negatives, Robotham blurted out: "Don't even *think* about me."

"...Finally there's Jasper whats-his-name from Culture and Sport. Who's a joke."

"So you're scraping the bottom of the barrel and my name came up," said Damian.

"What's bitten you?" asked Gerry, puzzled. "I'm offering you the ultimate prize and you're off in a huff."

"The poor boy is in shock," said Bessie. "He'll get over it. Leave it to me."

Support from the Chief Whip? Now he was really in shock!

"You tick all the boxes from our point of view," persisted Gerry. "Not part of the Tory establishment and a well-known supporter of fair votes."

"You forget one thing," said Damian. "Mistress Harding, our new Speaker, has ordered us back to the classroom in just a few hours: ten tomorrow morning. No time for us - or anyone - to put any pressure of the PM."

"That had occurred to me," said Farthing. "So we've prepared a delaying action. I wanted a few words so you'd be aware of our intentions. If Tichbold refuses to budge, we intend to remove him. I believe we can muster enough votes to do it. But we'd rather put things off for a few days and let you do the dirty work. However it's managed, this temporary PM must be....well, *very* temporary. When he's gone, we'd be happy to work with someone like you."

"Can you give me, say, three days?" asked Bessie, a gleam in her eye. Revenge was all the sweeter when served very cold - after a gap of forty years.

"Under the circumstances I'm sure Speaker Harding will allow us a little grace," replied Farthing. "Reckon you can de-throne Adam in that time?"

"I'll have a damned good try."

"Good girl," Farthing started levering himself into an upright position.

But Damian had regained control over his thoughts and indicated he wasn't finished: "One more thing, just a suggestion. At present we only have one item on our agenda, right?"

Farthing nodded: "A fairer voting system for the next election."

"Why just that one item?"

Everyone looked puzzled.

Finally Bessie answered: "Obvious, I'd have thought: we need another election to fill all those empty seats and my old opponent over there insists we do so under a new voting system."

"Let me put it another way," persisted Damian. "We are assuming those of us that are left have the power to change electoral law, so why stop there?"

"What else do you want to change?" asked Chloe.

"How long is a piece of string? Are you, Gerry, a fan of the House of Lords?"

"Good grief, no! Long past its sell-by date. A disgrace."

"And look at the way the House of Commons votes: first the division bells clang, *then* we rush into the division lobbies, *then* they physically count us - a monumental waste of time."

"You want electronic voting?"

"Of course! This is the twenty first century, for God's sake! Then there's the geography of the Commons chamber itself, designed for yelling at each other face to face: no one else does it like that any longer...."

"You appear to have let loose a rebel," said Bessie. "Sure you want him as our next PM?"

Farthing smiled. "If Damian carries on like this they'll think he's one of our lot. Anyway, Bessie, your job now is to fix Mr. Tichbold. Think you can manage?"

"You bet!" she replied with relish.

"Well, *mine* is to slow the election bandwagon long enough for you to achieve it," said Farthing. "After that, we might be able to consider anything else Damian has up his sleeve.

29

The meeting of the Interim Parliament next morning did not last long. The leader of the opposition asked for a further adjournment on the grounds of 'unexpected difficulties', which the Prime Minister, aware of the precariousness of his position, did not oppose.

At first Madame Speaker was reluctant to agree, so Farthing pointed out that some countries might go for weeks, even months, without any formal government, if they had difficulties constructing a coalition. A parliament, he reminded the House, was a legislature, not an executive, which in the UK comprised the prime minister and his cabinet, who were on call 24/7.

In a retreat from his previous call for an election 'in the shortest possible time', Farthing now suggested it would be wise to take a little longer and get it right. Speaker Harding had to agree and set the next meeting for the following Monday.

Both sides went back to their members for some hard figures on which way a vote for change would go. They also contacted the smaller parties who held the balance. On Saturday evening Bessie Robotham phoned her Labour opposite number to compare notes. They were a close match and put the matter beyond doubt. Any proposal to change the electoral system to a proportional one would be passed by a margin of about thirty. A decisive figure in their reduced assembly of 170.

Damian and Chloe were in his Pimlico apartment having dinner when Bessie rang to tell them the news.

"Where does this leave Adam?" asked Damian.

"In difficulties," replied Bessie. "We have a Prime Minister who says he is opposed to what is clearly the majority opinion of the House. He can either change his mind, depart gracefully or be thrown out. Someone needs to talk to him. That someone obviously can't be me. Nor Gerry. So you, Damian, have been volunteered. I've told Adam you would like to see him and he said that'd be fine. Go down to his place tomorrow and have a chat."

"Go down where? Isn't he in Number Ten?"

He's in Number Ten during the week - sort of. Trouble is, the old PM's widow wasn't expecting her husband to be flattened by a rogue flying object, so had made no provision for being thrown out of house and home. Adam has done the decent thing and let her stay on for a few days while she gets things sorted. She should be out by Monday, meanwhile Adam's off for the weekend to his Berkshire estate. He's awaiting your call to fix the details. This is his private number: Ready to copy....?"

Five minutes later Damian had been connected to the Prime Minister, who was all the gracious host. Of course he'd be *delighted* to discuss matters with him. Pack an overnight bag. And *do* bring that lovely little scribe of yours... what was her name again?"

"Chloe Pettigrew."

"Yes, Chloe. Also welcome to stay the night." With the flow of history running against him, Tichbold wanted events recorded to his advantage. He had usually been able to charm the media at least halfway to his way of thinking and this Pettigrew girl was young and therefore malleable; easily influenced by an alpha male like himself.

30

Damian didn't keep a car in London, where it was a hindrance rather than a means of transport, so he and Chloe took a train to Reading, the nearest station to the Tichbold estate. There they were met by a prime ministerial limousine, which took some twenty minutes to convey them to a large mock Tudor house set in rolling country. To the left were some outbuildings, probably stables, with an adjacent paddock; to the right an expanse of lawn; behind, well away from the house, was some rough ground which gave way to an area of woodland.

The car crunched round the semi-circular drive, coming to a stop by the front door, through which the prime minister emerged to greet them.

"One of the perks of office," he commented, pointing to the car and driver. "Come, let me take your bag." He grabbed Chloe's overnight grip, at the same time awarding her his most dazzling smile; the smile that made women go weak at the knees and won elections. Damian might have been invisible.

"Hermione - my wife - suggests we have a quick cold collation," he continued. "Then I'll show you around. After that, perhaps a brisk walk: it's such a splendid day...."

The weather had in fact turned up trumps. The storm which had inadvertently caused London's tower to lean had long since disappeared towards Norway and they were now enjoying a temporary ridge of high pressure. It was the sort of glorious English scene in which Inspector Morse or Hercule Poirot could have counted on for at least a couple of corpses by teatime. Unfortunately, the day would probably remain murder-less; arsenic in the prime minister's 'cold collation' would have solved a lot of problems, but Damian doubted whether he could get away with it. PMs these days had *security*.

In the hallway they were greeted by Hermione, tall, slim, dark-haired, an English rose, who in middle age retained much of her youthful bloom. She was wearing an apron with "THE BOSS" inscribed across her bosom. To prove the point, she took Chloe's bag from her husband and with a "Let's get rid of these" over her shoulder led the way up the stairs.

The house was more 'Mock' than 'Tudor', probably built during the 1930s. It had double glazing and rooms high enough for even Adam to stand upright in. Not a mediaeval structure. Damian was further impressed when Hermione showed them to their room, which was light and airy with a large *double* bed. Mrs. Tichbold, an avid fan of 'Strictly', was of the opinion that wife Mandy had been over-hasty and Damian hard done by: a man that could do with a new woman in his life.

Lunch was spent in idle gossip, Adam loath to open the Pandora's box of politics until they were alone. Just after two o'clock he led them to the back door, where a parade of green wellies, mud-less and sparkling, stood ready for use. Adam slipped his feet into the master's pair, inviting Damian and Chloe to find some that suited them.

"Still a bit soggy out there," he explained.

As they set off towards the outbuildings, Damian realised they were being shadowed by two bulky figures in their forties.

"I call them Bill and Ben", explained Adam. "Here to see no one bumps me off."

Bill and Ben smiled grimly and followed them.

"Let's say hello to the cavalry," suggested Adam, as they approached the head of a horse, who was viewing them from above a stable door. "Her name's Fidget and she's partial to sugar."

He produced a handful of sugar lumps from a pocket, gave a couple to Chloe and said: "Go on. You'll be friends for life. So says Hermione. Don't understand it myself. If a dog wants to be your friend for life he'll jump up and lick you. A cat will settle down on your lap and start purring. A horse...? Well, just look at Fidget here, munching away without as much as a thank you. They also crap all over the place, again unlike cats and dogs. Hermione says I'm insensitive to horses. She's probably right. Usually is."

Meanwhile Damian's attention had been caught by a red rosette pinned on the next stable door. Pointing to it, he said: "I thought you were true blue Adam? What's this sign of the opposition doing on your territory?"

"Ah yes. Very sad. It's Hermione's *in memoriam* to dear departed Clipper."

"Clipper?"

Her grey gelding. Hadn't been able to ride him much recently, that's why she bought Fidget. Why a red rosette? Well, at horsey shows they give out these baubles as prizes, so this is her tribute to him: red for first. For God's sake don't leak my guilty secret to the opposition."

Sugar lumps ingested, Fidget still showed no sign of being grateful, so they moved off. Adam led the way towards the deciduous woodland about a hundred yards away up a slight slope. Bill and Ben followed at a respectful distance.

"Don't suppose you've come to hear me talk about

horses," began the Prime Minister.

Damian laughed. "No, I've come as bringer of tidings - whether good or bad will depend. You've no doubt heard about the straw poll, which showed a clear majority in favour of change to some form of PR. Majority of about thirty it's reckoned, so no chance we'll be sticking to first-past-the-post."

"Did Gerry say *which* system they're talking about?"

"He wants STV, like they have in Ireland. Looks like he'll get his way."

"Bit of a dark horse, Gerry. Been around a long time, so more influence than you might think."

"Gerry and Bessie have asked me to come and sound you out. See if you'd be prepared to change your mind. The next election *will be* under a fresh set of rules, so why not jump on the bandwagon and lead the way?"

For a while the Adam did not reply. They reached the edge of the woodland, started up a path that was slippery with mud and exposed tree roots; just the job for green wellies. Bill and Ben, equipped only with shoes, were finding the going tough.

At last Tichbold said: "Every politician dreams of one day landing the top job. I got here by a quirk of fate. Looks like another quirk will make my tenure a short one."

"Not if you bow to the inevitable," said Damian. "Nothing wrong with U-turns if circumstances change."

"But circumstances *have not* changed. Just because we've lost most of the old guard doesn't mean we have to submit to those that are left. I've always said this next election should be held under existing rules, any change to those rules having to be passed by the *next* parliament. If I said anything else now it would be seen as opportunism."

"So what are you going to do?"

"Sleep on it. If I'm of the same mind tomorrow, my position will become untenable. I shall resign. The party will have to elect a new leader. And the country a new prime minister. Which may not be the same person. That idiot who crashed into parliament deprived us of our majority. Now any leader must enjoy not only the support of his own party, but also the House as a whole."

"Let's hope your sleep guides you in the right direction," said Damian. "In the meantime here's something else to think about. Do you have any pet hates? Anything in public life you'd like to change?"

"You must be joking! I'd change the whole shooting match. Tradition is all well and good, but it can become fossilised. I'd start again from scratch: keep the good bits, ditch what's out of date."

"Excellent! That's exactly what we'd like to do."

"What do you mean?"

"MPs usually spend their time pouring over details of coming legislation: first reading, second reading, report stage, back and forth to the lords. The whole thing takes forever. Now, just for once, we have no run-of-the mill stuff to consider. There's a clean sheet. Why not write something dramatic on that virgin sheet? Gerry wants to get rid of the House of Lords or at least radically change it. We have a once-in-a-lifetime opportunity to do something dramatic. Maybe many things dramatic."

They slithered up another hundred yards, Bill and Ben in town shoes struggling in their wake. Then the prime minister stopped. The rest of the party did likewise.

Adam stood there amongst the beeches and hornbeams, his height accentuated by being further up the slope. With a smile, he asked: "How does our little Lenin propose getting his ideas passed into law? Or are you thinking of calling out the red guard?"

Damian grinned: "We have no plans to guillotine His Majesty and the aristos. Just want to test the waters, see what can be done in these peculiar circumstances."

The prime minister paused for a moment, looking down at the little gathering amongst the trees. Then he said: "I like it! Shows promise. I need some time for thought, so let's go back to the ranch. We'll thrash out some ideas over dinner."

Tichbold led the way in an about turn, Bill and Ben stoically bringing up the rear, their town shoes now a sodden mess.

31

They reconvened at aperitif time in the Tichbold lounge, the oak beamed ceiling high enough for modern man to stand erect, the windows large enough to allow reading by daylight. The mantelpiece collection consisted of half a dozen items of travel memorabilia plus two small silver trophy cups. The pictures reflected the contrasting tastes of the owners: *hers* were of horses - one of them a Stubbs? Surely not; *his* some Edward Seago skyscapes.

Bill and Ben were not there, maybe busy patrolling the estate, so it was just the four of them. Hermione had produced some Tesco nibbles. Adam had dispensed drinks: G&Ts for the ladies, Scotch for the men. Chloe had changed into a beguiling long skirt and multi-coloured top, a hit with Hermione.

The prime minister's wife started things off by saying: "Don't know what you two have done to my husband, but he's spent the afternoon locked up in his study. And is now looking amazingly cheerful, considering the circumstances."

"Cleared my mind," Adam announced. "Earlier I didn't know what was best. Should I or shouldn't I? Go or stay? Things are now much clearer."

"So you'll stay?" asked Damian, assuming that was what his good humour meant.

"You'll have to wait a moment for the punch line," replied the prime minister with a smile. "First let me lead you through how I got there. Damian asked me if I had any pet hates, so I'll pass the parcel: what do *you* think they are, my dear?"

Hermione considered it for a moment. Replied: "You're forever on about *something* Adam, but if I had to pick *one* I'd say you're too impatient."

"I plead guilty. We live in age of paralysis where getting anything done is well-nigh impossible. When I say 'we' I mean here in Britain. Tiger nations like China take about one tenth of the time we do. It wasn't always so. When Mountbatten went to India in Forty Seven to arrange for independence sometime in the distant future, he was so appalled by what he saw that he had the whole thing done and dusted within six months: too fast some said, but my point is he didn't hang about. Then there was a lady called Ruth Ellis, in the Fifties if memory serves: shot her lover in April, tried and found guilty in June, hanged by the neck in July. No dithering there either. Again, maybe a little *too* fast. But now...? Well, there was a fellow called Chilcot, told to merely pen a few words about the Iraq war: it took him over six years! Six *years* to write a report! I rest my case."

"Difficult to ditch entrenched habits," said Damian.

"I thought that was what you were about? A complete makeover?" said the prime minister with a sly grin.

"Well, yes..... We already seem to have enough support to change the voting system. While we're at it, I thought we might try out a few more ideas. Getting things done faster is an excellent one. We'll add it to our agenda."

"There's one problem," said Tichbold. "I can't be the one to lead us into the promised land."

"Why not? Aren't you the prime minister?"

"At the moment, yes. But I carry too much political baggage. We're living in a strange new world where normal party differences have become blurred and the Tories no longer have an overall majority. The opposition don't trust me: quite rightly. And I don't trust *them*. We need someone from the middle ground."

"Like who?"

"Maybe like you, Damian."

"I'm far too young. And not well enough known." This was becoming absurd! First the Labour leader had suggested him for the top job, now it was the Tory leader.

"Pitt the Younger became prime minister at twenty four," Tichbold pointed out. "Compared to him you're geriatric. As for not being well known, maybe it has escaped your notice but virtually everyone in the public eye has been eliminated. Just three of us from the old cabinet are left: Bessie and I, who are ruling ourselves out; and Jasper from Media and Sport, who's is a cretin. Next one to take over is *bound to* be unknown."

"Actually, Damian is very *well* known," said Chloe. "Not as an MP perhaps, but when he was with West Ham: and then Strictly…."

"I *always* voted for him on Strictly," added Hermione. "I'll bet more people have heard of Damian than Adam."

Damian mumbled; "Don't know what to say."

Adam laughed. "A politician who doesn't know what to say? Get a grip on yourself, man!"

Hermione: "Don't be too hard on him, dear. The poor boy's had a shock."

"I spent the afternoon thinking…."continued Adam.

Hermione, softly: "….is that what you were up to?"

Adam, taking no notice of his wife: "And I noticed something interesting. At the end of the last war, when much of the world lay in ruins, which countries then did the best?"

Hermione: "America."

"Of course. But which others?"

Damian, thoughtfully: "Germany?"

"Exactly! The Marshal plan got their economy going again, but after that it was thanks to their own efforts. One day they were out for the count, the next they were flogging us VW Beetles. Same with Japan. No sooner had they been nuked, the country a wasteland, than they were turning out transistor radios at knock-down prices. Overnight transformations."

"What's your point?" asked Damian.

"That sometimes we *need* a good catastrophe to shake us up. Heard of the Black Death?"

Damian: "Yea, way back. Lots of people died. Nasty business."

"Nasty at the time, no doubt. But it killed off the feudal system by making the labourer worthy of his hire. It was the start of the modern world. That's one theory, anyway."

"So you think our political cull might be an opportunity?" asked Damian.

The prime minister nodded. "Fourteenth century plagues and twentieth century wipe-outs seem to have had unexpected benefits. We've now seen most of our top people annihilated. Disasters on such a scale don't happen too often. It would be a crime to let this one go to waste."

"So what do you suggest we do next?" asked Damian.

"We spend the rest of the evening enjoying my hospitality, then a good night's sleep. Tomorrow we travel to London in the prime ministerial limousine to attend the next meeting of our Interim parliament. Where, for the reasons just given, I will announce my resignation."

"Shock horror all round," said Damian.

"No doubt." Tichbold thought for a moment. "Madame Speaker will then have to announce another adjournment, so that a new prime minister can be found. Gerry Farthing has already said that his Labour party does not have sufficient support for the next PM to come from *his* party; indeed he's indicated that the next leader will *have to* be someone from our ranks."

"Another meeting in the Attlee suite?" asked Damian.

"I would think so." The prime minister smiled. "Where I shall nominate our member for Mid Oxfordshire, Damian White, as my successor. It will of course be up to the rest of the Conservative members to decide who shall take my place, but you must stand a good chance."

"I still don't get it," said Damian. "Why do you want *me*?"

"It's not that *I want you*," said the prime minister. "You're a rebel, who takes little notice of the party whip, so in normal circumstances you'd be my last choice. But the numbers now point to a coalition, where that sort of bloody-mindedness will appeal to other parties and so become an asset."

Damian smiled. "In spite of that two-edged compliment, I hope you'll still join us in our adventure. Speeding up Britain's creaking joints could be your baby."

"I don't intend missing it for anything". Adam Tichbold raised his glass. "Cheers!"

32

Next morning the prime ministerial limousine set off early to beat the rush hour, Adam in front with the driver, Damian and Chloe in the back. It was another beautiful morning, although the forecast was for more fronts to sweep in by dusk.

They made it to Central Hall Westminster by 9.30, to find the place already buzzing, Conservatives gathering to the right, Labour on the left. The press and TV were out in strength, keen to capture the moment Britain changed its electoral system. Prime Minister Tichbold was smiling and chatting to colleagues, so it was assumed he had overcome any reservations he might have had and would be leading the charge.

At 9.55 Speaker Angela Harding ascended the centre stage and sat down on the single chair behind the table. She was dressed in a corporate style blue suit and appeared to have recently paid a visit to her hairdresser.

At 10 am the babble of conversation began to die. Speaker Harding banged twice on the table and the room fell silent. She was opening her mouth to speak when she - and the rest of the House - saw that Prime Minister Tichbold was on his feet.

This was most irregular. The Speaker ran the business of the House, always had done. However, Tichbold was

134

clearly determined to have his say. This was only an *Interim* parliament after all, not a proper one, so the speaker did not argue the point, just said icily: "Yes, Prime minister?"

"I crave your indulgence, Madame Speaker, but before we start on today's business it's only proper that I make a personal statement."

"Very well." Harding was still not pleased.

Adam Tichbold turned to face his audience. As always he was immaculately turned out in a bespoke grey suit and triangle of blue peeping out of a top pocket. His long black hair had been trimmed to the millimetre and showed no hint of grey.

"Colleagues, ladies and gentlemen," he began. "There's just one item on today's agenda: that the system for electing our members be changed to the one known as the Single Transferable Vote. Were I leader of the party with the backing of most of us in this room, there would have been no problem. However, fate has cut a swathe of death through our ranks, most cruelly affecting my party. As a result we, the Conservatives, no longer command a majority amongst the living."

Adam paused. By now most people had guessed what was coming. TV cameras had zoomed in to close-ups of his face. Everyone held their breath.

"My views on today's motion are well known," he continued. "I'm against it. Our parliament has succeeded throughout the centuries by *not* changing things too hastily. Had we been afforded enough time to debate the matter properly, with a *full* - I repeat a full - quota of members, I might have been persuaded. But that is not the case. This motion seeks to radically alter the way we do business. It should not be approved without proper scrutiny. Or by a rump parliament denuded of full membership. I therefore have no option but to resign as prime minister." He sat down.

Let's now roll out that corniest of clichés: you could have heard a pin drop.

Speaker Harding finally broke the silence: "Mr. Tichbold, has your party had the chance to decide on your successor?"

On his feet again, Adam replied: "I only made up my mind on the way here, so the answer in no. However, the possibility has been discussed with close friends, so I would like to offer a suggestion: or rather two suggestions."

Speaker Harding nodded for him to continue.

"Normal practice is for the governing party to select its new leader and for that person to then be offered to parliament. However, these are *not* normal times. With no party enjoying an overall majority, my successor must be someone acceptable to a broad spectrum of opinion; in other words, he or she should be chosen from everyone in this room."

Speaker Harding: "Very well, that sounds sensible. And your other suggestion?"

"I would like to nominate the member for Mid Oxfordshire, Damian White, as the next leader of the Conservative party."

"Indeed!" Speaker Harding could not conceal her surprise.

Before she could say any more, Gerry Farthing was on his feet: "Madam Speaker, I would like to second that. Mr. White would also be most acceptable to those of us on this side of the House."

There was a stunned silence. When Madame Speaker found her voice again, she asked: "Are there any further nominations?"

It was in effect a rhetorical question. If a candidate

already had the support of *both* major parties, no one else was going to put their head above the parapet.

However, Adam Tichbold was not finished: "A final observation, Madame Speaker. Although I believe Mr. White is the person best suited to guide us through the present impasse, I reserve the right to challenge him for the leadership when we again have a full and properly functioning parliament."

"Observation noted." Speaker Harding was beginning to lose patience with him. She continued: "The motion is that the member for Mid Oxfordshire, Damian White, be elected leader of the conservative party. And Prime Minister. In the absence of division lobbies, we'll try a show of hands. Those in favour?"

A forest of hands went up. From every political area.

"I'd like this properly recorded," insisted the speaker. "Will the three main parties each select someone to do a count. When their figures tally, report back to me."

By this most interim method it was established that Damian White MP had the support of 103 surviving members of parliament, a clear vote of confidence.

"I hereby declare Damian White to have been duly elected to serve as our prime minister," said Speaker Harding. "He will see His Majesty the King to receive the seals of office at the first available opportunity. Meanwhile, may we get back to the matter in hand? Our one and only agenda item: a change in the way we elect the members of this parliament."

33

This was the cue for Gerry Farthing to get up and give a resumé of how STV would work, single member constituencies being replaced by larger ones that elected several members, typically between three and six. Instead of marking ballot papers with a cross, voters would be invited to indicate a numerical preference. To those that said this was too complex, the answer was simple: Ireland had been using the system for the past century. If Paddy could cope, so could we. STV was voter-friendly, fair and practical. He recommended it to the House, which immediately passed it: a first reading majority of 27.

Speaker Harding then asked Farthing how he was going to process his Bill through the Lord's for their scrutiny, seeing that the Nobles no longer had a chamber and had not met since the disaster. Although the imposing red-tiered benches of the Lords had escaped AfroAir's impact, Health and Safety had visited the scene and pronounced the whole Palace of Westminster unsafe, a decision some said should have been taken years ago. Whereas the Commons had immediately got back to business, the Lords, average age nearly 80, had simply dozed off and done nothing.

Gerry Farthing had long wanted to get rid of the second chamber and now saw his opportunity. He replied that the Lords appeared to be defunct. He saw no reason why his Bill need trouble an organisation that had died.

"You mean to ignore the Lords' scrutiny stage?" asked

the Speaker.

"I do," he replied. "If the next parliament wants to resuscitate the victim, that will be up to them. For now we have work to do and can't afford to wait."

As Farthing sat down, Tichbold rose to congratulate the leader of the opposition on his keenness to get things done. But surely, said Adam, the transformation of the electoral system could not be done *that* fast? It was a complex process that would take a while to complete. As he posed the question Adam was aware that he was in a quandary. He was looking forward to freeing up Britain's sclerotic bureaucratic arteries, but - ironically - this could not be done overnight. UK plc was not a Ferrari that could be accelerated from nought to sixty in four seconds: it was more like a twenty-year-old Ford that would need some coaxing to get it up to speed. So he was relieved to hear Gerry reply that they would seek to implement STV 'as fast as was humanly possible'. That was probably code for several months. Plenty of time, Adam reflected, to have some fun sorting out the sloths.

Speaker Harding wound up the meeting with the observation that the Report stage and Second Reading of the Bill they had just passed would now be completed without any reference to the Lords. Finally, was there Any Other Business?

Damian White, rising for first time as prime minister, replied:

"There is, Madame Speaker. Although STV is simple to use, its implementation will, as we have heard, take time. Constituencies will have to be merged, boundaries may have to be redrawn. As has been said, 'we need to get it right'. This will primarily be a job for the Whitehall Mandarins, leaving us, as representatives of the people, with time on our hands. I see no reason why we should remain idle. My cabinet will therefore seek to use this time profitably; see if there are further ways to haul this country into the twenty first century."

"So this STV Bill will not be our Interim Parliament's only piece of legislation?" asked the Speaker.

"No. I intend to find further work to keep us occupied," replied Prime Minister White. "My colleague Mr. Tichbold tells me he is an impatient man, so Secretary of State for Speed should be a title to suit him nicely. You will appreciate, Madame Speaker, that I wasn't prepared for the situation I now find myself in, so you will have to wait a day or two for details. I will only say this: don't go home and put your feet up. We shall meet again."

34

Speaker Harding finished their business in time for lunch, which for newly elected Prime Minister White consisted of a hastily eaten chicken and salad sandwich. There was much to do before bedtime.

His first task was to make the short journey to Buckingham Palace for the ritual of 'Kissing hand'. No such unsanitary encounter actually takes place. Nowadays it merely signifies the sovereign's acceptance of a new prime minister; a chance to have a chat and for both sides to size each other up. Damian thought the king was not ageing well, his facial colour too high, his demeanour harassed. The meeting was civil enough and ended with the monarch offering his usual opinions on how to run the country, an unconstitutional foible which everyone accepted and then ignored.

After that, it was back into the prime ministerial limousine to see his new London home, No.10 Downing Street. Over lunch, in fact as soon as his election became known, Damian had received a call from Jacob Wells, Director General of MI5, who had insisted he take up residence with immediate effect.

Recent events had taken their toll of the security boss. Never a large man, he seemed to have lost even more weight. The immediate aftermath of the crash had been bad enough. Jacob's complaint during those first hours of chaos that 'he'd had no one to report to' had been well founded. If Andorra or San Marino had suffered a similar cull of its upper echelons, the world would have continued to spin on its axis, but a state as complex and wealthy as the United Kingdom couldn't afford to be rudderless for even a few minutes, never mind hours.

When, by late evening of that terrible day, Tichbold had finally been confirmed as the country's next supremo, the Director General had breathed a little easier. But his problems were not over. His suggestion that Tichbold should make haste to take up residence in Number Ten had been casually received. Not only was the dead PM's widow in a state of collapse, thus in the short term immovable, but Tichbold had other things on his mind. A house move was not a priority. He had paid a brief visit to No.10 to be shown the ropes, but continued to live in his country estate.

Jacob Wells could not have cared less about a prime minister's domestic life. That No.10 was supposed to be his London home was beside the point. The crucial fact was that this was the place from where Britain was governed. It was a communications hub. It was fortress. It was *secure*. Or at any rate as secure as anyone could make it in this age of terrorism. Every prime minister should therefore consider it his castle.

At one time Joe Yokel, up in London for the day, could wander into Downing Street to be photographed standing outside Number Ten. Those days were long gone. The *whole* of Downing Street was now an armed camp, safe from any invasion below the strength of an army corps.

Jacob Wells had already suffered enough sleepless nights and was determined that this new prime minister should toe the security line. Do as he was told. The size and shape of his entourage didn't matter. He'd heard that White had split from his wife and had a new girlfriend. No problem. He could have every loose woman in London for all he cared, as long as Numero Uno was safely tucked up in Number Ten *with* her.

Prime Minister White wasn't interested in loose women, but he *was* interested in *his* woman. Whom, he realised with something of a start, was Chloe Pettigrew. Mandy had been gone too long from his life for there to be any hope of reconciliation; according to rumour she now had a live-in boyfriend. Damian still saw his children pretty regularly, but that was it. Under normal circumstances a new love would have been a big event, but so much had been happening that Chloe had crept up on him unawares.

Now he had to give her serious thought. He remembered her comment about having had two husbands and losing her men rather easily. Clearly not a clingy type. So although he was becoming more than a little fond of Chloe, if things should not work out long term, a parting of the ways would not appear to present a problem.

With the philosophy of enjoying their partnership while they could, he rang her mobile. She was still in Central Hall and he asked if she fancied being mistress of Number Ten. From an Oxford backwater to the seat of power in one go was enough to give any girl vertigo, but Chloe must have had a head for heights because she didn't hesitate to accept. Damian told his driver to divert and pick her up.

The front door of Number Ten is unlike any other in that it can't be opened from the outside; no keyhole, nothing. Just that iconic Number Ten in white. Damian and Chloe had to first negotiate the security barrier at the entrance to Downing Street, then knock on the door of their new home. Ask to be admitted. Pimlico this was not.

The duty housekeeper was there to welcome them and show them round. The deceased PM's widow and her belongings had finally been removed the night before. Tichbold's presence had never been more than a pair of pyjamas and a toothbrush, Hermione having insisted on staying in the country with her pet mare, Fidget. Number Ten was now empty and Damian's to do as he liked with.

He immediately delegated the domestic and social side of it to Number Ten's new mistress. A leader's success depends in large measure on how good he is at picking people. Whether Chloe would be any good at running Britain's version of the White House he had no idea. He had known her for only days, a time of turmoil when he had been preoccupied with other matters. But they got on, she was young and attractive and seemed competent.

Whether she could cope with Number Ten probably wouldn't matter too much, because Damian saw himself as a very temporary tenant. He was head of only an interim government and unlikely to survive when the real thing was elected in a few weeks. Chloe would be spared having to choose new wallpaper.

While Number Ten's mistress visited the kitchen and bedrooms and arranged for essential personal effects to be fetched from Pimlico, Damian was shown round the business end of the establishment. He wanted to get a feel for the house's geography; and make some essential phone calls. It was too late for anything more today, but he was scheduling his first cabinet for tomorrow at 2pm.

By 7.30 they had finished. Both declared themselves bushed.

"What now?" asked Chloe.

"How about a Chinese take-away?" replied Damian. "With a bottle of wine."

The new mistress of Number Ten grinned; "Think they can manage that?"

"Let's see," replied the new Prime Minister. "Their first big test."

35

MARCH 26th.

Damian decided that his cabinet should *not* meet in the Cabinet Room, which was too big and impersonal. The long table, with space for a couple of dozen chairs and more seating at the sides, was fine for a normal parliament with an extensive legislative programme, but not necessary for this temporary one with a limited remit.

He would not be having a string of ministers with impressive titles and large departments. Even Number Eleven next door was without a tenant, the previous Chancellor having been amongst the victims. There was no reason to replace him because the Treasury could easily keep things going for a few months; indeed it was whispered that matters would be vastly improved without a Chancellor around to meddle.

Damian had chosen instead a small anteroom, nice and cosy, with an oval table large enough to seat six - maybe eight at a pinch; more seating could be arranged at the sides, if that became necessary.

Shortly before 2 pm the TV cameras outside No.10 recorded the cabinet arrivals:

First was Adam Tichbold, tall and haughty, striding along briskly, as though in some parliamentary race. Damian had considered naming him Secretary of State for Speed, but had been persuaded this was too naff so had settled instead on 'Minister without Portfolio'. Adam was being given a roving commission to apply an oilcan to the rusty ship of state. A kick up the backside, as he put it.

Next came Gerry Farthing, *not* built for speed and wearing the sort of scruffy coat favoured by TV detective Colombo. Gerry was to be Secretary of State for Electoral Reform.

Then there was Bessie Robotham, also trying to give an impression of meaning business, but spoiling the effect by only achieving a breathless waddle. Bessie was to be Home Secretary, focussing on security.

The TV crews waited for the next arrival....and waited.

At 2.05 the door of No.10 opened and Prime Minister White appeared with his three colleagues. He approached the microphone and fiddled with the switch. In hushed tones the BBC commentator reminded viewers that Damian was Britain's first black prime minister - although in fact he was more a coffee colour. Black and White, The Whisky Premier. West Ham had instilled in him the need to keep fit, something he had not forgotten, having put on only a few pounds since those glory days on the pitch. He looked young for his age; absurdly young to be Prime Minster.

Having finally found how to turn the mike on, Damian began with the usual mantra of being 'honoured and humbled' by his new responsibilities. That bit out of the way, he continued:

"Yes there *are* only four of us. We're the slim-line team, with little more to do than deliver another parliament with a full quota of members. We've just passed the first part of that legislation. The next stage will examine the detail, crossing the 'Ts' and dotting the 'Is', making sure everything is as perfect as possible. This shouldn't take long, because we're already pretty much agreed. We're a team of all the talents, some of us Conservative, but it's *Labour* leader, Gerry Farthing, who's the brains behind our

146

election strategy."

Damian paused, aware that he was being economical with the truth. Those weasel words 'little more to do than' were camouflage, hiding his ambition to do as *much* as this short parliament would allow.

The break in his little speech permitted the man from ITV to put a question:

"Prime Minister, no one seems to understand how your new electoral system will work. It seems far too complicated..."

"Well, Mr. Donovan..." Damian had recognised the ITV reporter, a tall, thin man in his late thirties, with prematurely grey hair. "....Can you count?"

Donovan didn't know what to say. Everyone was flummoxed.

"Very well, let me show you: One... Two... Three... Four... Five....." As laughter took over, Damian stopped.

When it had subsided, he continued: "There, that wasn't too difficult, was it? That's all we're asking: that you count. Our present system was designed for illiterates - only have to make your mark: they say this should be a cross, which is pretty daft considering we normally put a cross when we *don't* want something; however, any mark is acceptable as long as your intention is clear. From now on, though, you'll be asked to write a number: one against your first choice, two against the second; and so on until you get bored or run out of ideas. Entirely up to you. Think you can manage?"

"Still don't see the point in changing something we're used to," persisted Donovan.

"It's so *you* get a fair deal," said Damian. "Remember Brexit? A close call but that was a referendum where all the votes went into one pot. No one could argue about the result. At present we put general election votes into six hundred different pots, where anything can happen. A party like UKIP can amass millions of votes but not a single MP, whereas the big parties, Gerry's and mine, tend to do rather better than we deserve."

"This new thing must be pretty difficult to count," grumbled Donovan.

"Longwinded, maybe, but not difficult. Ask Dublin. They've been doing it for a hundred years and seem well able to cope. But no more election night dramas with the swingometer, I'm afraid. You'll now have to wait a day or two for a full result."

More questions were brewing, but this could go on all day if he let them. He therefore introduced his team to the world and made a graceful exit. There was work to do.

36

The oval table in the anteroom was plenty big enough for Damian's little cabinet. He positioned himself at the head of the oval, letting the others pick their pitch. Adam Tichbold sat on his right, Gerry Farthing to his left. Bessie Robotham elected to sit beside Gerry, as far from Adam as possible: old enmities died hard.

"Well, who'd have thought it," began Damian.

Who indeed. Gerry smiled. Adam stretched his long legs. Bessie sat hunched, keen to get going.

"Let me start by stating the obvious," continued Damian. "The time factor. We're bypassing the Lords, so it should be fast track to the Royal Assent for our Electoral Reform Bill. But the practical problems will take longer. That's your baby, Gerry, so talk us through it.

Gerry Farthing glanced at a memo sheet in front of him, paused for thought, began:

"I already have a team in place from the Electoral Reform Society, which was founded in eighteen eighty four, so they've been waiting a while..."

"Plenty of white beards...," said Adam.

"...Yea, and they know all the wrinkles," continued Gerry, smiling at his little joke. "But they'll need one vital piece of guidance from us: how many MPs do went want to end up with?"

"America has a population of over three hundred

million, but only four hundred and thirty five Congressmen," said Adam. "I know we've cut back a bit, but even six hundred is far too much for our population of....what, seventy mill? I say go for a big cull."

"Will voters stand for that?" asked Bessie.

"Voters will be kissing us when they learn how much it'll save them," replied Adam.

"Let's pluck some figures out of the air," said Damian. "Who's for five hundred MPs?"

"Four hundred," said Adam.

"Pig in the middle, four fifty," said Bessie.

"Don't go for a round figure," said Gerry. "How about four hundred and sixty nine? Might fool people into thinking we know what we're doing."

"Good idea," said the Prime Minister. "Let the white beards and wrinkles know we're aiming for four hundred and sixty nine MPs. Ballpark figure."

They digested this for a moment, then the Prime Minster continued: "There are a couple of other election matters we should think about: like where will the new Parliament meet? The Palace of Westminster is clearly out for years...."

"Maybe forever," interjected Adam. "Never was much good, even for the likes of Gladstone and Disraeli. Now it's just a nostalgia symbol. Let's build something modern and fit for purpose. Ken and Boris got a fantastic new city hall in a prime location. We deserve the same. Convert the old wreck into a hotel: just imagine what we could charge for a room with *that* view."

"It'll take time," said Damian.

"All the more reason to start at once. Give me the green light and I'll scour London for a suitable site. I've got architect friends who'll make some preliminary drawings: not the bear-pit design we've been used to, instead I'll ask for the semi-circular model everyone else uses. Built-in electronic voting, the lot. Get the whole thing signed and sealed by the time the next parliament takes over. How about it?"

"It's all yours," said the Prime Minister. "Anything else?"

"The House of Lords," replied Gerry Farthing. "We've done away with it during the period of this emergency, but the new parliament might haven other ideas; we should give them some pointers. I personally think we *do* need a second chamber, but exactly what? An elected Senate, like the Yanks and Aussies? Or a small appointed body of real experts?"

"Okay, put something down on paper," said the Prime Minister. "Remembering we don't have much time. About three months, I think you said, Gerry?"

Farthing nodded. "That's what they tell me it'll take to get STV up and running. It also happens to be the magic hundred days, during which our masters, the people, are supposed to suspend judgement and allow us our heads. We're aiming to change the way this country is run, so we'd better get a move on before anyone notices."

Damian nodded, then turned to his new Home Secretary: "Anything we can do for *you*, Bessie?"

She shook her head. "Can't think of anything beyond trying to make sure no one tries to knock you off your perch. I'll talk to Jacob Wells, who's the expert."

"That's it then." The prime Minister looked around at his team. "Any other business?"

A collective shaking of heads.

As an afterthought, Adam said: "I suppose we've all seen today's Daily Mail?"

"You mean their 'Out of Africa' story?" asked Damian.

Tichbold nodded. "They've dug up a so-called expert, who's tipping a new plague from the 'Out of Africa' plane crash; due to bodies lying festering for days under the wreckage."

"Load of codswallop," said Bessie. "You know what the press is like – especially the Mail. Lives by lurid headlines, which have been harder to come by in recent days. It's just a wheeze to boost their circulation."

"You're probably right," said the Prime Minister. "But we don't want the Mail spreading panic. If the story becomes too toxic, can I rely on you, Bessie, to dampen the fires?"

The Home Secretary nodded and they left it at that. Thought no more about it.

37

The Mail's 'Out of Africa' scare was soon submerged by the torrent of requests and advice which next morning descended on the new Prime Minister. Although MPs lay down the country's policies, the actual job of running UK plc falls to a diverse band unelected organisations, the main ones being the police, armed forces and civil service.

The police and armed forces are happy enough to go away and do their own thing. Indeed, interference from on high tends to be a damned nuisance. The civil service is a different matter. Politicians and mandarins are joined at the hip, running the country in tandem, the biggest difference being that the unelected lot tend to be a good deal brighter than their political masters. If there's a major cock-up, the mandarin will usually manage to slide away with a knighthood and fat pension, whereas the politician finds his face on every front page and out of a job.

Although a strange alliance, this has been the British way from time immemorial and it was unprecedented for the mandarins to have been left out in the cold for nearly two weeks. Even as the drama was unfolding and no one knew what was happening, Jacob Wells had been bemoaning the fact that he had 'no one to report to'. During the following days the situation had stabilised but barely improved. Although Adam Tichbold had quickly been voted in as the new PM, he'd had his hands full sorting out the mess and trying to work out what to do next. The fact that the old PM's widow was prostrate with grief and difficult to prise out of Number Ten hadn't helped. Now at last the government appeared to have a reasonably permanent head. The pressure was on to get back to 'business as usual'.

Which was why Prime Minister Damian White found himself facing Cabinet Secretary Sir Justin Hopgood at the unusually early hour of 9 am. Pinstripes and bowler hats are no longer *de rigueur* for Civil Servants and Sir Justin favoured casual more than most. It being early and the meeting informal, he was wearing grey slacks, white shirt, blue pullover and blue tie. He reckoned that a subliminal way to oil the wheels of government was to dress in the appropriate colour: blue for Tories, red with Labour.

Sir Justin was a well built man in his early fifties, with blue eyes and a ruddy face that was almost exactly spherical; the sort fellow one might take for a farmer. Any impression of innocence would be misplaced, because no one reaches the pinnacle of the civil service without being formidably clever. Sir Justin's record included a Double First at Oxford and Fellowship of All Souls. He could digest and regurgitate at will more abstruse facts than most computers. Some people said that common sense did not match his other attributes, but such comments were probably mere jealousy.

With coffee dispensed, Damian led the way to his new-found anteroom, sat down and said: "I gather you're impatient to get things moving again."

The Cabinet Secretary took a sip of coffee and replied: "Number Ten has been like the Marie Celeste." His voice was unexpectedly high, almost soprano.

"Never known anything like it," he continued. "The place is usually a hive of activity. People coming and going; lots of action. Then suddenly…. Nothing. The ship of

154

state wallowing in a storm with no one on board."

"Just the grieving widow, sobbing in a corner."

"She didn't help. But Tichbold was quickly appointed and I saw him just twice. Briefly, at that."

"He had a lot on his plate. We all did."

"I understand your difficulties. But hopefully all that's behind us. Can we now expect a return to normality?"

Damian gave it a moment's thought. Replied: "No, I don't think you can. There won't be 'normality', as you put it, until we again have a full parliament. As you know, that won't be for a few weeks. Until then, you'll have to put up with the abnormal."

"Won't you even consider appointing people to some of the empty posts? Just *pro tem*?"

"You mean a new Chancellor?"

"No, I fancy the Treasury can keep things going quite nicely on its own for a while. I was thinking more of a Chief of Staff. We really could do with a link man here at Number Ten."

"Originally Tony Blair's idea, I believe," said Damian. "Governments before that seemed to have done well enough without a Chief of Staff."

"That was then. The world has changed. Take it from me, Number Ten needs a gatekeeper."

"If you insist, I expect Chloe….Miss Pettigrew could fill that gap."

"Pettigrew….!" The Cabinet Secretary's face became even ruddier. He wasn't often lost for words. Recovering, he said: "Chief of Staff is *usually* a political appointment. From amongst the PM's closest supporters."

"Miss Pettigrew is a *very close* supporter. Not politically, perhaps. In fact, I've yet to discover what her politics are.

If any."

"Then hardly suitable for the post. Chief of Staff is *very* political."

"This must be rather confusing for you, Sir Justin, but Number Ten is now almost *non-political* – at least in the party sense. I'm a Conservative, but our flagship policy of electoral reform is being spearheaded by the *Labour* leader. Don't worry: you'll have the old familiar world back in a few weeks. Won't have to put up with us for long."

"So you look upon yourself as the Night Watchman?"

A reference to cricket always seems to defuse an awkward situation; the game where one can stand at silly-mid-on, bowl maidens over and collect a pair of spectacles by scoring two ducks. For the uninitiated, a Night Watchman describes a tailender, put in towards the end of a days' play ahead of his usual position, so as not having to expose a better batsman. Is that also gibberish? Never mind.

Damian continued in similar vein: "An imperfect analogy, Sir Justin. In cricket they usually make an effort to dismiss tailenders, but I reckon I'm fireproof. At least until after the election. That's because no one wants my job. It's a political mix of arsenic, strychnine and cyanide: a poisoned chalice. Bessie Robotham and Gerry Farthing both claimed they were not PM material. Nonsense of course. Everyone wants the top job. Adam Tichbold's excuse was he could not lead a government whose main policy he had always opposed. Fact is, all my colleagues have calculated that their careers would be best served by having someone else take the flak for this apology of an administration."

"Probably go down in history as the 'Small Parliament'. To set against the Short Parliament of three weeks in the spring of Sixteen Forty; and the Long Parliament which sat for twenty years after that. An interesting trio." Sir Justin smiled to himself as more data went into the human hard drive behind those blue eyes.

"We're more like a Small-Short Parliament," said Damian. "But whatever you call us, I suspect they'll soon bowl out the Night Watchman when normal play resumes. The big hitters will take over again and I'll be on my way."

"Maybe." The Cabinet Secretary paused for another intake of coffee. "But in the meantime it would help if you could at least *pretend* you were in it for the longer term. Talk to the department heads. Organise Number Ten. You never know: even tailenders have been known to knock up a century."

"You're right, of course." Damian realised he had been so preoccupied by the Leaning Tower and its aftermath that he had been in danger of neglecting government's housekeeping chores.

"People appreciate a call from Number Ten," added Sir Justin. "Improves morale; makes them feel wanted. But try not to mention ships when talking to Horrocks."

"You mean Admiral Horrocks, the sailor?"

"That's the man. Admiral Sir Harry Horrocks, Chief of Defence Staff. Recently taken over from General Silvers. Buggins turn for the navy to get the top Services job. Nice chap, Horrocks. Most capable. But has a chip on his shoulder. About ships."

"Aren't Admirals supposed to *like* ships?"

"Oh they do, they do. Trouble is they never have enough of them. Same with the Raff: never enough planes. And our army could scarcely fight a war against the Isle of Man. Usual story. New lot comes into Number Ten, full of bright ideas, wouldn't hurt a fly. Next thing you know, we're off to war….. You're not planning a war, by any chance?"

Damian shook his head.

"Just as well. Take my advice: don't. We can't. We've virtually disarmed this country to pay for the NHS, railways and other worthy causes. Horrocks says that if Norway felt like a repeat of Seven Ninety Three we'd be unable to stop them."

"Seven Ninety Three?"

"Viking raid on Lindisfarne. Monks slaughtered. Start of a pretty beastly time. Horrocks says we'd have to let Norway keep Lindisfarne. Not enough naval power to stop them. He's very touchy about."

"Okay, I get the message. No war. I promise."

"Excellent, Prime Minister."

"But I *am* minded to let Miss Pettigrew run Number Ten."

The Cabinet Secretary made no comment. Stomped out. Life is full of compromises. In exchange for no war he'd have to put up with Chloe in Downing Street.

38

With legislation on track and the nation's top dogs chatted up, Damian could now turn his attention to the rest of the world, which was eager to know more about Britain's new young leader.

He spent nearly half an hour on the phone with President Galway of the USA. Likewise President Lacoste of France, who spoke good, if heavily accented English; and the German Chancellor, Heinz Freiwoller, whose English was near perfect.

To all of them Damian stressed he was just holding the fort until a permanent leader could be elected. In other words, it was nice talking to them, but not to expect any foreign affairs decisions. It would be way into the summer before Britain was again on the international map.

Chloe started learning how to navigate her way round Number Ten and getting to know the staff. Made a list of people she would like to invite round to dinner: might as well make use of her few weeks of glory.

Their honeymoon period lasted about 48 hours. Until Thursday's Daily Mail arrived, with a big black headline: LONDON PLAGUE.

It was the same story as two days earlier, but more strident and detailed. It hinted at a replay of the Great Plague of the 1660s, the cause this time not rodents' fleas, but a virus imported from the Africa, which had multiplied a billion times in the decaying corpses buried beneath the Palace of Westminster. A plague transported the modern way in an Airbus. The Mail's star witness was Sir Marcus Merton, an 'eminent epidemiologist', who agreed that 'a pandemic might be brewing.'

Damian and Chloe were into their toast and coffee, when the Mail's bombshell landed on their breakfast table.

"Looks like we'll have to barricade Number Ten and cancel your dinner parties," said Damian, with a flippancy he didn't really feel.

Chloe calmly took a sip of coffee. "Remember what Bessie said. The Mail loves lurid headlines. Tomorrow it will have found something else to entertain us: an alien invasion of Southend, perhaps; or transgender issues in our primary schools."

"Thought you journalists were sticklers for the truth?"

"We are. But we also have to sell our stuff."

Damian finished his toast. Then said: "I think we should find out what the Mail's tame boffin has to say for himself. Sir Marcus….whatever?"

"Sir Marcus Merton. Did a series on BBC Four called 'Invisible Bugs.' Talked about bacilli and viruses as though they were friends and neighbours."

"Neighbours from hell more like. Okay, let's see if we can persuade Sir Marcus up here for a chat."

Damian discovered that people did not need much 'persuading' if your address happened to be No.10 Downing Street. Sir Marcus, who worked in Cambridge, was ushered in just after lunch, an unlikely looking knight in a polo-neck shirt, hiking trousers and stout boots. He was an inch shorter than Damian, thus under medium height, slightly built with dark brown wavy hair and looked about twenty five, although Chloe's research had put him at forty four.

Number Ten has around 100 rooms to choose from, many rather large, but Damian was able to find one that was less intimidating, almost cosy. Sir Marcus had said 'yes' both to coffee and Chloe's presence; he didn't object to their talk being recorded as long as it was only for background: "on the record, off the record", as he put it.

"You seem to have stirred something of a hornets' nest," began Damian, when they had settled.

"The Daily Mail, not me," he said in a lilting voice that came from the valleys of Wales.

"No plague, then?"

"Who knows? I never make precise predictions. But the signs do suggest we could be in for a pandemic."

"So the Mail may be right?"

"It *may* be."

Damian took breath. This slippery scientist was beginning to…. yes, bug him was the appropriate expression. Trying for some clarity, he said: "A respected newspaper wouldn't be scaring the living daylights out of people without *some* reason."

Sir Marcus took a sip of coffee, put his cup down, said: "The Mail, like all the media, has been having a ball with the Leaning Tower of London. Circulation up, everyone happy. But that cash stream is drying up, so they're looking for something dramatic to replace it. When, lo and behold, they discover flu cases have risen sharply. With London attracting more than its fair share. A spike in flu deaths….. bodies under the Leaning Tower. Put two and two together and…. well, unfortunately for them that figure *won't* be four."

"There's no connection between flu and the Westminster disaster?"

"None. Pictures of such events always show rescuers wearing masks and it's assumed this is to ward off infection from the bodies. In fact it's because of the stink; the smell of decomposition. The safest place to be in a pandemic is surrounded by corpses. It's contact with the *living* that can kill you."

"Why has the Mail gone out on a limb if it's all nonsense?"

"Because it's not *all* nonsense. Apparently they'd written the story and were ready to go to print when they decided to check with expert opinion. Yours truly. They asked if there were signs of a possible influenza epidemic and I replied in the affirmative. Said it looked like we might be in for a big one. They didn't mention any Leaning Tower connection."

"So eggs on Mail faces?"

Sir Marcus shook his head. "Not really. They have a column in an inside page for 'Corrections and Clarifications', where banner headline blunders can be amended in the tiniest possible type. Happens all the time. Anyway, the paper is correct in its main argument: We *do* seem to be in for a pretty bad bout of flu."

"If not Leaning Tower corpses, where's the virus coming from?"

Sir Marcus shrugged. "We always have our home-grown variety, usually worst in winter. But on top of that millions of people are always on the move. From starving Africa, the war-torn Middle East, everywhere. Some will-of-the-wisp infection is always ready to ambush us. We've become pretty good at tracking and fighting these enemies, but the battle is never over. Our worst defeat was the so-called Spanish flu of nineteen eighteen, which killed over fifty million people: more than all the guns of World War one put together."

"That was before antibiotics," said Chloe. "Now we have proper medical defences."

"Maybe," said the scientist. "Except we've thrown these defences around like confetti – to fatten livestock, cure every petty pain. Result is many of these life savers no longer work terribly well. The flu virus is a clever little bugger, ready to disguise himself with new mutations. If he manages a really effective fancy dress which hides a potent armoury, he could kill a lot of us before we unmask him."

"So we have a problem?" asked Damian.

Again Sir Marcus shrugged, his favourite silent reply. "I can only say the potential is there for something pretty nasty."

"It seems I'm temporarily in charge of this country," said Damian. "What do you advise?"

"Damp down any panic that may appear. Which won't be easy when even a single death can produce the most extreme reactions. Remember Princess Di? Just imagine what could happen if large numbers of people start dying. The country will be knee-deep in floral wreathes; the sound of wailing deafening; roads turned into rivers by the tears of grief. Forget the British stiff upper lip; we now can't stop emoting."

"What sort of numbers are we talking about?"

"Haven't foggiest. But to give you a rough idea, let me throw some figures around. Ever heard of Eyam?"

"Rings a vague bell," said Chloe. "Village up north somewhere…?

"In Derbyshire: pretty little place, but known as the 'Plague village', because out of a population of three hundred and fifty, two hundred and fifty perished. Way over fifty percent mortality. In those days diseases were often pretty choosy, missing some places entirely while destroying others, like Eyam. Overall, the Black Death of the mid thirteen hundreds killed between thirty and sixty percent of Europe's population."

"I hope you're not forecasting anything like that?"

"No, no. Although some antibiotics may be losing their punch, modern medicine should protect us from the worst. Even so, things could get pretty scary. Best guide is probably the one I just mentioned, the Spanish Flu. A little over a century ago, so almost modern, it was a mere nothing compared with the ancient stuff, top estimate being about five percent of the world perishing. But just think about that for a moment. In Britain it would mean about three million deaths. Crammed into just a few months."

"Should I be buying shares in crematoria?" asked Damian.

Chloe grinned. "They'd impeach you for insider trading."

"We may be needing some gallows humour," said Sir Marcus. "But it's a good point. Disposing of bodies becomes a big problem. And the hard pressed NHS will pretty much collapse. You might like to make a few discreet plans."

"You said that flu epidemics are usually worst in winter," said Chloe. "We're almost into April, so surely things should now start improving?"

"I said 'usually'. Unfortunately, the canny little flu bug doesn't always do 'usual'. The nineteen eighteen epidemic peaked in summer. And was worst amongst those in the prime of life, rather than the young and elderly, which is the norm. You never can tell."

Sir Marcus finished his coffee and got up. "Now, if

you'll excuse me, it's time I returned to my tiny friends…"

Damian shook his hand. "Thanks for dropping in."
"You've been a great comfort," added Chloe.

"A speech extolling the virtue of stoicism might not be
a bad idea," said the scientist as he left. "And buy some
crematoria shares. Can't go wrong."

39

MARCH 31st.

Damian left it for a couple of days to see if the Flu story would go away. It did not. On Saturday evening he was warned that next day's Sunday papers would be headlining the story. The new mutation was proving disconcertingly deadly, with doctors' practices already in danger of being overwhelmed and pharmacies running out of antibiotics.

The prime minister knew he should be doing something: 'giving us a lead', as the Sunday Telegraph put it. But what *could* he do? He wasn't a magician. It was time to spread the blame should things to seriously pear-shaped, so he phoned his inner circle: Adam Tichbold, Gerry Farthing and Bessie Robotham.

Damian suggested another meeting at Number Ten, but Adam had other ideas.

"It's a weekend, so why not come down to the Tichbold ranch again," he suggested. "Guaranteed pest-free air. Hermione's excellent cooking. And Chloe can fatten up Fidget with more sugar lumps."

Which was how Prime Minister White and Number Ten's new Chief of Staff, Chloe Pettigrew, came to be heading Berkshire-wards, again attended by Bill and Ben, who had shifted the security focus from Adam to their new master.

The prime ministerial limo made its now familiar

crunching arrival around the Tichbold drive, to be greeted by the master of the house. There the similarities ended, because there had been a role reversal, Adam no longer prime minister merely an acolyte of his young leader. He was dressed in brown trousers and an open necked chequered shirt, it being unusually warm for late March.

"Bessie and Gerry are already here," he explained as Damian and Chloe got out of the car. "In the lounge devouring the Sunday papers. Not, I suspect, fitness fanatics. However, I could do with some exercise before the cerebral stuff, so how about a quick stroll?"

"Good idea," replied Chloe. "But we'd better not hang about. Looks like rain before long." A depression with humid Caribbean air was hovering over southern England, promising a mix of sunshine and heavy showers; they could already hear distant rumblings.

Chloe was looking suitably rural in a pair of tight jodhpur-like trousers and her hair let down. She was attracting admiring glances from Adam who, unlike the Cabinet Secretary, considered Number Ten's new Chief of Staff to be an excellent appointment.

"This time I've come prepared," said Chloe who had persuaded Bill – or it may have been Ben – to open up the car's boot. From it she extracted a pair of green wellies and a packet of sugar lumps.

"Let's go, before we get drowned," she announced, leading the way at a brisk trot towards the stables.

Horses can't be rushed, so they felt obliged to watch Fidget enjoy her treat. Perhaps 'enjoy' was the wrong word, because the animal just chomped away with a deadpan expression. 'Like watching paint dry', as Adam put it.

Their equine duty done, they set off up the slope towards the woodland at the far end of the estate. Adam with his absurdly long legs set a cracking pace, but they were all naturally fast walkers. Just as well Bessie and Gerry had opted out. Bill and Ben, this time equipped with proper footwear, had no difficulty keeping up; 'security' usually means ex-army or police and a decent degree of fitness.

They were well into the forest when a loud clap of thunder brought them to their senses. It was suddenly very gloomy. As one, they turned tail and stampeded down the slope. It's remarkably difficult to run in gumboots, so their pace was not exactly Olympian. Adam wondered whether government slaughter by AfroAir was to be followed by a further cull from lightning. But they made it. Just. Hailstones the size of marbles were beginning to attack as they exploded breathless through the back door.

Hermione, cool as ever, tut-tutted them a greeting for going out in such inclement conditions. Announced that Sunday lunch was in preparation and would be ready whenever they had finished saving the country.

Still panting, Damian Adam and Chloe joined the other two, who had been briefing themselves with the newspapers in the Tichbold drawing room. Gerry was surrounded by a chaos of discarded pages from the Observer, while Bessie was making a neater job of it with the Sunday Times.

Slumping into a vacant chair, Damian commented: "Not good news, I take it?"

"Armageddon," replied Gerry. "The Observer is calling for your resignation"

"If a Tory's in the hot-seat the Observer will be demanding his head on the block every weekend," said Bessie.

"Even so, we must do *something*," said Damian. "Which is why I suggested we meet."

"We must be *seen to be* doing something, even if we actually *do nothing*", said Gerry cryptically. "A fireside chat would fit the bill nicely."

There was a moments silence. Then Damian said: "It's nearly twenty degrees outside. Hardly fireside weather."

"I didn't mean literally. Neither did FDR. Like you, President Roosevelt found himself in the top job at a time of crisis, in his case the economic depression of the nineteen thirties. So he took to the 'wireless' as they called it, with a series of talks to the American people, known as fireside chats. Faced with a banking collapse, a world war, anything nasty, FDR's answer was usually a fireside chat. Now of course we have the telly, which is one of your strengths, so why not tell the BBC to book you a slot."

"No time like the present," said Bessie. "The press is acting over-excited, so the sooner we calm things down the better. I fancy it's time for Chloe to earn her keep, so come on Chief of Staff: see if you can fix something with the BBC. Or ITV. If that's okay with you, Prime Minister?"

Damian nodded, bemused at the pace of events. He would barely have time to gather his thoughts, never mind get anything down on paper. But they were right. He had to say something.

Chloe fumbled in her handbag for a mobile and was about to leave the room when Gerry said:

"Make sure they don't hype it up. The media loves to over dramatise. 'Chat' is a nice soothing word. Impress on the BBC -or whoever - that the purpose of the talk is to pour oil on troubled waters, not fan the flames."

Chloe nodded and left to make some calls.

"A fireside chat on the telly won't be enough," said Damian. "We also need some action."

"Bring on the army," suggested Adam. "That's the usual answer in a crisis."

"I promised Cabinet Secretary Hopgood not to start a war," said Damian. "Don't tell me there's a conflict somewhere out there that everyone's forgotten about."

"None that *I've* heard of," said Adam. "No doubt there'll be the usual SAS undercover stuff in the Middle East, but apart from that zilch. Most of the boys in brown will be marching up and down parade grounds in Aldershot or playing with their tanks on Salisbury plain. Ready for action."

"What sort of action did you have in mind?" asked Bessie.

"That'll depend," replied Adam. "If an infection starts to take a serious toll, there'll be fewer people around to do the usual jobs. The survivors will then tend to hunker down in their homes, rather than risk going out to face a deadly virus. Gradually planes will cease to fly, trains will stop, food remain undelivered. The army is an additional source of manpower if normal life starts to break down. To say nothing of facing down angry mobs demanding we work miracles."

"Squaddies can't fly planes or drive trains," said Gerry.

"They *can* drive lorries and keep essential services going."

"The army is not going to like it," said Bessie. "Not what it was trained to do."

"The army is trained to do most things," said Damian. "And will do as it is told. They call it discipline."

"Any of you Sharpe fans?" asked Adam.

No one answered.

"A fictional character I'm rather fond of," he continued. "Peninsular war hero, lot of blood and gore. I mention Sharpe because when asked what his job was he had a simple answer: to kill the king's enemies. Forget the

170

fancy uniforms and high faluting flummery, if you take the king's shilling it's for one purpose only: to kill his enemies. The downside is that the king's enemies will also be out to kill you. Join any of the armed forces and you accept a higher than average risk of dying."

"From bullets maybe, but not bugs," said Bessie.

"Bugs are also the king's enemies," said Damian. "Not a glamorous form of warfare perhaps, no VCs or other gongs on offer, but a soldier's job is still to fight and if necessary die for his country. When we're done here I shall phone Admiral Horrocks, and tell him to put the armed services on standby.

Bessie was about to say more but never had the chance because Chloe now returned, a smile on her face. Announced:

"You're on BBC One tomorrow at six thirty, after the news. They could have done tonight, but advised twenty four hours of publicity to make sure you had a good audience. They've only given you five minutes – like a party political broadcast - but that should be enough."

"Thirty seconds should do if it's just to tell them I'm putting the army on alert, but not to panic."

"Try to relax," said Chloe. "Imagine you're on Strictly – but without the dancing."

"In fact, I might take the opportunity to announce a few more changes," said the Prime Minister. "If forecasts are only half right, the NHS will be under serious stress…"

Adam: "…Totally unable to cope, more like."

Damian: "…So charging, say, two pounds to visit the doctor might be a small disincentive."

Gerry: "Here we go again! The Tories trying to put the clock back."

Damian: "I was only thinking of an honesty box as

171

patients come in. Therefore voluntary and no admin costs."

Gerry: "In that case no one will pay."

Damian: "*Some people* will certainly pay. How many I've no idea. They say there's no such thing as a free lunch: equally, there's no such thing as free medicine. That little honesty box might remind people that *everything* has to be paid for one way or another. Could also help fill the black hole of NHS funding."

No one said a word, so Damian added: "Almost everyone can afford two quid, but if you *really* can't manage you don't have to. Worth a try."

Adam slapped his thigh: "Three golden words! 'Worth a try'. It's the reason homo sapiens is no longer living in a cave hitting his woman with a club. *Of course* we must try charging for doctor's visits. Even if it doesn't work. Every small step forwards is built on failures."

"We're far too scared of the dreaded 'U-turn'," agreed Damian. "It's the worst abuse the media can throw at us. But I'd like to see 'U-turns' built into our manifesto, to be used when necessary. When that canny old operator Harold McMillan was asked why he had changed his mind, his reply was 'Events, dear boy, events'. So let's wear our U-turns with pride. Use them when we have to."

"I think a small charge for seeing the quack *would* work," said Bessie. "Should have done it years ago."

The Labour leader sniffed sceptically and asked: "Does the Prime Minister have any other quaint ideas up his sleeve?"

Damian grinned. "How about making prisoners work for their keep?"

Gerry: "Back to sewing mailbags?"

"I was thinking of something more useful. Like clearing litter."

"One way of easing the pressure on prisons, I suppose," said Gerry sarcastically. "No longer any need for dodgy escapes over the prison wall, the bad boys can just wander off when the warder is busy having a pee."

"It would not of course apply to anyone dangerous," replied Damian. "But most inmates are pretty harmless. Look upon clearing litter as a sort of semi parole, with the bonus of being able to repay society for any wrongs that put you in inside in the first place."

"Very laudable, I'm sure," said Bessie. "But I doubt the prison officers would wear it. Too many extra duties."

"With a bit of persuasion they might welcome the change," said Damian. "Can't imagine many worse jobs than being a prison warder. Give them a choice of getting out in God's fresh air… add a few pence to their pay. I reckon they'll jump at it."

"In the current catch-phrase, 'worth a try'", said Adam, with a smile.

"Okay, I'll get the legislation underway," said Damian. "But we'll have to be quick about it. After all, we're an *interim* parliament and the public won't tolerate too much delay before they have something more permanent."

"If we get a really good plague the public might have so much on its mind that it *does* forget about it," said Adam, ever the cynic.

"We can hardly bank on mass deaths helping us out," said Damian. "Must plan on circumstances being normal. The second reading of our Electoral Reform Bill is up for debate next week, so that only leaves its implementation. What's the latest on that, Gerry?"

The Labour leader made an effort to sit up straighter in Tichbold's all-too-comfy chair and replied: "The Single Transferable Vote is based on large multi-member constituencies, so we have to merge our current six hundred into.... I'm not sure of the precise number, but it will be somewhere between eighty and ninety bigger ones. Your constituency of Mid Oxon, Damian, will fit nicely into Oxford county, returning three members."

"Must complicate matters that we are also reducing the number of MPs," said Bessie.

"Not really," said Gerry. "Whether we use the old figure of six hundred or our new target of around four hundred and seventy MPs, these still have to be juggled into the new scheme. I'm told the job is pretty near done. Computers think nothing of merging electoral rolls, so that's near completion. It's the human element that takes time. Voters have to be weaned off the old habit of putting a cross and instead educated into inserting numbers. Not exactly rocket science, but no one likes change, so every household will be sent an instruction leaflet. The most difficult part is ensuring that the people running the show know *exactly* what to do. An STV count takes time and is quite different to what anyone has been used to, so all returning officers will need to do a training course and pass an exam."

"I'd like to get back to normal as soon as possible, so can we nail down to an election date?" asked the Prime Minister.

Gerry Farthing gave it a moment's thought. "Should be able to manage early June."

"So can we pencil in the first Thursday in June?" Damian looked around for agreement.

"Why Thursday?" asked Adam.

"Because we *always* go to the polls on a Thursday," replied Bessie.

"The French do it on Sundays," Adam pointed out. "So what's so special about Thursdays? Aren't we supposed to be breaking the mould?"

"Let's just say early June," said the Prime Minister. "Precise date to be decided. And decided soon."

"Can we now decide to have lunch?" asked Adam. "Hermione has prepared a Sunday roast, Yorkshire pud, all the trimmings. I'm starving."

The motion was carried unanimously.

40

All Fools day. The papers usually had a suitable jest hidden within the genuine news, but Damian couldn't find anything. Maybe they thought it wasn't the time for jokes. Flu cases were mounting rapidly, with mortality rates *much* higher than in a normal epidemic. There was as yet no clear pattern, but, as in 1918, those in their prime seemed to be suffering at least as badly as the very young and elderly.

The business of the day was the Interim Parliament's second reading of The Electoral Reform Bill. Unlike the old Commons Chamber, where TV cameras could focus on both speakers and audience, the Central Hall Westminster was a normal conference venue, with Speaker Harding on the raised platform at one end, looking down on the ranks of MPs below. Members wishing to make a brief point usually did so from their seated position, while longer speeches were done from the front, facing the audience. There was much neck twisting to retain the tradition of addressing the Speaker, but no one had yet tried the more obvious method of mounting the platform. Speaker Harding had made no ruling on the matter, the Interim Parliament still playing things by ear.

On one point Speaker Harding *had* made her wishes clear. The press and TV cameras were to remain at the back of the hall. This was fine for filming the speeches, but meant viewers could no longer see audience reaction.

176

Prime Minister White in the front row was therefore a long way from the cameras, with only the back of his head visible.

This advantageous geography was enabling Damian to sit out the debate while actually doing some homework for his coming talk. The Electoral Reform Bill would be remembered as the Labour leader's finest hour, so no need to spoil his party. Guaranteed a comfortable passage, it was more a triumphal procession than a debate, the few who spoke against some minor point being mere puppets. Damian's conscience was clear as he surreptitiously scribbled notes on the back of an old envelope. And remained silent.

The Bill was finally approved just after 4.30 pm by 98 votes to 54, the larger than expected number of absentees being due to members confined to bed with the dreaded bug. Now only the spidery signature of the king was needed for elections by The Single Transferable Vote to become law.

Damian offered Gerry Farthing his hasty congratulations, then left by the back door for the short walk to Downing Street. Chloe was 'at home', as he now had to call Number Ten, hopefully with the kettle on for tea, but also supervising the BBC team, who wanted enough time to record his talk before transmission at 6.30.

He had pondered a good deal about how to present the talk. Standing or sitting? If sitting, formal or casual? He had eventually settled on the study as the venue, seated behind a simple wooden desk, his face lit by the window at his two o'clock position. Over his right shoulder, above the fireplace, was a painting of Maggie Thatcher, to his left a large bookcase. A message from the seat of power, yet not too formal. A fireside chat British version.

After a quick cup of tea, Chloe and the TV team assembled in the study. The prime minister was behind the desk, a few salient points to remember scrawled on a single sheet of A4 in front of him. He envied politicians across the pond who always seemed to start off with the phrase 'My fellow Americans'. Anything like 'My fellow Britains', worse still 'fellow Brits', would probably reduce his audience to helpless laughter, so he set off rather lamely:

"Ladies and gentlemen. If you're surprised to find yourselves watching what appears to be an episode of Strictly Come Dancing from Downing Street, let me assure you no one is more surprised than me. It's been quite a ride from West Ham football club, via the dance floor to Number Ten.

But I'm not here today in my usual role as an entertainer. No muddy claret shirt after a bruising game at Upton Park: no glitter and sequins from Strictly. Today it's business. And not very pleasant business at that.

I am of course referring to the flu virus that's decided to pay us a visit. It's around most years, but this time it's more than usually active. Tonight I want to put this nasty little fellow into perspective."

The Prime Minister took a sip of water from a tumbler on the desk, glanced at his notes and continued:

"First let me say that most of you will remain perfectly healthy. It may seem like everyone is getting it, but going down with flu is actually a minority occupation. Every autumn we spend a hundred million pounds of your money giving the elderly flu jabs, so we're already doing our best. And pharmacies will sell you all sorts of tablets if you think they will do any good.

But jabs and pills are only partially effective - some say even a waste of money, which leaves us with the uncomfortable fact that there's not much modern medicine can do. We're back to the age-old remedy of a day or two in bed.

However, large numbers of people off work for even a few days does cause problems. Trains and buses may have to be cancelled, essential services come under pressure. I have therefore told the service chiefs to make manpower…" the Prime Minister smiled "…and womanpower available to fill any gaps that may appear. I ask for your understanding and cooperation if this happens where you work.

If you come down with this flu of course take a few days off, but the rest of us should be prepared to make allowances. Work longer hours, perhaps. Be flexible. We must keep the country ticking over. Remember the British stiff upper lip. Good luck. And thank you."

The TV crew shut down, relaxed.

The cameraman, smiled to himself and said: "No mention of what really scares people: which is dying. No one minds a bit of flu if they recover."

Damian got up, stretched his legs. Said: "It's like that episode of Fawlty Towers where they have German guests and Basil keeps saying 'don't mention the war'. Now the unmentionable is death. So I don't. Just skate diplomatically round it. The show we've just put on was designed to talk down the grim reaper."

You did a pretty good job," conceded the cameraman. "Whether it'll work, I'm not too sure."

41

APRIL 5th.

The phone woke him. He scrabbled for the bedside clock, which showed 6.50. Fumbled for the receiver. Put it to his ear and managed some sort of noise to show he was awake.

"Hopgood here," came the words from the other end. "Sorry to ring so early, prime minister, but I thought you should know. Give you a chance to formulate some words. I'm afraid the Labour leader Gerry Farthing has just died."

"Good God! How? When?"

"Not sure of the details. Only just been woken with the news myself."

Damian was finding the Cabinet Secretary's eunuch-like voice disconcerting. Probably sang counter tenor in the local choir. Had he been emasculated at school? Did he have a wife?

With an effort he forced himself to attend to the matter in hand. Which was poor old Gerry.

"Farthing seemed fit and well on Monday. Big day with his Electoral Reform Bill. Most cheerful."

"He was in his early seventies, so perhaps a heart attack," suggested Hopgood. "Or a flu victim. No doubt we shall find out in due course. It occurred too late for the morning papers, but Breakfast TV and the radio will be full of it. So expect a call soon from the media."

"I will, Sir Justin. And thank you for warning me."

"Gerry gone?" Chloe was sitting up in bed rubbing her eyes, hair all over the place.

It was a scene Damian would normally have found exciting, but death dampens the ardour, so he just nodded, got himself vertical and headed for the bathroom, saying: "I'd better shave before the world wakes up. Could you see what TV has to say. And field any phone calls."

Ten minutes later he joined a dressing-gowned Chloe in front of the screen. On the table a mug of tea and bowl of fruit.

The news presenters were in full flow, so Chloe pressed the mute while she brought Damian up to date:

"Sounds like flu. He took to his bed on Tuesday. By Thursday the infection had gone to his chest. And he died this morning just after five. Frighteningly fast."

"They say this flu strain can do that." Damian started peeling a banana and continued: "But what a way to go! Gunned down in his moment of glory, finally victorious with Electoral Reform. Almost Nelsonian."

Chloe: "One way of looking at it, I suppose."

"After Trafalgar, Horatio Nelson was pickled in a cask of brandy, sent back to Blighty, buried in St.Pauls's cathedral and then put on London's highest pedestal," continued Damian. "Don't suppose they'll go that far with Gerry, but he's certainly timed his exit to perfection. After last Monday anything else he might have done would have been an anti climax."

Chloe gave a shiver. "Listening to Marcus rattling off his statistics was…well, just lots of figures. But Gerry is personal. Makes you realise anyone may be the next. You… me….."

"Gerry *was* getting on a bit," said Damian, trying to find words of comfort he didn't really feel.

"Marcus said this flu bug can hit anyone. At any age."

Before they could talk themselves into a deeper pit of depression the phone rang. Damian was expecting someone from the media, but it was Home Secretary Bessie Robotham. After some perfunctory words of regret for Gerry Farthing and an apology for disturbing him so early, she came straight to the point:

"We're starting to have serious problems with bodies."

"What sort of bodies?"

"Dead ones. They're piling up. Waiting times at most crematoria are now over two weeks. Facilities inadequate."

"What do funeral directors say?"

"That's why I'm ringing. I've had their Association's Director on my back. A Mr. Douglas Withy. Says his members have a reputation for excellence, which is being put sat risk by bottlenecks in the system. Says no one is listening to him, so he must talk to you."

"You mean the crematoria can't burn people fast enough?"

"Something like that. No doubt he'll have the full story when you see him. As I hope you will."

"Of course. Fix a time this afternoon and ring me back."

Damian and Chloe returned to their breakfast in the hope that the day might improve. If anything it got worse.

The morning was dominated by Gerry Farthing, all the usual eulogies when someone well known departs. But the subplot was the growing realisation that if the Labour leader had been struck down, it could happen to *anyone*. It could happen to *you*.

182

Most people have a defence mechanism against danger. Troops going into battle tell themselves it can't happen to them; it'll always be the other guy, even though logic says everyone will be equally exposed. If danger becomes especially acute, some may go to the other extreme of resigned acceptance: nothing they can do, so what the hell, a short life but a merry one.

In the absence of any defence mechanism, things could turn ugly. With panic. By afternoon Britain's mood was looking increasingly jittery. Damian's 'fireside chat' had been designed to calm things and had seemed to work. For a while. Now he was less sure.

At 3.45 Chloe told him Douglas Withy had arrived. An offer of a cup of tea had already been accepted, so Damian suggested the informal anteroom, which had a small table and some easy chairs.

In his mind's eye he had Withy down as large, solid and imposing, dressed in funereal black – maybe arriving in a carriage drawn by four black horses crowned with plumed feathers, Pompes Funèbres, French fashion. His guest turned out to be disappointingly normal, mid fifties in age, about the same height as Damian, with a plentiful head of dark hair parted down the middle. He was dressed in a smart grey suit, striped shirt, and a mottled brownish tie, that could have been a stage prop for the snake in the Sherlock Holmes story of the Speckled Band.

"I believe you have a problem," began Damian, as they sat down.

"No, Prime Minister. *You* are the one with the problem." The voice had a touch of north country. Geordie perhaps.

"A blockage in the works?"

Withy nodded. "I represent our Association, the NAFD, the nation's funeral directors. As you may imagine, the

183

current situation is rather hectic. And distressing. When grandma or grandad goes, it's a time for grateful contemplation. A celebration of life. Often gets quite jolly. But we're now seeing all too many people cut off in their prime. A lot of children. That means real grief. We are professionals and can normally handle our emotions, but we're being stretched to the limit. Overtime has become the rule rather than the exception and our members are becoming exhausted. The quality of our product is having to be reduced and corners cut. Which lowers morale even further."

"What do you expect *me* to do?"

"I expect you to get things moving, prime minister. We can't go on like this. We are coping – with difficulty, I'll admit, but coping. But the end users – the buriel grounds and crematoria are not. They are still trying to keep gentlemen's hours; kick off at ten thirty, forty five minutes per service, then knock off in late afternoon. While this emergency lasts we need a conveyor belt operation, twenty four seven, religious services limited to ten minutes."

"Is that possible?"

"Of course. A full religious ceremony could be held anywhere, so reducing the crematorium part to the bare minimum would be no hardship. Fortunately, we have one of the world's highest rates of cremation, around seventy five percent of all deaths, so making use of this to its full capacity should solve the problem. Although there's little we can do about the burn time of about ninety minutes, at present there's little or no night work, and many crematoria have excess capacity they rarely use."

"But like you, they would have manpower problems," Damian pointed out. "They may be able to run the machinery day and night, but the operators will need some rest."

"Use the army," said Withy. "Your own solution, as I

recall. The crematoria professionals would be around to train and supervise, but the extra hands could come from the armed forces."

"Wonder if burying the dead is included in the Sandhurst curriculum," mused Damian.

Withy cracked a half smile. "Bound to be. If you're in the business of killing, they must surely include a few lessons on how to clear up the results."

Hit by a sudden brainwave, Damian exclaimed: "This is just the job for Adam!"

"Adam....?"

"Tichbold."

"The ten minute premier? Fellow you took over from?"

Damian nodded. "My Minister without Portfolio. Well, now he has one. A portfolio. Minister for burning people more rapidly. I wanted to call him my Minister for Speed."

"So a fast worker?"

"Impatient, certainly. By his wife's admission. Fast? We'll see. I'll put him to the test."

"When can he get going?"

"Yesterday, I hope. Haven't been in touch for a couple of days, but I'll do so soon as you're gone. You should hear from Adam shortly."

The Director of the National Association of Funeral Directors rose to his feet: "So I'll liaise with the Minister for.....?"

"Crematoria and cemeteries.....?" Damian thought for a moment, then shook his head. "Better be boring and stick to Minister without Portfolio."

Mr. Douglas Withy nodded: "A wise decision Prime Minister."

42

Inexplicably, Damian felt more cheerful after his joust with Britain's head dealer in death. Perhaps it was that a decision had been taken. Hopefully progress had been made. Or it might have been that death had again been reduced to talking about numbers. Gerry Farthing was personal, therefore unsettling. Best try and shove him somewhere down in the subconscious. Concentrate instead on the numbers.

Who better to play the numbers game with than their bug man, Sir Marcus Merton. They had only met in person once, Sir Marcus being too busy with his microscopes and Petri dishes up in Cambridge, but Damian had kept in touch by phone to check on the plague's progress.

Their conversations had always been stimulating. Even uplifting. Sir Marcus, in that lilting Welsh voice of his, was like a kid with a new toy. A froth of enthusiasm. And no wonder. How many scientists are granted a real live example of their speciality on their own doorstep? This was Britain's worst epidemic in over a century and Sir Marcus was in his seventh heaven.

Damian had to wait five minutes before the scientist came to the phone, Britain's prime minister having to play second fiddle to a bunch of test tubes. A sensible order of precedence.

"Can you tell me the latest?" Damian asked, when there was finally signs of life from the other end.

"Trend still upwards," came the reply. "Can hardly expect anything else if nineteen eighteen is anything to go by. But there are also fascinating differences. People this time seem to be dying rather faster."

Sir Marcus sounded so enthusiastic that Damian was tempted to exclaim 'Jolly good show'. Instead, he asked: "Any reason for this?"

"Too early to say. But it's a virulent little beast."

"Any chance of getting more antibiotics? Or other medication?"

"Not really my field. You'll have to ask the NHS. But with the numbers I'm seeing, I suspect it'll be a Mother Hubbard situation."

"Cupboard bare?"

"If not bare, certainly looking sorry for itself. Anyway, many antibiotics are now of doubtful efficacy. Weakened by excessive use. Some hardly worth spending money on."

"So we're back to our primitive defences, the human immune system?"

"Yes and no. Sometimes our immune system over-reacts and is *itself* the problem. They reckon that's why so many young and healthy people died in nineteen eighteen. They suffered from a surfeit of health."

"So whether we live or die is a lottery?"

"That's how it may appear. But every epidemic has a pattern, a reason, if only we can unlock it. That's what makes this puzzle so absorbing. Solving the conundrum."

"Any nearer to solving where it came from?"

"Let's say that the Daily Mail was not wrong when it headlined Africa. That continent is in such a dire state you hardly notice the odd epidemic. We wake up if it starts spewing ebola, but other diseases like malaria, dysentery, sleeping sickness, general malnourishment are so pervasive that the odd flu epidemic makes little impact."

"A few million of them then head for Europe in makeshift boats, bringing these presents with them," said Damian.

"Exactly. They say the severity of the Spanish flu was due to population movements at the end of the Great War. Today *everyone* seems to be on the move. Take the Haj, for instance. Every year two million people from around the Islamic world meeting up in Mecca to exchange diseases. They then return home to hand them on to friends and family. ISIL terrorists may make the headlines, but I bet they kill fewer people than the virus-bearers of the Haj."

"A comforting thought," said Damian drily, adding: "Any clue when this present plague will start dying down?"

"Not the foggiest. The nineteen eighteen version drifted on until the end of nineteen twenty, so we can expect plenty more fun. Whoever wins the next election will have their hands full."

"Keep me posted," said the Prime Minister. And rang off.

43

They ended the day with another Chinese takeaway and a bottle of Australian Sauvignon Blanc. Crazy, of course. Here they were in Number Ten Downing Street, nerve centre of a rather diminished British Empire. They were masters of one hundred rooms and a posse of staff, but were behaving like a hard-up couple in a suburban semi.

However, it had been a tough day emotionally. First Gerry Farthing. Then discussing the nation's growing pile of corpses with the leader of the funeral mafia. Finally Sir Marcus's forecast that the show might continue for another couple of years. A day of death, with barely a respite.

In all this gloom there had been only two glimmers of light: in spite of media forecasts of mayhem, the British public seemed to be achieving a degree of stoicism: as yet no riots or signs of disaffection: and Adam Tichbold had jumped at the chance to get the nation's crematoria up to speed.

By 6.30 Damian had had enough. There was little more he could do that day. After all, he was only the *interim* prime minister. The Night Watchman. No mass of legislation to worry about. His only job was to keep the ship of state from sinking until the next lot took over. No one could begrudge him an evening off with his new girl friend.

Girl friend: Chloe Pettigrew. Could there ever have been a weirder romance – if one could use that word. Still only... what was it, less than two weeks? Fourteen...

thirteen days since chance had placed them in the same room the moment the earth had shaken for them. AfroAir had hit with a helluva wallop.

Thereafter, she had used him to access the biggest story of her life. He had used *her* because… well, he had recently been chronically short of female company. And she was turning out to be a very smart lady: many talents wrapped up in an attractive package.

It had been a chaotic scramble from one crisis to the next, so opportunities to murmur the traditional sweet nothings had been reduced to brief moments in bed between passion and unconsciousness. Days had been so hectic they had slept the sleep of exhaustion.

Damian was beginning to realise he had been very lucky with his new companion. She was not only beautiful and sexy, but also competent, having fitted into the job of Number Ten Chief of Staff as though tailored for it. Chloe was a people person. Got on with everyone in Number Ten. Got on with everyone, period.

For the first time since wife Mandy had abandoned him, Damian was beginning to feel human again, so it might be worth an effort to try and hang on to his new treasure. Which was why he had set aside this evening for relaxation. A 'get to know you better' evening. No TV, just a candle-lit dinner. The bait should perhaps have been something more exotic than a Chinese takeaway, but there was plenty of wine in the fridge to enhance the eating experience.

Chloe took the king prawns with ginger and spring onions, sweet and sour chicken, special fried rice, and stuck them in the microwave. From its temperature on arrival their dinner appeared to have travelled the length of London.

Damian lit a couple of candles, arranged Number Ten's chopsticks artistically on the table, opened a bottle of

Barossa Valley's best and drew the curtains.

When the reheated food had been served and the wine poured, they clinked glasses and looked soulfully into each other's eyes. His beloved was dressed in a revealing maroon dress, hair flowing over her shoulders, a hint of some unknown scent.

"Another crap day at the office then," she said, having been brought up to date on the day's events.

Damian nodded. "Not a lot of laughs. But probably brilliant for your best seller."

She smiled. "Give me a day of disasters and I'll never complain."

"So your editor, what's his name…?"

"Forrester."

"Yea, Forrester. He's happy for you to keep playing truant from Oxford?"

"Of course. We hacks follow the news, which is now being made right here. I'll probably return to the dreaming spires after the election."

"Prime ministers have been known to sack their Chief of Staff," said Damian mischievously.

"Maybe. But never a Chief of Staff who attends to other needs." Chloe leant over and stroked his hand, causing a king prawn, wedged precariously between his chopsticks, to take a dive onto his lap.

He recovered the wandering crustacean, which had made a nasty mark on his trousers and conceded: "Very well. No reshuffles." He then retired to water down the prawn stain, which made it look as though he had done a pee in his pants.

On his return Chloe said: "Talking of Oxford, while you were entertaining that funeral fellow, I had a call from an old pal of yours: name of Warbeck."

"Alec Warbeck. With all that's been going on, I'd almost forgotten him."

"Well, he hasn't forgotten *you*. Asked me to remind you what he'd said: that the last shall be first. Whatever that might mean."

Damian sat back, wiped his mouth, remembered: "It's thanks to Alec I'm sitting here now. He rang me at once when the previous Mid Oxon candidate died unexpectedly, did a rush job to get me selected, then became my election agent. Said that Tony Blair had been the last candidate in the country to be selected when he first stood in Sedgefield and it wasn't long before he was standing in Number Ten. Joked that I also could be the 'last one that came first'."

"Seems he was right."

"Blair was here for ten years. I'll be lucky to last ten weeks. But I don't suppose Alec was ringing to remind me of old times."

"No, he wants to advise you not to neglect your home patch. Power corrupts and absolute power…that sort of stuff."

"I've hardly had time to get corrupted," said Damian grumpily. "Give me ten years and yea…. by then I might enjoy a bit of corruption."

"Alec also pointed out there's an election coming up and nothing can be taken for granted," continued Chloe. "Especially with this new system you've let yourselves in for. No more shoo-ins for Tories in safe seats. You'll now have to work for it."

"He's right," admitted Damian. "Seems I've been seduced by Westminster." He grinned. "And by one of Westminster's visitors. But I really should get back to my roots in the provinces. I'll give it my attention."

"Alec thinks you should give it your attention pretty

smartish…."

"…Alec *has* been free with his advice…."

"…Says the natives are becoming restless. Not happy to wait forever for your fancy new election. Want to get the job done pronto."

"Funny he should say that. I've been thinking along the same lines. It was Gerry who suggested early June. Seemed to think we needed that long. But the Electoral Reform Bill is now an Act of Parliament. Legally we could have the election next week."

"So only the practicalities are holding us up?"

Damian nodded. "Except I wouldn't use the word 'only'. The old system was absurdly easy. First count all the votes to find the turnout. Then separate them into piles for the various candidates. Agree any questionable voting slips with the returning officer – not everyone put a cross in the space provided. And that was it. Unless it was so close you needed a recount. Constituencies racing to be first to declare could manage the whole thing in about an hour flat. Even those working at a more sensible tempo could often do the job in three or four hours."

"Compared with how long for STV?"

"In difficult cases maybe the same in days. It's not so much complicated as tedious. But done to a formula. Gerry wanted to make sure everyone was fully trained to use it, but he's no longer with us and I wonder whether perfection on this first outing is really necessary. If a returning officer runs into difficulties, he only has to call in the experts. The bits of paper – the votes – won't go away. If necessary shut up shop for the day, sleep on it, come back refreshed. I think Alec may be right; we should accept possible hiccups during the count in exchange for more rapid implementation."

"I'll bet your Minister for Speed would agree."

Damian thought for a moment, then got up and went to the phone: "Let's see."

Chloe: "Won't Adam be busy making the crematoria burn faster?"

"Maybe. But it's getting late, so he should be back by now. Anyway, I'm only asking for his opinion, not more work."

His call was answered on the fourth ring by Hermione: "Oh…it's you again."

Damian laughed. "Is that the way to greet your prime minister!"

"You've got Adam working his socks off. Only arrived home half an hour ago. Go on like this and he'll be a *customer* for one of those burners."

"Bet he's enjoying it."

Hermione sniffed: "Says if he's not re-elected he'll go into the funeral business. A licence to print money."

"No danger of a recession, that's for sure. And in boom times like now he'd be making a killing - pardon the pun. But my impression is it's pretty much a close shop. Family businesses going back generations. Don't like outsiders feeding at the trough."

"Damian, dear boy!" Adam cut in from the upstairs extension. "What can I do for you?"

"I'd like a few words about the timing of the election…"

"Excellent idea. But not now. I'm just back from a day dealing with death. Gasping for my snifter. I need one more session to put some real rockets up their backsides, so let's say the day after tomorrow. Sunday here at the ranch again? Becoming quite a habit."

"I'll do another roast," interjected Hermione, now back to her usual self. "And of course bring Chloe."

"And don't forget sugar lumps," added Adam. "Sugar lumps for Fidget."

"I'll make a note of it in my diary."

Britain's population may have been dying fast, but the prime minister's priority had to be treats for a horse.

44

APRIL 7th.

The trip to the Tichbold estate was becoming almost routine: Damian and Chloe in the PM's limo, with security boys Bill and Ben on hand to make sure they behaved themselves; the familiar crunch round the gravel drive to be greeted by the master himself, the Minister without Portfolio – alias the Minister for Speed.

"Slight change of plan," announced Adam as they got out. "The weather man is forecasting a postprandial deluge, so Hermione has seen fit to take her charger for a gallop while it's still dry. Affairs of state must defer to my domestic schedule, which now places the prandial bit at one fifteen, when the carving knife is now due to meet the roast."

"Don't see why your wife's nag should be the only one to benefit," said Damian. "Could do with a gallop myself. Too much sitting around recently. Hardens the arteries."

Like many a former athlete, Damian's departure from top flight sport had still left his body with the need for stimulus. It had rebelled at going straight from a tightly-strung instrument to a couch potato. The life of an MP was hardly conducive to maintaining a fitness regime, but even when parliament was in session it *did* have long weekends, when members were expected to make their presence felt back in their constituencies. Damian certainly did that, but he also tried to keep in shape by joining a squash club; made an effort to play every day during his release from Westminster: Friday evenings and at some stage during Saturday and Sunday. Squash is one of the most intensive sports known to man and just about satisfied his craving for exercise.

That worked fine when life had been normal, but the past couple of weeks had been anything but. During this time he had not once been on a squash court, hardly even walked any distance. He was going to seed.

He heard Chloe say: "Looks like it'll stay dry for another hour or two. Why not go off on your gallop? Might even meet Hermione and Fidget."

Although clouds were gathering in the west and the wind strengthening, Chloe was right. Even if he *did* get soaked, it would hardly matter, indeed would cool him down. He immediately discarded the absurd notion of asking Adam if he had any sporty clothing to borrow. His Minister for Speed was at least a head taller, so nothing would fit.

"Yea, I could do with a workout." Damian took off his pullover and gave it to Chloe. He would have to go off in what he was wearing.

"What about us?" wailed Bill – or it might have been Ben.

"What *about* you?" replied Damian.

"We're supposed to be your security." He clearly didn't fancy his chances of keeping up with a man credited with once having some of the fastest legs in the country."

"The chance of an assassin lurking in Adam's undergrowth must be pretty remote. I'll take my chances. Everyone heard that?"

They all nodded.

Adam smiled and said: "Prime Minister's statement

197

noted. We are hereby absolved from any harm that might befall him."

Damian grinned: "If anyone does get me, I aim to be the fittest corpse in the morgue."

45

He started his gallop at little more than a trot. Although running was a bit of a bore, he had done a fair bit of it during his top sporting days and always took care to warm up. No need to pull a muscle. He reckoned his best distance had been the non-olympic event of twenty yards, where he'd have given Usain Bolt a run for his money, but stamina had also been on the agenda: not a full Marathon, but certainly ten to fifteen miles.

The Tichbold estate and its protective undergrowth did not last long. Within minutes he found himself in a country lane, lined with trees wondering whether it was time to burst into leaf. With intermittent sun, clouds racing across on a brisk westerly, temperature around eight Celsius, it was ideal running weather. It was also ideal running country, England being covered in a maze of public footpaths and bridleways. He soon managed to get off the road, along muddy lanes and edges of fields still awaiting their spring growth. All the while gradually upping his running tempo.

After a little over an hour he estimated the Tichbold estate to be three or four miles over to his right: somewhere. He had a good sense of direction, but they had always approached the Tichbold's in a chauffeur driven car, so he had taken little notice of the route or surrounding area. He knew he was somewhere in Berkshire, but that county meandered in a confusing fashion, from rural uplands in the west to England's industrial silicon valley in the east. On their first visit the drive from Reading station had not taken too long, but beyond that…..

The most frequent arguments with his ex, Mandy, had been over a reluctance to ask for directions when 'unsure' of his position: that's to say, lost. He was now 'unsure.'

A few minutes later the footpath he was following emerged into a B-road lined by a gaggle of houses. Hardly even a village, but it *did* have a newsagent, where middle England was busy collecting its Sunday papers. It was time to swallow his pride and fix his position, so he approached a man who had just emerged from the shop carrying a copy of Mail on Sunday.

"Tichbold? Nah, never heard of the place," he replied.

"Tichbold is the name of a person," Damian explained. "Not where he lives."

"You mean you don't know this guy's address? Or the name of his village?" The man peered suspiciously at Damian and added: "Ain't I seen you before somewhere?"

"Probably on a Police Wanted poster."

Uncertain whether this was meant as a joke, the man hesitated, then blurted out: "Sorry, mate, can't help you. Ask inside." Then departed as if pursued by a thousand devils.

Damian did as suggested and found the newsagent temporarily without a customer. The middle-aged man behind the counter was well built with thinning sandy coloured, wearing a navy blue pullover and striped *tie*. Who on earth would wear a *necktie* on a Sunday morning?

This time the reply to Damian's question was positive.

"You mean Tichbold, our local big noise," he confirmed. "Something to do with the government. Large house, lots of land."

"Can you tell me how to get there?"

"You in a car?"

Damian realised he couldn't have been a reassuring sight: hot, sweaty and out of breath; long sleeved shirt rolled up to the elbows; hair all over the place; muddy town shoes. A runner, perhaps, but not one geared for running. He shook his head and replied: "No car. I'm trying to keep fit."

"Got it!" The man waved a finger triumphantly. "Knew I'd seen you before, the moment you walked in."

Shit! thought Damian. I've been rumbled.

"In my younger days I was a big Hammers fan," said the man gleefully. He was well-spoken and quite pukka, as if he had come down a few notches in the world. "Never forget a face. You were their star striker back in…. well a while ago. Am I correct?"

Damian nodded, bemused. No mention of Strictly Come Dancing, when he'd been on view to the whole world. And no mention of politics. This fellow was running a newsagent, for goodness sake, a place where Damian's face had hardly left the front pages for days, yet he appeared to only connect him with football. Maybe it was a context problem: as prime minister, Damian was always well groomed and in a suit, whereas this scarecrow apparition could only be someone from sport; a former West Ham player minus his claret shirt.

"I follow the team's fortunes even now," continued the man, still into identity failure. "This season's been a bit of a disaster – as always. They'll need to buy some decent players on the summer transfer market. As for their manager…."

Damian let him rabbit on for a short while, answering the odd question, but becoming increasingly impatient. He was saved by the rumble of his mobile. With an apology, he extracted it from his pocket.

"Where the hell *are* you?" It was Chloe.

"Don't know exactly. I'm trying to find out."

"Bill and Ben are in hysterics: want to alert the police, close all borders, summon the Cobra team. How soon will you be back?"

"Just a mo. I'll check."

He found the newsagent eyeing him with a grin: "Your good lady not happy?"

"Lunch is on the table. Threatening to start without me. Any idea how long it'll take to get back? To Tichbold's?"

"*I* would need at least half an hour, but *you*… if you're half the man you once were…maybe ten minutes."

"How do I get there?"

"See that pub on the corner….well, take the footpath on the far side, follow it for about a mile….."""

Damian tried to lock the stream of instructions into his head. Cut the man short when he reckoned he'd got it. Time for a sprint down the home straight.

"Thanks for your help!" Damian waved a goodbye and shot out of the shop. The last thing he saw was the dawning of full recognition in the newsagent's face.

46

Halfway home the heavens opened. By that time Damian was going full blast, so the cooling effect was welcome. But it was a sodden and out-of-breath scarecrow that finally burst through the Tichbold's back door.

"Off with those clothes! Into the shower!" Chloe was becoming quite bossy.

"Can't have nude dining," said Adam. "We must be about the same size round the nether regions, so he can have a pair of my boxer shorts."

"I'll lend him a spare dressing gown," said Hermione. "Rinse out the clothes; put them in the airing cupboard. With luck, he should be presentable for the journey home."

"If not, I'm sure you can let him have your robe on an extended loan, my dear," said Adam. "Prime minister arrives back in Number Ten dressed for bed! That should keep the gossip writers happy."

Damian took the ribbing in good part. Little else he could do. But in truth *he* was also happy. Hadn't realised how much the past two weeks of physical sloth had taken its toll. He needed exercise like a druggie depended on his daily shots, so the run had returned him to top form.

Now scrubbed and smelling civilised, dressed in his host's underpants, his own pullover left behind before the run, and his hostess's robe and slippers, the prime minister made his entrée to the Tichbold drawing room. Went straight to Bessie Robotham and gave her a hug. When arranging the get-together Adam had at first not mentioned Bessie, which Damian suspected had been deliberate: if their past history gave Bessie problems with Adam, the converse must also be true. Neither would be comfortable in the other's company. But Damian had insisted on her presence and Adam had immediately agreed. Bessie had arrived while Damian had been on his run.

"We're already running late," Hermione pointed out, giving Damian a reproachful look. "The sooner we eat the better."

"In a moment, my dear." Adam was approaching Damian, offering a glass of wine. "We're having sirloin of beef, so I trust red will be acceptable?"

"Of course."

"A Nuits St.Georges, nine years old, so should be quite drinkable." Tichbold was a wine traditionalist: Burgundy or Bordeaux for preference; some German whites were almost acceptable: Italy, Spain…? Maybe. The New World…? Perhaps one day. His cellar was legendary.

"Before going in to lunch, I would like to reflect for a moment. Remember an old friend and in my case…." Adam smiled. "…In my case an old opponent. Ladies and gentlemen: Gerry Farthing."

"To Gerry."

Silence, except for the slow intake of Burgundy. No eye remained dry.

Damian was the first to find his voice, although there was a catch in it: "Have they selected another leader yet?"

"You know the Labour party," replied Adam. "Choosing a leader takes forever and is more painful than childbirth."

"Come on, we'll continue this discussion round the

table," ordered Hermione, leading the way in.

"I hear Iran has chipped in with some nice words," said Bessie. "Maybe we are no longer children of Satan."

"Gerry espoused some interesting causes," said Adam, as they sat down. "Some were lost causes, but all were interesting. He was Westminster's unchallenged expert on Iran; knew much more about the country than me and I was supposed to be foreign secretary."

"They won't be remembering Gerry with their best booze in Teheran," said Damian.

Adam laughed: "Orange juice, more like. I'm something of a wine buff and remember once tasting an Iranian vintage. From the Shah's time, of course. Thousand and One, they called it. Pretty nasty stuff, but I was amazed they even had a wine industry. No doubt now classed as the devil's brew: the Mullahs won't allow it."

Reminiscing about the deceased's quirks had lightened the mood. Hermione's excellent cooking and Adam's Nuits St.Georges did the rest. The hammering of rain on the windows and Britain's population plummeting under the worst plague for a century, all for the moment forgotten.

47

It was after three by the time they extracted themselves from the dining room and ambled into the lounge, where Hermione had dispensed coffee. Hermione herself had more important matters to deal with than running the country: clearing up after the meal and making sure Fidget was happy. So the quorum on that April afternoon was just four: for the government there was the Prime Minister, Minister without Portfolio and Home Secretary. Representing the Fourth Estate was a reporter from the Oxford Herald, now in the position all journalists dream of but rarely achieve, so much part of the scenery that no one questioned her presence.

"So you want to bring the election forward?" asked Adam, placing his coffee carefully on a small table and easing himself into a deep chair.

"I've been advised it might be a good idea," replied Damian.

"Advised by whom?"

"My election agent and guru, Alec Warbeck."

"Oxfordshire starting to wobble?"

"Alec thinks the whole *country* may wobble if we dither much longer. I've called this meeting to canvas opinion. As all good prime ministers should."

"Back again to the example of India in forty seven," mused Adam. "History has not been kind to Mountbatten; says he panicked, gave away the jewel in the crown far too quickly; the partition riots and slaughter all his fault. But it's one of those stupid 'what if' arguments. We'll never know. My view, for what it's worth – probably not much – is that waiting any longer would have been even more disastrous. A quick surgical amputation was the lesser evil."

"I don't thing Gerry would have approved any similar butchery," said Bessie.

"Gerry is no longer with us," said Damian quickly, keen to quell any argument between the two old protagonists. "We're the ones left carrying the baby, even if Gerry was the one who gave it birth. And I tend to agree with my friend Alec – and Adam: we have to get a move on."

Bessie: "How fast exactly?"

Damian: "I like the French idea of Sunday elections. So let's say three weeks from now: April the twenty eighth."

Bessie: "That's *much* earlier than Gerry would have wanted."

Damian: "Gerry was never a Speedy Gonzales. But I am. If the training of returning officers and all the machinery of our new system is not fully rehearsed in another three weeks, so be it. An STV count is tedious at the best of times. We'll have experts on hand to help if things get sticky and just take a little longer."

"What about all that interesting legislation we're trying to push through before the curtain falls?" asked Bessie.

"We have a blitz," said Adam. "Do what we can in the time available. I believe Damian's keen to save the National Health Service?"

Bessie: "Don't be silly! People have been trying to save the NHS since the day it was invented. All have failed."

Damian: "So we try again. Most MPs are too scared of losing their seats to do anything adventurous, so I'm prepared to carry the can for anything we try. After all, I'm the Night Watchman. Expendable. Just holding the fort until the higher order batsman can take over again. That's you, Adam."

Tichbold squirmed. "I wouldn't put it quite like that."

"I believe you once did. Said you reserved the right to challenge me for the leadership once we had a full parliament."

"Actually, you've been doing pretty well….."

"Cut the flannel, you old rogue." Damian was grinning, not a bit put out. "We all know the score. It's a fluke I'm here. You're the political heavyweight. When normal service is resumed, you'll take your rightful place at the head table."

Bessie, softly: "The scum always rises to the top."

"Shut up, Bessie!" Now Damian was angry. "We're in this together, so keep personal squabbles out of it. The point is if *I* take the flak for any contentious legislation, it'll leave you two in the clear for the next parliament."

"I don't like that word 'contentious', said Adam.

"Few people do," said Damian. "But we're living in a brief window of opportunity when radical change may be possible…."

Bessie: "You can't live in a window…."

Damian ignored her and continued: "…After a struggle lasting a century and a half, we've at last managed to bury our ancient voting system. Let's try and kill off a few more sacred cows while we're at it."

"If your proposals are too crazy, you won't get them through parliament," Adam pointed out.

"I might. Our interim parliament is not only much slimmer than the previous model, it's also very different. When AfroAir demolished the House of Commons, it removed the cream of its inhabitants. You two and Gerry were almost the only ones from the old lot to survive. The masters and prefects have mostly gone, leaving the new boys and girls to run the show. Kids like me might take the opportunity to indulge in a little rebellion. As kids do."

"What changes would you like to make?" asked Bessie.

"Actually, nothing 'crazy'. Just sensible. But they'll be unpalatable, which is why they've been funked for so long."

Bessie: "Spell it out."

"Today's NHS is a world away from the original concept, which was that good health should not depend on having a good bank balance. It's now seen as a bottomless pit of goodies which everyone has a right to plunder. If a woman can't have kids, she's off to the fertility clinic for treatment costing a fortune; if you eat yourself silly and reach thirty stone, there's an obesity clinic to sort you out for nothing – actually not for *nothing*, because *someone* has to pay and that someone is the rest of us who are not into self harm; as for the legions of hypochondriacs, most GPs are only too ready to get rid of them with endless prescriptions – again at our expense."

"So no more IVF, no more fatty clinics, no more free pills?" asked Bessie.

"You've got it," replied Damian. "The country can't afford it. We're effectively bust and need to re-establish some basic principles. If you are genuinely skint, then the state will continue to provide necessities like food and basic medicine. Beyond that, if you want something, you pay for it."

"There'll be rioting in the streets," said Bessie.

"Probably," said the Prime Minister. "With the ringleaders summoning their troops using the latest smart-phones. We now have a new definition of 'poverty'."

"The Roman Empire collapsed because the plebs got

hooked on free bread and circuses," mused Adam. "Perhaps we're headed the same way."

Damian nodded: "We either reform or go under. Not only should you pay for what you want, there should also be an obligation to work for any money received. Again, apart from a safety net for the genuinely disabled."

Bessie: "So no more benefits?"

Damian: "Any fit person receiving unemployment benefit will have to turn up for work should they be needed. Fruit picking in season, removing graffiti and litter picking any time…."

Bessie: "I thought litter was reserved for those doing porridge?"

Damian: "You know what I mean, Bessie. The elderly and decrepit, those that have done a decent life's work, will have earned the right to sit in front of the telly all day. But we're breeding a generation of perfectly fit *youngsters* who think it's their right to develop square eyes in front of the box. A generation that believes money grows on trees. A generation with an idleness ethic. Maybe we're only talking about a minority, but there's enough of them to cost us a fortune. And they could turn dangerous. If you've grown up believing you have a divine right to eat the state's sweets and then the state suddenly takes these treats away, you'll probably throw a tantrum."

"You may be right, but this is Contentious with a capital C," said Adam. "Next thing we know there'll be guillotines in Whitehall."

"I aim to draft two bills," said the prime minister, unperturbed. "A National Health Service reform bill. And a Benefits reform bill. Try and get the House to accept them. If they're rejected, at least I'll have tried."

"You won't have time," said Bessie. "Not if you also want an election in three weeks."

"It's amazing how fast you can get legislation through the House if you really try," said Damian. "Remember the Fixed Term Parliament? One of the wheezes dreamt up by Cameron and Clegg. That disappeared, like a puff of smoke, overnight."

"You're in a double bind," Adam pointed out. "Taking on not only complex and….." he grinned "…. contentious legislation. You also need to get yourself re-elected. Or don't you intend to hang around after this brief moment of glory?"

"I certainly *do* mean to 'hang around'." Damian gave the other two a long hard look. "Maybe not from Number Ten, but making life a misery for Bessie from the back benches was such fun I'd happily go back to that."

"In that case, you can't afford to neglect our lords and masters, the electorate," said Adam. "Under the old system we three were lucky enough to have safe seats. Come an election, we'd put on a bit of a show and prance around the constituency saying the right things, but we knew nothing we said or did made the slightest difference: the bookies were laying better odds on an alien invasion than us losing. Gerry's new dream-child has changed all that. There's no longer any such thing as a safe seat."

"True enough," admitted Damian. "My patch of Mid Oxon has been merged into the bigger constituency Oxfordshire, which will return three MPs: would have been four had we not also reduced the number of MPs. The main parties will all put up three candidates, but which of the three emerges top of the poll, with the best chance of going to Westminster, will be up to the voters."

"Any idea how thing are shaping up for you?" asked Adam.

Damian: "The rural areas are heavily Tory, while the city of Oxford is equally solid for Labour: academics and students love to dream the socialist dream. Who will win the third seat is an interesting question. Certainly not Labour, so it'll be a scramble between the Lib Dems and us."

"Meanwhile, we're fighting like cat and dog amongst ourselves to be the one to top our own poll," said Adam.

"Which is as it should be," said Damian. "With a preferential system most voters will not only get an MP from their favourite *party*, they'll also be able to influence which *individuals* of that party go to Westminster."

"In that case it's time to pack our bags and take the first train home," said Chloe.

All eyes turned to reporter Pettigrew.

"You've been pretty quiet," said Adam. "Thought you hacks were wordsmiths."

Chloe smiled. "We're merely recorders of events. It's not our job to *influence* those events, although that's what some of my colleagues try to do."

"You're the Homer to our Odyssey", said Adam. This produced some bemused looks, so he added: "Sorry about that. Eton gave me a classical education: not much use in the modern world. Homer was a hack who recorded events in blank verse. I trust you'll be equally poetic with us, Chloe."

Chloe smiled: "Of course, Adam. But as most of us did not go to Eton, I won't be doing it in Greek. Just plain English. If that's okay?"

Bessie: "What she means is she's taking everything down to use in evidence against us," said Bessie.

"No harm in that," said Adam. "If you can't stand up to the press, you shouldn't be in this job."

Seeing another Robotham-Tichbold feud brewing, Damian cut in quickly: "Ccan we settle on Sunday the twenty eighth of April for the election?"

Tichbold: "Done!"

Robotham, after a pause: "I suppose so."

Damian: "In the meantime I'll bulldoze what legislation I can through the House. Call for dissolution at the last possible moment. And that….would seem to be that?" He looked around questioningly.

There was a moment's silence. Then Adam said: "We meet at Philippi."

More blank stares, so he added: "That damned classical education again! Shakespeare's words from his play Julius Caesar, when the conspirators agreed to meet up again at Philippi."

If you're planning to stick a dagger into Damian's toga, I'll thank you to leave it until after the election," said Chloe. "Never mind Philippi: we're off to Paddington. To catch a train home."

Chloe was wrong. She had forgotten that her lover's current job, like Caesar's, carried the bonus of possible assassination. They would be returning to Wheatley in the Prime Ministerial limo, guarded by Bill and Ben.

48

The Prime Minister was bushed. But happy.

It had been a hectic eighteen days, but in that time he had managed to steer most of his legislation through the House. There had been compromises, of course, never got one's *entire* wish list, but the essentials had passed their second reading. Tomorrow the king would add his scrawl, making the NHS Reform Bill and Benefits Reform Bill, Acts of Parliament. The law.

The Great Plague had also settled into a routine, so much so that the media had more or less lost interest. Every few days Damian had phoned Sir Marcus Merton for an update, enjoyable chats because the epidemiologist was always so cheerful.

"Mortality rates are holding at about eight percent," Sir Marcus would say breathlessly, as though commentating on a horse race. "Although that figure can only be an estimate. People are panicking less, just taking to their beds until they recover. Or don't. So we can only guess at the total number of cases, which makes any sort of statistical survey rather suspect."

"But your graphs have hopefully stopped rising?" asked Damian.

"Indeed. They're flat-lining. As in those hospital dramas, when someone snuffs it. Lots of bells go off, heart

214

monitor flat lines." Sir Marcus giggled.

"Any signs that your graphs might start going *down*?"

"Dear me, no! If nineteen eighteen is anything to go by, this epidemic still has lots of life left in it."

"Or death."

It took a moment for Sir Marcus to catch on. When he did, he was contrite: "An inappropriate phrase I'm afraid. Yes, I regret that several million souls are still due to die from this virus." He did not sound too regretful.

I guess what keeps people going is the knowledge the odds are heavily stacked in their favour," mused Damian. "For a start, most people will *not* catch the bug. And if you do, there's less than a one in ten chance of dying from it."

"Exactly," agreed Sir Marcus. "By the time it fizzles, I'd expect the virus to have accounted for maybe three percent of our population: five percent tops. No comparison with the devastating plagues of the Middle Ages. In fact, hardly worth bothering about. The last substantial cull of civilians in this country must have been the German bombing raids of the nineteen forties. People soon grew to accept them. Life continued almost as normal. And you seem to be doing a good job disposing of the extra bodies."

"Credit for that must go to the Chief of Defence Staff, Admiral Horrocks," said Damian. "At first he didn't like being diverted from playing with his boats, but I must say he's come up trumps. Thanks to his troops, we now have conveyor-belt crematoria. Corpse to cinder in a couple of hours. Twenty four, seven."

"Brilliant!" said Sir Marcus. "I like things nice and tidy. No loose ends. Allows me to continue gathering data with a clear conscience."

"I imagine you'll eventually have plenty of figures to work with."

"Unprecedented, I hope. Trouble with those Middle Ages plagues is lack of reliable information. Records sketchy, no proper attempt at collation. Even with the Spanish flu, little more than a century ago, there's a lot of guesswork."

"I thought you said this present outbreak was also guess-prone," said Damian, perhaps unkindly. "Due to not knowing how many people actually caught the virus."

"We'll never reach perfect knowledge, but record keeping is now so thorough we'll know with precision not only *how many* have died, but also their sex, age and location. A breakthrough in epidemiology."

"And doing your reputation no harm."

Sir Marcus laughed. "We live and die by our reputations, prime minister. You, of all people, must know that."

"Too true. And in three days time I'll have to defend that reputation in an election. So, if you'll excuse me…."

As he put down the receiver, Damian reflected that his future in parliament, never mind as prime minister, was looking increasingly precarious. He had always wanted to get rid of First-Past-the-Post, which was grossly unfair, highly unpredictable and on two occasions had left the party with the most votes as number two in seats. He had therefore been one of the main supporters of Farthing's Electoral Reform Bill. Unfortunately, it could also be the vehicle for kicking him out of parliament.

Under the old system, he'd had the constituency of Mid Oxon sewn up. A solid mass of Tory blue plus many floaters won over by his fame and personality. A majority of at least twenty thousand in the bag.

But Mid Oxon was now history and his agent, Alec Warbeck, was saying that new constituency of Oxfordshire would return three MPs, where the projections for Damian were not good. Tory and Labour would almost certainly win one each, leaving Tories and Lib Dms battling for the third.

There would be an even more ferocious *internal* fight to head the polls in one's own party. In the old days, this would have been decided by a handful of the faithful in a smoke-filled room, but now it was up to the voters, who no longer had the task of just putting a cross against one name from a short list, but could select as many preferences as they felt like from a much longer list. Most people would go 'One-two-three' for candidates of *their* party, then maybe further down the list 'four-five-six...' until they got fed up. Or they might venture across party lines. Unless they were fans of the Monster Raving Loonies, they should end up by electing *someone*. More fun than the old way. And simple enough.

Not so for the people running the show, which was why Gerry Farthing had wanted a long training period. To get elected a candidate had to achieve 'the quota', calculated by a formula involving total votes caste and seats to be filled. As it was rare for anyone to reach the quota on their first preferences, votes would then be transferred from the no-hopers at the bottom of the pile and then excess votes from those already elected until, in the case of Oxfordshire, three candidates had reached that quota.

It was a complex business, which would probably cause hiccups on this first outing, but experts were on hand to sort things out. The full result would probably not be known for several days, but so what? They would get it right in the end.

Damian had quite another worry. Maybe it was hubris, maybe not paying attention, but he had started off by assuming he would easily sail into the Tory's pole position, therefore guaranteed a place in Westminster. After all, his had been a household name for years, first with West

Ham, later with Strictly Come Dancing. And now he was Prime Minister. What could go wrong?

What was going wrong went under the name of Rupert Delahaye, another of the Tory candidates. Damian, sitting smugly in his Mid Oxon bubble, had been slow to realise that he now had the rest of the county to consider. Not only the largely Labour city of Oxford, but more importantly the rest of the shire, which was as true blue as his part, but ruled by a seigneur of impressive lineage, Rupert Delahaye.

The Delahayes claimed descent from a knight who had landed in Pevensey Bay with William Duke of Normandy in 1066. This first De la Haye must have wielded his sword to good effect, because he soon found himself the proud owner of several thousand acres north of a city called Oxenford. His descendents still lived there, albeit under reduced circumstances, now with a mere three hundred acres.

Damian White, the one they called the Whisky Man because his name was white while his skin was black, could only offer an ancestor that landed with the Empire Windrush in 1948. In the snobbery stakes it was no contest.

Had family background been Damian's only handicap it might not have mattered, but there were more serious obstacles. From their estate just west of Banbury the Delahayes had controlled the constituency of North Oxon since….well, it seemed like since 1066. Cedric Delahaye had entered parliament in his late twenties and was tipped to one day become the 'Father of the House', it's oldest serving member. AfroAir had put paid to that.

Cedric had been the perfect constituency MP, not so ambitious that he was too often absent on affairs of state, instead he was assiduous in attending to the needs of his domain: patting equine muzzles at gymkhanas; snipping

218

ribbons to open new buildings; speaking at Rotaries, Lions clubs, Women's Institutes. The best type of country squire. A man respected and loved.

You don't survive as a family for a millennium without taking seriously the business of procreation, so when Cedric had been confirmed as one of the Leaning Tower victims, the next in line was there to effortlessly step into his shoes.

Colonel Rupert Delahaye was in his mid forties, well into a distinguished military career and tipped to go all the way to the top. Unlike his father, Rupert *was* ambitious, so when he promptly resigned his commission in mid-stream to follow the family trade of politics, he was in no mood to take any prisoners. Rupert Delahaye was going flat out to be the voters' first Tory choice. The signs were that he would succeed.

Damian and his election agent Alec Warbeck had thrashed the problem around over countless drinks until they were punch-drunk.

"Rupert is so damned sound!" grumbled Warbeck, implying that Damian was not. The ultimate political insult is to be labelled as 'unsound'.

"His dad *always* followed the party line," continued the election agent. "And I'll bet Rupert will do the same. Sandhurst training. Discipline and all that."

As opposed to Damian White, who had made his name by *defying* the party.

The Whisky Man might have been the darling of West Ham fans, a Strictly winner and currently prime minister of the United Kingdom, but all the signs were that he would be pipped to the post as top Oxford Tory by Colonel Delahaye.

After a week crunching the numbers, moaning to himself and dithering, Warbeck had finally delivered his verdict: "I reckon your best bet – maybe your *only* bet – is to make a play for that third spot."

"I thought Elwyn would get that?"

Elwyn Evans was the leading Lib Dem candidate, considered to have a decent chance of making it as number three.

"He won't if you pull your finger out," replied Warbeck. "Although Mid Oxon will vote you solid number ones, in the county as a whole Delahaye looks to have you beat. So you need to set your sights on Elwyn; fight for those second, third, fourth preferences, when they start transferring votes from the rubbish at the bottom and left-overs at the top."

"How do I do that?"

"You're a rebel at heart, Damian, so go for the rebel vote. Take a trip home to Blackbird Leys, rebel territory if ever I saw it. And spend some time in the dives of Oxford city. Students normally detest Tories, but they *love* you. In their eyes you're hardly a Tory."

The prime minister had taken his election agent's advice and hit the Oxford highspots. And lowspots. On Saturday he was due to visit the Kassam stadium, for an Oxford United end-of-season home game. Some fans had not forgiven him for deserting his sporting homeland for the brighter lights of London, but most realised that no one with true ambition signed up for Oxford; the Kassam would be sure to welcome a famous local lad – hopefully also with votes.

It had been an exhausting period, Chloe a tower of strength by his side. Now it was nearly over. Three days to go until the election. He'd done his best. Couldn't do more.

49

It was still dark when the phone rang. Which in late April meant *early*. Damian thrashed around for the receiver and succeeded in knocking his alarm clock on the floor. Chloe turned in her sleep and mumbled what sounded like an obscenity. Could one dream obscenities?

At last he found the receiver: "What the hell is it?!" Although they were not in Number Ten, but on the campaign trail in Damian's Wheatley flat, he had made the usual arrangement to be disturbed only in an emergency. This had better be an emergency!

It was Home Secretary, Bessie Robotham: "Sorry to wake you, but I've just had a call from Jacob…" She sounded as groggy as he felt. "You know….Jacob…"

"Jacob Wells? The spook?"

"S…right. He says there's been an invasion."

"Christ! Not Afghanistan again?"

"No, Hampshire."

"How can anyone invade Hampshire? That's in England."

"Exactly. That's why Jacob rang me. And why I'm telling *you*."

"Admiral Horrocks said this might happen. Said our

221

armed forces were now so feeble, the Vikings could take Lindisfarne if they felt like it."

"This lot don't sound like Vikings. Call themselves the Heroes of Hattin."

"Heroes of Hating, what the hell does that mean?"

"Not Hating: Hattin. That's Hotel, Alpha, Tango, Tango, India, November."

"Okay, Hattin. I'm none the wiser."

"Jacob says it's an Islamic thing. Going back a thousand years. Bottom line is they've taken over Fort Brockhurst."

"Fort where?"

"Just shut up and listen…." Bessie had forgotten she was speaking to the prime minister. *Damian* had forgotten *he* was the prime minister.

She continued: "…Some time during the night a group calling themselves the Heroes of Hattin broke into Fort Brockhurst. Claimed the place for the Islamic republic of Hattin. Said they were heavily armed and would repel any attempt to remove them. That's all we know."

"What….where is this Fort Brockhurst?"

"Hampshire. Gosport."

"How many…. 'invaders'?"

"No idea. When you've woken up, turn on the telly and find out. BBC, ITV, all the media's there. They'll know a fat lot more than we do."

"Any sign that these…heroes of wherever are planning to march on London?"

"Don't think so. Sounds more like they're digging in for a siege."

"In that case there's not much I can do at the moment.

Give me a couple of hours more kip; ask Jacob to call me at, say, seven-ish. Suggest you do the same. *Good night, Bessie!"*

He replaced the receiver gently, trying not to wake Chloe, a needless precaution because she was one of those girls who could sleep for England. Once gone, nothing seemed to disturb her.

Damian himself was not so lucky. He tossed around for half an hour and dawn was breaking when he finally gave up. Dragged himself out of bed, put on the kettle for coffee.

And turned on the TV. Might as well get himself up to speed on events.

He surfed the channels, but all offered much the same fare. Something dramatic had occurred, but then everything had gone quiet, so reporters were desperately trying to stretch what little information they had.

Which amounted to the fact that the inhabitants of Gunners Way Gosport had been woken shortly after midnight by the sound of heavy vehicles thundering outside. No attempt had been made to keep quiet, so it was assumed the noise was deliberate. Annoyed by the disturbance, some sleepyheads had got up and drawn back lace curtains to see what was going on. A Mr. Fred Smith described how he had seen some dark figures break the locks on Fort Brockhurst's landward gate, after which the convoy of nineteen - he had counted - army type lorries had driven over the bridge that crossed the moat, through the main gate and into the fort.

Just after 1am the BBC had received a message from an organisation calling itself 'Heroes of the Horns of Hattin', announcing that Fort Brockhurst was no longer part of the United Kingdom, but had been captured by the Islamic Republic of Hattin. Any attempt to retake the fort would result in what they described as 'a thousand infidel

223

corpses'. A similar message had appeared on social media networks. No ransom demands had been made, nothing more said, except to stand by for further announcements.

These stark facts being the sum total of actual knowledge, reporters had fallen back on speculation. A dip into the history books established that the Horns of Hattin had been a notable victory for the Moslems against Christian Crusaders during the twelfth century. So motivation appeared to be the all too familiar one of Islamic extremism.

Beyond that, guesswork reigned supreme, in particular as to how well equipped this invading 'army' might be. Military experts were hauled out of bed for clarification, but this was an impossible task seeing that the trucks had been battened down to hide their cargoes. Nineteen large vehicles could accommodate an awful lot of soldiers and military hardware. Almost anything, really. One expert even flirted with the notion of a 'small nuclear device.'

On one fact the experts were all agreed: the Heroes of Hattin could hardly have chosen a better target to attack and then defend. Getting in had been absurdly easy, the fort apparently uninhabited, its landward approach guarded only by a ramshackle fence with a lock any child could break. After that it had been a matter of moments for the convoy to drive across a narrow bridge that spanned the moat, through the main gate and into the fort.

On the other hand, removing the invaders would *not* be easy. Looming behind the moat, which was wide and surrounded the fort on all sides, were ramparts, not that high, but immensely thick and pierced by slits designed to give an all-round field of fire. Trying to gain intelligence about the occupying force would also be difficult, because only the bare and forbidding walls could be seen from the outside. Fort Brockhurst may have been designed in another age to stop the French, but the basics of infantry assault had barely changed in two hundred years: it would

224

still be a difficult and dangerous place to re-take by conventional means.

In an effort to find something interesting to talk about, the media then turned their attention to the strip of cloth that had been hoisted on the fort's flagstaff. As night turned to day and a breeze sprang up, the design began to reveal itself: a green background with what looked like a curved silver sword in the centre. The Saracen sword of Saladin.

After half an hour telly watching, Damian reckoned he had learnt as much as he was going to, so went off to shave and get dressed. After that, he gave Chloe a dig in the ribs and a 'wakey wakey' in the ear. They were a reasonably compos mentis couple having breakfast by the time Jacob Wells rang at the appointed hour of seven.

"I know as much as the BBC does," was Damian's reply to Jacob's opening query. "Anything more you can tell me?"

"We've had the Heroes of Hattin under low level surveillance for about a year," replied MI5's Director General. "Didn't appear to be a threat, which is why it was only low level."

"Nothing appears to be a threat until it strikes," said Damian wearily. And immediately regretted being critical. The security services did an amazing job under impossible circumstances.

"You'd be horrified if you knew how many crazies there are out there," said Jacob. "But we're not the Stasi or KGB and don't have the manpower to keep a proper eye on all of them. To say nothing of the uproar there'd be if we started arresting every nutter that came to our attention. But we *do* know who's the leader of this little lot."

"That's something, I suppose."

"Name of Hamid Khan, born in Birmingham thirty

eight years ago to parents originally from Pakistan. Now goes under the name of Salah-ud-Din."

"A resurrection of the Saracen hero?"

"That's right. Hamid Khan – let's call him that – is older and better educated than the usual terrorist. After leaving school he took an economics degree at Birmingham University. We then lost sight of him for a while: these guys lead shadowy lives. We think he went off to fight for IS – Islamic State, after which he probably spent time in his ancestral homelands in Pakistan. Four years ago he was definitely back in the UK – he's a British citizen, remember - and started to acquire a following, almost exclusively of unattached young men from the third world."

"Perfect cannon fodder."

Jacob sighed and continued: "It's difficult to exaggerate the plight of these lost souls, millions of whom have been pouring into Europe for at least the past two decades. No homes, no roots, no women, no money, no jobs, no prospects. No wonder they flock to any pseudo messiah that offers them the slightest hope."

"Enter Hamid Khan."

"A clever chap, Hamid, I'll give him that. You can no longer get away with blatant hate preaching, so the message of Salah-uh-Din, as he calls himself, is all about past glories. No arguing with that. The Islamic world of a thousand years ago was more civilised, even more tolerant than its Christian counterpart. Brainwash impressionable minds with such stuff and those not already Muslims will soon be signing on the dotted line."

"The seventy two virgins must help."

Jacob sighed again: "I think the media makes too much of those virgins awaiting the martyrs in paradise. I believe Salah-ud-Din's biggest attraction is giving these men a purpose in life. A sense of belonging. Something they've never known before. Something worth dying for."

"But we don't know what this lot might be prepared to die for?"

"No we don't. Which is a puzzle. Our best brains have been working on this and no one's yet come up with a convincing answer. But our modern Saladin has promised us more information, so we can only wait. It's part of the game. Meanwhile, might I suggest, prime minister, that you'd be better placed in the centre of things in London. I realise the election is important, but Oxford is rather out on a limb if this turns into a real crisis. I would also strongly urge a meeting of Cobra."

"Good idea. I first need to tie up a few loose ends with my election agent, Alec, but we should be able to get away by ten."

"So back in Downing Street well before midday? Allowing a break for lunch, can I set up Cobra for two o'clock?"

"Do that. I'll see you in the Cabinet Office a few minutes before two."

50

Damian and Chloe finished breakfast, after which Alec Warbeck arrived to discuss their election campaign, which now had to be cancelled for the day because of Saladin. This might cost him a few votes, but needs must.

Damian had left the BBC news channel on in case of further developments, which was just well because Chloe suddenly exclaimed: "Something's happening!"

He turned the sound back on to hear the reporter say in excited but hushed tones: "....there's to be a statement. Which will be made from *inside* the fort. They've promised us safe conduct, but are only allowing *one* camera team in and only a basic crew of two, the cameraman and myself. So the quality may not be…..ah, here we go."

They saw the fort's main gate open and two men in military fatigues emerge. One of them beckoned the BBC team forward. As they approached the gate they were quickly and expertly frisked, then allowed to continue.

For the first time viewers were able to see Fort Brockhurst from the inside. The walls, which seemed even more solid from this angle, enclosed a wide open space, with a two-storey building in the centre. About half of this open area now served as a parade ground, with a platoon of maybe thirty men drawn up on one side. They wore the type of camouflage dress common to all armies and ranks, with forage caps on top and AK-47 rifles by their sides. In front of this group stood three men also dressed in khaki but less smart, unarmed and bareheaded. In front of *them,* making the arrow head of a wide V-shaped pattern, was what appeared to be a single NCO: the sergeant major? Apart from the small group of three, everyone was standing at attention, clean shaven and smart. Impressively military.

After being allowed to film the men on parade, the BBC team was ordered to stand to one side and face towards a small rostrum in the centre of the square. When everything had settled, what was obviously the commanding officer appeared from the far side, striding briskly towards the platform. He was about six foot tall, sharp featured with brownish skin, his face sporting about a week's growth of designer stubble. He was dressed in camouflage, like his men, but on his head wore a green beret adorned with a small silver scimitar. A real sword, the scabbard decorated with an intricate pattern, swung by his side.

The Commander mounted the platform and eyed his men.

The NCO yelled: "Prese..e..e..nt arms."

Which they did. Surprisingly well.

NCO saluted.

Commander returned salute.

NCO yelled: "Orde..e..e..er arms."

Again pretty well done. Not the Brigade of Guards, but good enough to show this was no rabble. Which was the purpose of the exercise.

The Commander spoke for the first time: "At ease, men." Everyone relaxed.

Looking directly at the camera, he said: "My name is General Salah-ud-Din, leader of the Islamic Army of Hattin. Before going any further, let me just say that the men you see before you are only a small part of my occupying force. The rest are at their posts, alert and ready to repel any attack. I suggest you do not try."

Hamid Khan, alias Salah-ud-Din, had thrown off any Brummie accent he might once have had, his accent classless, educated.

He continued: "There are now six million Moslems living in Britain, about ten percent of the population. In some city areas we make up the overwhelming majority. Many people grumble about ethnic ghettoes and I agree with them. This is a problem and I am here today to offer a solution."

"There is a precedent to what I'm about to propose. My parents came from Pakistan, which was carved out of British India so that they could worship in their own way in peace. The purpose of the Hattin army is to ensure a similar outcome for Moslems in Britain. An area to call our own. We will leave this fort as soon as there's a satisfactory agreement."

"My earnest hope is that this can be arranged amicably, but realistically I know we may have to fight for it. I've taken the name of a famous warrior from the past, Salah-ud-Din, who threw the Christian interlopers out of the holy land. My ancestors, the Khans, are also know as fearless warriors. My men….well, you see them before you, all ready to die for the cause."

As he said this, the Commander stepped off the platform and strolled towards the camera.

A smile on his face, he continued: "There's a nice story, you may have heard it: about an admiral called Byng, who lost a few ships and….to everyone's astonishment was executed for it. It was done, they said, to encourage the others."

Salah-ud-Din beckoned the BBC camera forward. It followed him as he came to a halt in front of the three men who formed the separate group.

Turning to the camera, he said: "We raided an army depot on our way here and these three were foolish enough to try and stop us. As with Byng, life isn't always fair…."

Salah-ud-Din pondered for a moment, then pointed to the man on the left. "You!"

Two men from the platoon came up and frog-marched the prisoner a few paces forwards.

The memory of millions watching the broadcast in real time had one thing in common: the events of the next few seconds happened with lightning speed, yet agonisingly slowly.

The NCO grabbed the prisoner and ordered: "Kneel."

The prisoner, an ordinary looking man in his thirties, looked too bemused to refuse – not that it would have done him much good.

Salah-ud-Din drew his sword from the scabbard, stepped back two paces and took aim. The scimitar whirred. It was such a clean cut that the head rolled a few feet across the parade ground before coming to a stop. For an appreciable instant the torso remained upright, gushing a fountain of blood to a brain that had departed. As the body collapsed, a dark red stain, unnervingly like a map of Africa, spread slowly over the parade ground.

The Commander handed his weapon to the NCO: "Clean it, Sarn't Major."

"Sir!" The NCO took a cloth from his pocket and wiped the blood off the blade. Handed it back.

Salah-ud-Din replaced the scimitar in its beautifully crafted scabbard and turned to the camera.

Smiled and said: "To encourage the others."

51

The journey to London in the government limo was the most miserable Damian could ever recall making. Like biblical Job, he felt overwhelmed by the catastrophes that kept cascading down on the country. And on him. The AfroAir crash had been a shock, but in a strange way stimulating; a crisis to set the adrenaline flowing. The flu epidemic had crept up on them more slowly, but again he felt they had done what they could. The first had been an accident, the second an act of God. These things happened. But this outrage was different. This was pure evil. How could one cope with wickedness on such a scale?

"Why didn't the BBC pull the plug when they realised what was about to happen?" murmured Chloe. "We could *all* see what he was going to do."

After the upcoming Cobra meeting Damian would have to remain in Downing Street overnight, so Chloe had offered to come with him. An offer he had accepted gratefully. The thought of sleeping in Number Ten alone, with nothing but the nightmare of a decapitated head rolling across the tarmac to keep him company, was beyond contemplating.

Damian answered her question: "The BBC did nothing because, like everyone, they were in shock. Couldn't believe their eyes. Rabbit in the headlights effect. Happened so damned fast."

"I'll bet he planned it like that."

"Of course he did. Islamic extremists have a long

history of using the sword as a terror weapon. Quite often these executions have been filmed, but watching them is so horrific they've never reached a wider public. This was planned specifically to make sure the *whole world* would be watching. Women, children, everyone. Hamid has 'encouraged us' with a vengeance."

"What happens now."

"Cobra happens. That's when we decide on the details. People are not merely angry, they're incandescent, so I can promise one thing: Salah-ud-Din and his filth will be wiped off the face of the earth."

52

The government Crisis Management room, sometimes called the Cabinet Office Briefing Room, or COBRA, is conveniently situated in Whitehall, just down the road from Downing Street. It's an oppressive bunker-like place, lit by a harsh overhead strip light, with room for about twenty people round an oak veneer table. At the end are large screens for video links and power-point displays.

At two o'clock precisely they were ready to go, Prime Minister Damian White in the chair. Others round the table included:

Director General of MI5 Jacob Wells, slightly built and donnish, specs perched on the end of his nose.

Home Secretary Bessie Robotham, a buxom northern lass in a tweedy outfit, as though about to go for a ramble on the moors.

Minister without Portfolio Adam Tichbold, long black hair coiffed to perfection, blue hanky positioned to the inch in his breast pocket: languid and suave as they come.

Cabinet Secretary Sir Justin Hopgood, whose farmer's looks and squeaky voice disguised Britain's best brain.

Chief of Defence Staff Admiral Sir Harry Horrocks, all gold braid and medals, as though auditioning for a Gilbert and Sullivan opera.

There were about a dozen others, most unknown to Damian, but they would doubtless reveal themselves if necessary.

The Prime Minister tapped on the table for silence. The hubbub died. He began:

"First I'd like to clear up some points that have been bothering me: Fort Brockhurst. Who owns it? Was it really empty? And why was it so easy to gain access?"

Jacob Wells, adjusted his glasses and glanced at his notes: "Fort Brockhurst is one of the forts built during the late eighteen fifties to guard Portsmouth against a French invasion by Napoleon…." He paused. "That can't be right. By the mid eighteen hundreds Napoleon had been dead for ages and we were allied with France in the Crimea."

"Different Napoleon," came the falsetto tones of Sir Justin Hopgood. "We're talking about Napoleon the Third, who in eighteen fifty one became over-excited. Soon settled down and we were chums again by the time the Crimean war came along. But Palmerston carried on with his forts anyway; damned silly waste of money, but then he was the Gunboat Diplomacy chap….."

An insistent and ever louder banging on the table stopped Sir Justin.

The Prime Minister had suffered under too many chairmen unable to stifle waffle: "Gentlemen, please! We don't have all day. My question was: 'Who owns Fort Brockhurst?"

"English Heritage," replied Jacob. "It was empty because they can't find anyone to run it. Even on an ad hoc basis. At one time they had tours once a month in the summer, but in recent years not even that."

Prime Minister: "And it had poor security because there was nothing of interest inside?"

Jacob Wells: "I presume so. The cluster of buildings we saw in the square house a museum, but I don't suppose it has much of value. Anyway, I don't see how *anyone* could have foreseen what this Saladin fellow would do."

235

"You're right, Jacob. Thank you." The Prime Minister paused for a moment, then continued: "We come now to the tragic victim. What was his name again?"

Admiral Horrocks: "Corporal John Smither."

"Married?"

I'm afraid so. With two young children."

"Not his lucky day," said the Prime Minister. "How come he found himself facing a homicidal maniac?"

"Hamid and his army were able to buy most of their equipment quite legally," replied the Admiral. "Vehicles, clothing, that sort of thing was no problem. We think they were also able to get hold of some arms and munitions from abroad, then smuggled in on a lonely beach. But they must have still been short, because on their way down, earlier last night, they broke into Longmore Camp on the A Three."

"An army camp?"

"An *ex-army* camp. Borden… Longmore… there'd once been quite a military presence straddling the A Three road, but these places have been closed now for some years. All that remained was a small storage facility. Containing some arms and munitions."

"Guarded by the unfortunate Smither?"

The admiral nodded. "And two privates. All very low key and hellishly boring. Nothing ever happened."

"No chance for them to even sound an alarm?"

"Apparently not. First thing anyone knows is Smither without a head."

Well…. That seems to explain *how* it happened. So unless there are any more questions…?" The Prime Minister glanced around the room. No reactions. "….We come now to the more pressing point of how to handle Hamid's infamous proposal. Are we agreed that his demand is effectively that the United Kingdom cedes part of this country to what he calls the Islamic Republic of Hattin?"

There was a general buzz of consent.

"Treason pure and simple," said the Cabinet Secretary. "Not even worth discussing."

"Pity we no longer hang people for treason," said Adam Tichbold. "Then we could string the fellow up and everyone could watch it on the telly. Poetic justice."

"We could adopt the Quisling solution", said the Cabinet Secretary."

"The what?"

"Norway abolished the death penalty even before us, but then came the war and invasion. The government escaped to London, where they enacted a law making treason a capital offence. Returning home after Hitler's defeat, they tried Quisling for treason and duly shot him. We could do the same."

I think we may leave that question to the incoming government," said the Prime Minister. "*Our* problem is not what to do with our criminal, but how to first catch him. We can't simply obliterate Fort Brockhurst with a large bomb; first because it's surrounded by suburban Gosport, which would suffer collateral damage; and secondly because of the two surviving prisoners still in their hands. I have therefore asked the army's director of Special Forces, General Quilter, join us. Can you help us, general?"

General Freddy Quilter was about Damian's size, so not large, probably in his late forties, but looking younger and very fit. Unlike the admiral, he was in standard battledress, a normal day at the office. Although his published CV was fairly ordinary, it was rumoured that the unexpurgated version included several black operations with the SAS.

"This must necessarily be a preliminary assessment," began the general in a precise and clear voice; he had spent a career giving briefings. "All we know so far is what we saw on TV. That they have some AK Forty Sevens, the world's most popular rifle. And, by inference from the parade Hamid put on to impress us, that his so-called army is probably well trained and disciplined."

"Not an easy nut to crack?"

The general nodded. "Especially as we are completely in the dark as to what he has up his sleeve. No accurate idea of his strength, nothing on what was hidden in those trucks. However, with the Prime Minister's permission, we have already taken the first essential step...."

Quilter gestured towards Damian, who nodded, then continued:

"Which has been to quarantine the threat. Seal it off. My men have Fort Brockhurst surrounded and are confident Hamid cannot get out to wreak further havoc. Like taking more hostages."

"So now we have to bring him to justice," said the Cabinet Secretary.

"Indeed," said the general. "But that won't be easy because of the moat. Water barriers may be old fashioned, but they remain extremely effective. My Special Forces rely on stealth penetration, then, depending on circumstances, perhaps a sudden stun-and-storm, but here it will be difficult to get close without being spotted."

"What about an airborne assault?" asked the Prime Minister.

"Again I'm afraid not much has changed," replied Quilter. "The pioneer here was the German, Karl Student, who received a lot of positive publicity but was in fact remarkably unsuccessful. His failure to take The Hague in nineteen forty was almost the only setback in the German campaign in France. The following year, again in a campaign that succeeded, Student lost so many men in Crete that Hitler banned all future airborne adventures. On the allied side, we have only to look at the disastrous 'bridge too far' episode at Arnhem. Airborne attacks *can* succeed, but the risks are great and casualties can be heavy. I would not recommend it in this instance, especially as Hamid is bound to be on the lookout for it."

"But we must do *something,*" said the prime Minister. "There's no question of any sort of bargaining with such an outrageous proposal."

"These situations take time," said Quilter. "Very frustrating, I know, but that's how it works. Plenty of posturing. Demands going back and forth. Can go on for years."

"You're not hearing me, general," said the Prime Minister. "I said *no bargaining.* And I've no intention of waiting for *years.* We get rid of this blot on our landscape immediately. Within days."

For a moment Quilter was silent. Then: "Very well, Prime Minister. On your head be it. I will draw up a plan for an assault on Fort Brockhurst. But if there is to be any chance of avoiding a massacre - a massacre of *British* troops, I will need some sort of diversion. Maybe you'd like to talk to this Hamid fellow yourself."

There was a hush. One did not speak to a Prime Minister like that: even an interim Prime Minister. Everyone waited for the inevitable explosion.

Instead, the Prime Minister grinned: "An excellent idea, Quilter. I might even do that."

The general's natural tan turned a deeper red: "I didn't mean my remark to be taken literally, sir. Your personal involvement won't be necessary."

"But it's a brilliant idea, Quilter. I don't mind *pretending* to bargain. Just a brief chat to the ogre in his den, while you bring on the cavalry."

"You can't do that." The Cabinet Secretary's voice was up another octave. "A British prime minister handing himself over to terrorists. We won't allow it."

"The *main job* of any country's leader was once to do battle on their behalf," said Damian.

"Henry the fifth at Agincourt and all that…" said Adam.

Sir Justin: "…And Bosworth in fourteen eighty five…."

Adam: "…where King Richard failed to find a horse, according to the Bard…."

Sir Justin: "…and consequently lost his head. A salutary lesson, I'd have thought."

Damian smiled. "That was a while ago. I'm talking about now."

"When we're faced with a man who has already shown a predilection for decapitation."

"Enough." Damian held up his hand. "My mind is made up. I may only be an *Interim* prime minister, but that means I'm also expendable. A mere Night Watchman. In two days there's an election, so by the time I get talking to Hamid I may not even be prime minister."

"I must say this has possibilities." General Quilter was smiling. "But a word of advice. Wait for Hamid's next move, which is bound to come soon. All he's done so far is lay out his stall. Next comes the squeeze. *That's* when you bend under pressure."

"Maybe I could help." It was Adam Tichbold again. "It's no secret that I have ambitions for the next parliament. What if I state, loud and clear, that if *I* find myself leading the country next week – I'm sorry Damian, but that's certainly a possibility – I shall lose no time blitzing Hamid's pathetic little army? Might persuade him to talk to you while he still has the chance."

The prime minister was about to reply when a figure at the far end of the table said: "We have a news flash, Prime Minister. Okay to put it up on the screen?"

Damian nodded. The big TV at the end of the room came alive to show a BBC reporter outside Fort Brockhurst:

"….In a new twist to the ongoing drama here, General Salah-ud-Din, leader of the self-styled Islamic army of Hattin, has just announced he will execute another prisoner if we don't start what he calls 'meaningful discussions' by nine o'clock on Sunday morning. That, of course, is the day after tomorrow: election day……"

The reporter started elaborating without adding anything of substance, so after a couple of minutes the prime Minister said: "I think we've heard enough."

The screen went dead.

"Seems we're running out of options," said the Prime Minister. "I now need to be talking to Hamid Khan by Sunday morning. Polling day will also have to be D-Day for Fort Brockhurst. Please draw up plans to that effect, general, and let me have the first draft by tomorrow morning I realise this is a rush, but our hand has been forced."

General Quilter nodded. "We're used to rush jobs in the army. I'll have a preliminary plan to you by nine o'clock tomorrow. I do have one request, though. Despite the probability that Hamid has night vision equipment, our best chance of success remains a night assault. If you still insist on a personal confrontation with this man, can you keep him talking for twelve hours or so?"

The Prime Minister smiled. "His demand is only that 'meaningful discussions' should start. He can't possibly expect a rapid agreement. Don't worry, general, I'll keep him busy."

"I need hardly add that everything we've just said must be accorded the highest level of secrecy," said Quilter. "Careless talk could cost lives, including that of our prime minister."

"Can't even tell Chloe," said Adam, with a grin.

"*Especially* not Chloe," agreed Damian. "She'd do her damnedest to stop me. Now, if that's all….."

The prime minister glanced around the Cobra room. There were no more offers.

"….Okay, let's get to work to rid the country of this pestilence – and I'm not talking about the flu bug."

53

A reply was immediately sent to Salah-ud-Din, accepting his demand for 'meaningful discussions'. But on three conditions: that no further executions took place; the talks be in secret with no publicity; and a promise of safe conduct for 'a government representative'. No indication was given as to who this person might be, only that he would have plenipotentiary powers to negotiate.

The Prime Minister brushed aside the Cabinet Secretary's suggestion that the election be postponed: democracy could not be seen to be giving way to violence.

The rest of the day was a strange hiatus. Until General Quilter presented him with a plan for disposing of Hamid Khan, there was nothing more Damian could do in that direction. However, from now on his full attention had to be on defending what amounted to an attack on the United Kingdom, so political campaigning would have to take a back seat.

By now it was getting late and the Prime Minister found himself in London rather than Oxford, so he could do little except return to Number Ten, where he arrived pondering how to tell Chloe that....well, that he could tell her *nothing*. However, her antennae must have picked up the vibes because she greeted him with a kiss and the comment: "I don't want to know."

Emotionally drained, he was dithering about what to do next when Chloe continued: "Looks like you need a night out on the town."

Still playing out possible military outcomes in his head, Damian replied absentmindedly: "Oh….yea? Like what?"

"A slap-up meal, then home for some TLC."

So while the rest of the country battled out the remaining hours of the election campaign and Quilter's team plotted the demise of Salah-ud-Din, Prime Minister Damian White's girlfriend took him to the 'Sole's Delight', a fish restaurant in Covent Garden. Here they indulged themselves with the chef's special, allegedly caught at Dover, polished off an expensive bottle of Chablis, gorged themselves on an obese-making gateau, and finished with a brandy (for Damian) and a Benedictine (for Chloe).

Just after 11 pm they returned to Number Ten, where Chloe administered her promised Tender Loving Care. Then they both slept like babes.

54

Next morning, much refreshed after a good night's sleep, Prime Minister Damian White greeted General Quilter's emissary at the appointed hour of nine. His visitor was a man of solid build and medium height, hair so close-cropped it was impossible to say what colour it might be if allowed to grow. His handshake was vice-like, his smile just for the record.

"Compliments of General Quilter, sir. I'm here to brief you." He offered no name, the only clue to his identity being the single crown of a Major on his uniform. Special forces are not trained to socialise with outsiders, even prime ministers. Damian led the way into a small anteroom, simply furnished with four chairs and an oval table.

As they sat down at opposite sides of the table, the Major opened a slim briefcase, extracted a map and spread it out. Said: "The boss was most impressed."

"Oh?"

"That you were prepared to put yourself in harm's way like this."

Damian felt embarrassed. "Least I could do. Besides, it sounds interesting. Better than chairing some boring meeting."

"Different certainly. Boring definitely not."

The Major evened out the creases on the map, then began: "Our target: Fort Brockhurst. Property of English Heritage, who are responsible for its upkeep, so it is not derelict. However, we understand there have been no regular visitors for the past several years. You can't take this map with you…." The Major managed a wintry smile. "…So try and remember the general geography."

"Let's start with the fort's location in the middle of suburban Gosport, which lies across the harbour from Portsmouth. It's bordered on the west by the A Thirty Two road from Fareham, which ends a couple of miles further on at the tip of Gosport. At this roundabout…." the Major outlined the path with his finger…. "Gunners Way goes off to the northeast. The Fort sits in the Vee between these roads."

"Overlooked by a lot of building," said the Prime Minister.

The Major nodded. "To the east, yes. First a row of houses; then, at the junction of Wingate road, an industrial estate. This is the public face of Fort Brockhurst, the only way in being via two narrow bridges over the moat: here and here. It's also the only aspect from where you can actually see *out from* the fort without clambering onto the ramparts."

"Very public."

Again the Major nodded. "Which is both good and bad. Good because there's a constant stream of legitimate traffic, allowing us to set up base on the industrial estate without them noticing."

"Are you sure they don't know?"

"We're pretty good at blending with the local scenery. Even if they *do* suspect something – and they *must* know we won't be simply sitting on our backsides – they'll have no idea where we'll actually deploy our forces."

"Not from this direction, then?"

"No, that's the bad news. An assault from the eastern side would be suicidal. However, the northern and western perimeter is made up of thick earth-covered ramparts with no view out. Here they are effectively blind…"

"…Except for lookouts on the ramparts…"

"Of course. But lookouts can be distracted. Or neutralised by snipers. Our problems start when we're over the ramparts come down into the central open area, which is a classic killing ground. We can expect fire from the museum complex in the middle as well as from all the rooms that face inwards from under the ramparts."

"I'm beginning to see why General Quilter was not too keen on this idea," said the Prime Minister, a guilty conscience creeping up on him at the possibility of serious casualties.

"It's the boss's job to spot problems," said the Major. "But we don't get many chances of practising our trade for real, so the lads wouldn't miss this for anything. Our team have spent hours assessing the situation and we're sure this is do-able."

"And what's my role?" asked Damian. "Apart from keeping our terrorist talking."

"That's about it," replied the Major. "But it's an absolutely vital role. We can't do this in daylight, so you *must* try and keep him occupied - and not executing any more prisoners - until darkness falls and we can get to work."

"Hope you don't mistake me for a terrorist", said Damian, beginning to wonder why on earth he had agreed to this crazy scheme.

"I'm coming to that," said the Major. "We need you to wear a tracer, a gadget that tells our troops exactly where you are. We can expect Hamid to be on the lookout for

247

this sort of thing, so we've developed an *invisible* device: one you swallow."

The Major extracted from his briefcase a small black box, which he opened to reveal a white cylindrical pill about 20 millimetres long.

"Looks like the sort of thing just about everyone over the age of sixty takes these days for some ailment or other," he explained. "But this is no slow release tablet. On the contrary, it will *resist* all attacks from your digestive system, passing through your gut and emerging the other end exactly as you see it here."

"Charming! Does it keep burping away inside me until I eventually fart it out?"

The Major allowed himself a smile. "Depends whether you're constipated. The homing device has a life of about three days. After that it becomes an inert and harmless object."

"Also harmless when active, I hope?"

"Of course. Goes without saying."

"Even so, nice to hear you say it. Do you have any more surprises for me?"

"One more thing you should know, sir. We're planning a little post-election celebration."

"What do you mean?"

"One of my men came up with the idea that we could make use of the fact tomorrow happens to be election day. I believe the polls close at ten, so shortly after that there'll be signs of some local whoopee."

"We never celebrate the polls closing."

"In the past, that's so. Now we will. Nothing official, just parties generated by Social Media to celebrate having a proper government again. Gosport is organising a fireworks display."

"Which you hope Hamid will be expecting?"

"We're sure of it. Terrorists live on the oxygen of publicity, so they gobble up all incoming stuff to see how successful they've been. Some words from you would also help."

"And you'll be organising *our noise* at the same time?"

"Exactly."

"What do you then want *me* to do?"

"Keep your head down. Play it by ear. We have a plan of course, but it's a corny old saying that no plan survives first contact with the enemy."

"But you'll know precisely where I am because of my little pill?"

"That's the sum of it. We'll tell Hamid *someone* will be arriving at nine, but not who. We'll drive you in, sitting in the back of an ordinary car - no government limo - blacked out rear windows, so no one can see who's there. The British public might not take kindly to the idea of their leader trying to cut a deal with a man who chops off people's heads."

"I have one condition," said Damian. "I must be able to cast my vote first."

"I was afraid you'd say that. But it should be okay as long as you're at the polling station soon after it opens at seven. We'll have a helicopter waiting nearby to whisk you to our safe house near Fareham. From there you'll go on in a car via the A Thirty Two road, which has a bad reputation for congestion, but shouldn't be too bad early on a Sunday. No reason why you can't be at the fort by nine. Any more questions, sir?"

Damian shook his head slowly.

"In that case you have our thanks - and the thanks of our country. Have a good day. See you tomorrow."

The Major's briefing ended with another paralysing handshake - a friendly fire injury.

55

The rest of the day disappeared in a blur. As soon as the Major had left, Damian and Chloe eased themselves into the official limousine for the drive back to Wheatley. He was still Prime Minister, so Bill and Ben were on hand to make sure no one took a pot shot at him.

On the last day of campaigning everyone was expected to pull out the stops in a final frenzied burst of energy, so his agent had arranged to throw him straight into the fray with a visit to the Cowley motor works. But Damian felt strangely detached, so much so that as they left Cowley Warbeck asked if he felt okay.

"Of course, Alec. Why do you ask?"

"You seem, well…. Not quite with it. Not your usual self."

"Affairs of state. A lot to think about."

"Affairs of state should now be on hold. You need to focus on the final push. Unless you do, you can forget about any more 'affairs of state'. Looks like Delahaye has the number one Tory spot sewn up. Labour is a shoo-in for number two. Which leaves you and the Lib Dem fighting it out for number three. Where, I have to tell you, it looks far too close for comfort."

"Fingers crossed, then," said Damian casually.

An election seemed of minor importance beside the recurring image of Salah-ud-Din's scimitar severing a head in one clean sweep. Would more heads roll tomorrow?

Would it be *his head*? Could he rely on safe conduct from an animal like Hamid Khan?

Damian did two more meetings before telling Alec Warbeck he'd had enough. No, he was *not* going to complete his schedule. He was going home to Chloe. Warbeck knew better than to argue. Something was clearly amiss and that was the end of it. Anyway, a couple more meetings would make little difference. The die was cast. All they could do now was to await the verdict of the people.

Chloe also knew something was going on and, like Warbeck, was wise enough to keep her counsel.

But she did allow herself one statement: "If you want to tell me, go ahead. If not, that's also fine."

Damian pondered for a moment, then: "You know my lips are sealed. But tomorrow promises to be an interesting day. All I ask is that you don't believe *everything* you may hear. I've got an early call - need to be at the polling station soon after seven, so let's have an evening at home. A Chinese take-away, perhaps….?"

""While watching House of Cards….?"

"Brilliant!"

They were hooked on the American version of this political murder and mayhem. Rather farfetched perhaps. Couldn't happen in real life.

Could it?

56

APRIL 28th.

The Prime Minister was airborne, having caste his vote, shortly after 7.30. He and Chloe had put a brave face on their farewells. He didn't know whether it was worse for her, not knowing, but suspecting; or for himself, in no doubt where he was heading, but without a clue how his maniacal host would react.

It was a fresh morning, high cloud drifting in from the west, but dry. Beneath him England was starting to turn green as winter gave way to spring. They flew low down, due south, to begin with over home territory, close to where he'd grown up. They crossed the Thames at Dorchester, the Wittenham clumps standing out like tufts on a bald pate. After that it was almost all fields, apart from the strip of M4 motorway, busy with rush hour traffic. Despite a population reckoned to be over seventy million – no one knew the true figure – it was amazing how much of England remained rural. No question of giving away even an acre of this to anyone – let alone to a guy who enjoyed removing heads.

After half an hour the chopper landed him on the lawn of a large country house he did not recognise. As the rotors slowed, two khaki-clad figures emerged from the house and walked briskly towards him: General Quilter and the Major.

"Welcome, Prime Minister". The General shook his

hand. "You've made good time, so there's enough slack in the schedule for a cup of coffee."

"I'd rather get going….."

"With respect, sir, I think coffee might be a good idea."

From his pocket the general extracted the same black box the Major had shown him the day before: looked as though it was designed for an engagement ring, whereas in fact it held a small cylindrical object.

"Ah, yes….my tracer."

"Goes down better with some liquid," said the General.

"Reminds me of those suicide pills they give spies in case they're tortured," said Damian. "Maybe I should have one of those as well?"

""Hamid has no interest in harming you," said the general. "You're his one hope of getting what he wants."

Just as long as he kept that hope, thought Damian. But if he realised the game was up…. that holding the Prime Minister was no longer of any use to him….?

They entered the house through some French windows into what looked like a drawing room. The place was obviously a home, but there appeared to be no one else around. Maybe the army had borrowed it on a one-off basis as a convenient launch point.

The general poured a mug of coffee from a thermos, which stood on a table together with some Danish pastries.

"Help yourself," said the general. "Might be a while until lunch. Hamid has not told us about his catering arrangements."

The Prime Minister downed his tracer pill, selected a Danish and asked: "Any more developments I should know about?"

The general shook his head. "Overnight we've been

refining the plan. It's now as good as we're likely to get it."

"Zero hour still ten this evening?"

"Within five minutes. Soon as the little celebration we're organising reaches sufficient volume."

"What about the surviving prisoners? Presumably they won't have tracers?"

"Unfortunately, no. We've given these men a lot of thought, but it's well-nigh impossible to guarantee the safety of hostages during a shoot-out. Just as well there are only two – although that's small consolation if you happen to be one of them."

"What happens now? How to I get to the fort?"

"Sergeant Brady drives you there. Into the fort, so no one can see who you are, then comes back here."

The Prime Minister spread his hands: "The perfect plan. Can't go wrong."

"In theory," agreed the general. "Trouble is practice rarely follows theory."

57

His driver was a surprise on two counts: Sergeant Brady was female and in civvies.

It was not as though ladies in uniform were anything new. During the war the late queen had been an army motor mechanic and since then females had infiltrated almost every nook and cranny of the armed services. So why was it that if someone mentioned a rank and a name, he always assumed that name to be of male gender?

No easy answer, so Damian turned his attention to the other unexpected feature:

"I see you're in disguise this morning, Sergeant."

"Sir?"

"Not in uniform."

"The general thought it best not to advertise the service angle."

Damian had only managed a brief look at Brady before being bundled into a white saloon that had been manufactured somewhere east of Singapore. He had the impression of a solid-looking lass in her thirties, middling height, brown hair, experienced enough to be on Quilter's staff; white blouse and jeans, standard stuff so as to not stand out in a crowd Now, with plenty of time to study the back of her head, he could only register the female equivalent of the army's coiffeur rules, which appeared to be not-too-long-back-and-sides.

"They're hoping Hamid will be less suspicious of a lady driver?" asked Damian.

"That's the idea."

"And especially if she's not in uniform?"

"Yessir. So when we arrive it would be helpful if you could avoid addressing me as 'Sergeant'. Miss Brady will do nicely."

"Understood Miss Brady."

"General Quilter has tasked me with keeping my eyes open and reporting back on anything of interest."

Damian rolled his eyes: 'tasked me'. Why did the army have to turn nouns into verbs? Politicians were even more guilty of jargon…. But what was he doing worrying about such irrelevancies? Must be getting jittery.

"How much longer 'til we're there?" asked the Prime Minister. He *was* getting jittery.

"Base are keeping a running check on traffic density and our progress through it. Reckon we'll reach Fort Brockhurst at six minutes to nine."

"Excellent." He sat back, tried to relax. And failed. Started biting his nails. Hadn't done that since he was about twelve.

It was stop-start, with endless traffic lights and roundabouts, through urban scenery that had seen better days. Eventually they came to a roundabout where they did *not* carry straight on. Took a left, bringing them face to face with a low redbrick structure hiding behind a water hazard: Fort Brockhurst. His watch showed 8.55.

In fact, the low redbrick structure was only partially visible through a forest of gawpers, with nothing better to do this Sunday morning than watch what was going on in their real-life drama. The police had the mob well under control, having cordoned them back to allow vehicle access and keep them clear of the army - the British army - who had mounted a very public encirclement of the fort.

Brady was guided through, while Damian cowered in the back behind darkened windows. Although he had accepted the need for anonymity, he had spent his life playing to the gallery and hated the idea of skulking.

"Now we wait until someone shows," announced Brady, coming to a halt.

The Prime Minister tried to relate what he was looking at with the Major's map. Across the bridge spanning the moat was the main gate, which led into a small circular keep. On either side, shaped like an irregular rectangle, stretched the main part of the fort. Facing them was the aspect with windows and narrow vertical slits, so it was a dead cert that critical eyes were even now giving them the once-over. But not a single face could be seen.

At 8.58 the large main gate opened and three figures in battledress appeared. Two carried rifles at the ready, the third, with sergeant's stripes, was unarmed. Damian was almost sure this was the man who had cleaned Hamid's bloodied scimitar after the execution.

They marched across the bridge to the landward side gate, no longer padlocked, because the moat was like a WW1 no-man's-land: anyone venturing into this zone risked a bullet in the head. Here the United Kingdom ended. Beyond lay the Islamic Republic of Hattin.

While the two armed privates kept a watchful eye, the sergeant approached their car. He was a tall fit looking man in his thirties, skin colour much like Damian's, so his folks would originally have come from somewhere south of Dover.

With the driver's side window down, the sergeant poked his head in.

"Well, well, there's a turn-up for the book!" He

couldn't hide his surprise at finding himself looking at the Prime Minister.

Damian reckoned Hamid's sergeant was a native English speaker from north of Watford, closer than that he wasn't prepared to say. During his West Ham days, when visiting the footballing fortresses of Old Trafford and Anfield, it had sometimes been easier to find the back of the net than to understand what they were talking about.

"Out you come, then," said the sergeant, almost genially.

"We've been told we can drive in through the gate," said Brady.

"Told what!"

"These talks are confidential, so I am not getting out here," said the Prime Minister.

"My orders is to escort you in on foot," said the sergeant.

"Well, you'd better go back and get those orders amended," said the Prime Minister.

The sergeant hesitated then said: "Stay here." And marched back into the fort with his escort.

"No plan ever survives first contact with the enemy," murmured Damian.

"Do you think they'll eventually let us drive in?" asked Brady.

"Doubt it. This is all a game and if hanging around here wastes some time that's fine. My only job is to keep Hamid occupied."

"Might also annoy him."

"He's expecting to be annoyed. If I roll over too easily it'll make him suspicious. It's a delicate balance: I need to be *a bit* bloody minded, but not so much that it tips him over the edge."

"If you have to walk in, the whole world will know it's you talking to them," said Brady.

"True. But I never did really buy into the anonymity angle. If I have to ditch it, I won't be that upset."

"Might even turn out to be a good thing," mused Brady.

"Might indeed," agreed the Prime Minister. "Life's a lottery."

Damian's watch showed 9.18 before the escort detail reappeared and marched briskly towards them. There was a buzz of anticipation from the crowd.

"The general don't know what you was talking about," said the sergeant, bending down at the open car window. "No foreign vehicles allowed inside. That's the rule."

"Hmmm." The Prime Minister pretended to ponder. "Then I'd better go back and consult my colleagues. The agreement was that I could be driven in. If Hamid changes his mind on that, I can't trust him on anything."

"I'm just obeying orders," said the sergeant. "But I'll tell you this for nothing: the general ain't the sort of man you'd want to cross. Enjoys giving his sword a bit of exercise." The sergeant grinned. "And *I* don't mind cleaning up after him."

Damian decided to chance his arm. It was a risk, but this election day was teetering on the brink in every way. So he said:

"Tell this Hamid fellow I'll come in on foot if *you* announce, loud and clear, so everyone can hear, that I'm promised safe conduct. You might also remind him that by tomorrow I might no longer be Prime Minister. At least *I am* prepared to talk, but my most probable successor is a chap called Tichbold, who likes to whack you first and ask questions later."

The sergeant nodded and for the second time led his men back into the fort.

"That was rather strong," said Brady, when they were out of earshot.

"It's called negotiation," said the Prime Minister. "Let's hope it wasn't too 'strong'."

"And he didn't like you calling his general 'that Hamid fellow'."

"Tough. I want to make it clear that the British government considers all talk of armies and generals as a load of rubbish. They're criminals and I'm only consorting with them because I have to."

"Hope it doesn't push him to swing his sword again."

"So do I. I doubt it, but can't be certain. I'll be walking the tightrope."

This time the wait was even longer, nearly 9.50 by the time the trio from the Army of Hattin reappeared.

Through the open window the sergeant told them: "The general said yes."

"Excellent!" The Prime Minister did not move.

Neither did the sergeant.

"Off you go then," said Damian. "Tell them what we've agreed. Best parade ground voice."

The sergeant turned to face the expectant crowd: "General Salah-ud-Din, commander-in-Chief of the Islamic Army of Hattin, announces that he grants safe conduct while in Hattin territory to the British Prime Minister."

These words were received with puzzlement by the waiting throng. While there had been a media deluge about the Islamic Army of Hattin, the reference to the Prime Minister was far from clear.

Then Damian stepped out from his back seat purdah.

There was a gasp from the crowd. The Prime Minister in person!

He gave them a cheery wave before strolling with his Hattin Army escort across the no-man's-land of the moat into Fort Brockhurst. Into enemy territory.

58

As the main gate clanged shut behind him, the Prime Minister realised he was now a prisoner, dependent on the whim of a man whose favourite pastime was relieving people of their heads. Hamid *might* honour his promise of safe conduct. On the other hand…

They walked through the small circular keep and entered the parade ground, where the world had watched the execution of Corporal Smither. In the centre of the square, but occupying less than a quarter of it, lay the low building he knew from the map to be the museum. Round the periphery, built into the walls of the ramparts, were rows of rooms that could hide an army. Actually, they *must* hide an army, because the square itself was empty except for a handful of soldiers, one of whom was walking up a ramp that led to the top of the ramparts, probably to relieve one of the men on prone sentry duty: Hamid's eyes on the outside world.

The sergeant led the way towards the left hand area of the inner rampart. Damian glanced at his watch: coming up to 10 am. Twelve hours to keep Hamid at bay: keep him from executing any more prisoners. Twelve hours until General Quilter would hopefully obliterate him.

As they approached one of the rampart rooms that had a large window area, a door opened. A man in standard camouflage dress emerged. Even without the green beret or dangling scimitar, he was unmistakeable.

"Welcome to my country." Salah-ud-Din held out his

hand. 'My Country' obviously meant the Islamic Republic of Hattin, not Britain.

The Prime Minister ignored the outstretched hand and looked his opponent up and down: well built, wavy black hair, hawk-like features that probably originated in Pakistan's northwest frontier. On his lapels the crossed sword insignia of a general. But his most arresting feature was the eyes, which were a disconcerting milky blue.

"At least accept a cup of chai," he said, withdrawing his unaccepted hand and inviting the Prime Minister in.

"That would be nice." Damian followed him into the room, where the big windows gave the feeling of a conservatory.

Inside was a sofa, a low table surrounded by four white metal chairs; and half a dozen etchings of Nelson-era naval battles on the walls.

One of his men started filling two cups from a samovar-type tea dispenser. Hamid indicated Damian should take a seat.

Choosing to remain standing, the Prime Minister said: "Before we even *start* talking there's one essential preliminary: I must see with my own eyes that the two prisoners you have so far not murdered are alive and well."

Hamid nodded to the sergeant, who departed on his mission, then turned to Damian:

"You don't seem to understand, prime minister: in war there will be casualties."

"And *you* don't seem to understand, Hamid Khan, that wars are normally fought under the rules of the Geneva Convention, which specifically prohibits the murder of prisoners."

"A rule regularly ignored. Even, on occasions, by your country."

Continuing this argument would be fruitless and probably counter-productive, so Damian accepted the cup of tea and wandered back outside. The armed minders eyed him warily, but Hamid made no sign for them to interfere.

Fort Brockhurst's parade ground was empty save for a few soldiers at the far end. Most of their ordnance and manpower remained hidden, no doubt ready for rapid deployment. From this low angle Damian could only see a small part of the upper ramparts, but just visible were hints of Hamid's first-line defences, probably machine gun posts. These defenders would have an excellent field of fire *down* on any attackers, whereas he could see no hills or high buildings that might give a corresponding advantage to Quilter's men.

His amateur assessment of the fort's defences was cut short by the approach of the sergeant, followed by two of his men, each manacled to a prisoner. Still in their army shirts and trousers, the prisoners appeared subdued but unharmed.

They entered the room, where the sergeant came to a smart halt, saluted and barked: "Prisoners and escorts, sah!"

"You see!" Hamid smiled and waved at them, as though producing rabbits out of a hat. "In mint condition."

'Mint' might be over-egging it, but they certainly appeared to be physically unharmed.

Damian went up to the first one, a tall fair haired teenager and asked: "Been treated okay?"

He nodded dumbly, plainly terrified.

The other prisoner was older, medium height, starting to go thin on top. Damian put the same question to him.

This one managed to find his voice: "Suppose so. Haven't tortured us. Yet."

Damian was turning away, when the prisoner added: "Yea, they treated us great! Apart from fucking killing our corporal!"

A swipe from the sergeant's fist sent the prisoner crashing down, bringing his manacled escort with him. For a few moments they lay in a heap on the floor, before managing to untangle themselves and return to upright.

"That happens once more and I walk out." Damian was seething.

Hamid did not reprimand his sergeant but seemed to grasp that striking prisoners did not help his cause, so merely grunted and said:

"Take them away. We've seen that they're fit enough."

"They stay!" said the Prime Minister.

"Who do you think gives the orders here?" Sneered Hamid.

The situation was becoming tense, so Damian decided something soothing might be called for:

"I thought you wanted to negotiate. You must have hundreds of men on your side. Even with these two I'm heavily outnumbered."

His real reason for wanting to keep the prisoners close by was that this might give them a better chance of survival. If they were back in their cells when Quilter attacked, they would be indistinguishable from the defenders, who would hopefully be slaughtered to the last man; but in the same room as himself, in whose gut resided a tracer, they should stand a fighting chance.

Hamid considered the idea in silence for maybe a couple of minutes. Ambled around the room, finished his cup of tea. Finally he said:

"Very well. They can stay. But so do mine: The Sergeant, two guards and both the prisoner escorts. You'll be outnumbered six to three, with all the firepower on my side, so don't even think of trying anything silly."

"I'm not suicidal. Don't have seventy two virgins waiting for me." The Prime Minister selected one of the white metal chairs and sat down. "Now, can we get started?"

59

The two handcuffed pairs – prisoners and escorts – sat down on the sofa, where they made an odd sight. The armed guards remained standing, one of each side of the room, ever watchful. Their commander, self-styled General Salah-ud-Din, sat down facing the Prime Minister, with the sergeant, also ever watchful, between them.

For the next twelve hours Damian would have to put on an act: pretend to be negotiating, whereas his true role was merely to spin out time without provoking Hamid into more killing. Talk, talk and more talk. What they discussed hardly mattered, because by midnight his opposite number would hopefully be dead.

"All we know is that you have illegally occupied Fort Brockhurst and have made some demands," began the Prime Minister. "Let's start with what you hope to get out of this crazy scheme."

Hamid Khan put his elbows on the table and fixed Damian with those strange milky blue eyes. He must be mad, surely – whatever 'mad' might mean, so how had he been able to recruit so many followers? There must be some fault in the wiring of the human brain that makes the combination of insanity and brute force so inexplicably appealing. Stalin, Hitler, all dictators you care to mention, have only been able to operate with a degree of popular support. As yet Hamid did not command a force the size of the Wehrmacht or Red Army. It was up to Damian to ensure his efforts do so were strangled at birth.

"We live in an age of fragmentation," began Hamid. He might be bonkers, but his voice was cultured and persuasive. "It started after the first war, when three great empires, the Hapsburgs, Hohenzollerns and Ottomans, all disappeared, spawning a kindergarten of new nations. After world war two, it was the turn of the British, who, unlike the French, didn't try to hang onto the red bits on the map, but donated it piecemeal to the new United Nations. End of the cold war and now the Soviet Union and Yugoslavia exploded into ethnic shrapnel."

Damian set his face to show interest. Hamid could talk all day if he wanted to, as long as the clock kept ticking towards ten.

"Now it's the small country that's beautiful. Maybe we'll soon be living in our own little versions of Andorra or Liechtenstein." Hamid laughed at his own joke.

Damian managed a wan smile.

"The Islamic Republic of Hattin merely seeks to follow this trend," he continued. "A modest piece of mother earth we can call our own. There's yet another way we're in tune with the times: Britain may be godless, but - praise be to Allah - that's not the case everywhere. My ancestral homeland of Pakistan is proof that a state can be created by God. So is Israel. Both Iran and Saudi Arabia also live by God's word."

"What happens if I decide to take a holiday in sunny Mecca?" Damian could contain himself no longer.

Hamid looked puzzled. "You couldn't. Mecca is restricted to those of us of The Faith."

"Exactly. So tomorrow I shall advise His Majesty, as Defender of *our* Faith, that forthwith only Christians shall be allowed into the English holy city of Canterbury."

Hamid was not amused. "That's quite different."

Damian: "On the contrary, it's an exact comparison."

There was an uncomfortable pause. Damian realised he might have gone too far. His job was to let Hamid waffle on, not antagonise him. So he asked:

"This 'modest piece of mother earth' you talk about. Fort Brockhurst isn't much of a country. Smaller even than the Vatican. Do you have anywhere else in mind?"

"Doesn't really matter where we start. Places where Moslems are already in the majority - Bradford, Leicester - might seem the obvious choices, but it could be anywhere. With Fort Brockhurst as the nucleus, the Islamic Republic of Hattin could even be born right here in Gosport. Access to the sea, good trading propects….."

"The citizens of Gosport, who's families have lived here for generations, might object."

"That didn't seem to bother the Brits when they allowed to Jews to take Palestine. In the late eighteen hundreds Jews made up five percent of Palestine's population - less than ours now in Britain. Look what happened to the poor Palestinians: still waiting for the homeland that was taken from them."

Hamid had shot himself in the foot with this argument. It confirmed that the Army of Hattin had to be stopped right here, before it got ideas for taking over the whole country. But Damian couldn't afford to be too controversial, so just said:

"You've got the wrong culprits. When the League of Nations gave Britain the hopeless task of running Palestine, we made a reasonable fist of it between the wars, keeping the factions apart and limiting immigration. After world war two, bankrupt and knackered, with the holocaust pouring huge numbers of Jews into the Holy land, we simply gave up and went home. If you want to blame anyone, look to the surrounding Arab states – Egypt, Jordan, Syria – who refused the United Nations partition plan and then, after the ceasefire, kept the lands they'd taken."

"All history," said Hamid, airily. "Give us Gosport and I'm sure we could do a population swap for anyone not happy to stay on. After World War Two, umpteen million Poles, Germans, whatever, were relocated. A few thousand Gosportians would be a doddle."

The dialogue of the deaf went on and on, Hamid rolling out his fantasies, the Prime Minister buttoning his lip, when these became too outrageous. Anything to keep the charade going until the magic hour of ten.

They broke for lunch, a cold buffet brought in on a trolley by a couple of Hamid's boys, everyone eating where they sat. This was not easy for the manacled couples on the sofa, but they managed. The two armed guards ate in shifts, one dining while the other kept watch.

Eating now took precedence over talking, of which there had recently been a surfeit. Damian was left wondering where all this was heading. Hamid didn't appear to be a fool and must realise it could only end in tears. Instead of sudden death by suicide vest, Salah-ud-Din's chosen martyrdom looked to be a more prolonged affair. But martyrdom it must surely be. He couldn't expect any British government to accept such absurd demands.

Did his men also realise what was in store for them? Some must have an inkling. Damian was at a loss to understand how, in an age of science and progress, so many people could still welcome death for a religious belief. For centuries the Christian church had been torn apart with schisms, where heretics could be cured by the simple expedient of burning them at the stake. Cleansing by fire made sinners fit for eternal life. Now Moslems were the ones seeking trips to paradise. Arguing with such fanaticism was impossible, but he had to try and keep it going for a few hours more. Until darkness and election firework time, when Quilter's men would have a chance do their stuff without being massacred.

60

As lunch was cleared away, the Prime Minister realised their discussions were running out of steam. Hamid would soon tire of having his suggestions dismissed or put on hold. It was still only early afternoon. How the devil was he to occupy the next few hours?

The brainwave came to him out of the blue. The clue was Night Watchman: the tail-ender promoted in the batting order towards the end of the day. Batsman. Cricket. Of course! Would it work? Worth a try.

So before Hamid could get going again Damian said:

"Interesting Test Match. Pakistan in command, it would seem."

Hamid's face lit up. Martyrdom could be delayed if the subject was cricket, the colonies' most prized gift from the Raj.

"Yea, the boys haven't had such a good day against India since... well, maybe since the Champions Trophy in two thousand and seventeen. Remember that?"

The Prime Minster shook his head. Actually, he did have a vague recollection, but pleading ignorance should really get Hamid going. It did:

"Fakhar Zaman was let-off early on, then slammed a century. After that, Mohammad Amir skittled India out. Only one-day stuff, I know, but it was magic!"

"Now you have India on the ropes again...."

"Yep. This time in a test match. Babar Ali and Asad Zaman both with centuries. Pakistan declared at four hundred and fifty two for six. In reply India are seventy nine for three."

"Looking good."

"But early days. India are no pushover."

Babar Ali is a left-handed opener, right?"

Hamid said that was correct and went on to elaborate on Pakistan's chances. Not only did all this use up valuable time, it also subtly altered the atmosphere. Could you kill a fellow with whom you'd just been talking cricket?

They then turned to other sports, including football and Damian's time at West Ham. Hamid was an Aston Villa fan. As the afternoon wore on, discussions still mundane, Damian began to feel schizoid. Here he was having parlour-room chat with a terrorist, who had personally beheaded a man with half the world watching.

Eventually even this parlour-room chat started to dry up. Hamid's demand that Britain should cede land to the Islamic republic of Hattin had been noted by the Prime Minister. Nothing more. They had then whiled away the afternoon with what amounted to idle gossip. Terrorists are often credited with diabolical cunning, whereas in fact they are usually wounded souls with limited abilities. By raising and training this private army Hamid Khan had shown himself more capable than most, but now cracks were starting to appear.

Earlier Damian had pointed out that 'General Salah-ud-Din's proposals were so serious that nothing could be agreed without a full meeting of the British cabinet. The 'general' had accepted this and promised no further executions until he had an answer.

It was approaching six o'clock when they finally ran out of chat and Hamid said:

"Well, Prime Minister, you're free to go. Discuss what we've talked about with your colleagues and come back with an answer by this time tomorrow. It had better be favourable. Otherwise....." He smiled at the prisoners and made a throat-cutting gesture.

Normally Damian would have been out of Fort Brockhurst faster than ripping apart an opposition defence for West Ham, but there was a problem: the prisoners. Although Hamid had pledged their security for the next twenty four hours, General Quilter's assault was due in a mere four hours. If the prisoners were back in some unknown cell they would be in danger from friendly fire. However, if they remained close to Damian, the tracer currently making its way through his gut should greatly improve their survival prospects.

So the Prime Minister responded: "You put me in a difficult position. Because you didn't allow me to drive in, as agreed, the British public now know I've spent the day talking to a terrorist. Which they won't like. I therefore need to hang around for a few hours more until the crowd outside becomes fed up and goes home."

Hamid grinned. The notion that he had succeeded in making a British Prime Minister scared of his own people was immensely appealing. With a great show of magnanimity, he spread his hands and said: "Be my guest!"

61

In 1973 a convict on parole called Olsson raided a Stockholm bank and took four hostages. The stand-off lasted six days, during which Olsson treated his victims brutally, so the expectation was they would turn against him when freed. Instead, the ex hostages refused to testify against the bank robber and started to raise money for his defence.

The shrinks got to work on this conundrum and gave it a name: Stockholm syndrome. It can occur when hostages spend so long with their captors they start bonding with them.

There was no danger of Britain's Prime Minister bonding with the terrorist Salah-ud-Din, even though they had spent an unexpectedly convivial afternoon discussing Pakistan's cricketing prospects. But Damian was interested in the reverse side of the Stockholm syndrome: the effect contact with hostages might have on their *captors*. There are numerous examples of hostages being killed after quite lengthy incarcerations, but logic suggests that the odds on a lethal outcome should diminish the longer the two enemies are together. If it had been relatively easy to kill Corporal Smither, whom they had only just captured, it might be more difficult to do the same to men they had recently eaten lunch with. Or so Damian hoped.

Hamid departed as soon as he had announced Damian could stay a while longer. There an army to run, a defence to maintain. More chat, even cricket chat, was something he could ill afford. The guards were told that the Prime Minister could leave at any time, but to keep a careful watch on the captives. Damian had been scared these two might have been taken back to their cells, but fortunately this thought had not occurred to Hamid. With no orders to do anything different, the set-up in the room remained the same, except for the absence of the commander: two handcuffed couples on the sofa; two watchful armed guards. And the Prime Minister.

Damian got up to stretch his legs. There had been too much sitting around; as an exercise-aholic, he craved his fix. The guards eyed him warily, but made no comment. Pacing the room might be permitted, but he was doubtful whether he could go much beyond that.

Stopping in front of the tall teenaged prisoner, he asked: "You okay?"

A guard: "No talking!"

"I didn't hear the general ban talking."

The guard didn't reply.

They had been locked in the same room for hours. Tiring and boring. Damian decided to test the Stockholm syndrome in reverse: see if he could make the guards bend a little. So he said:

"Opening our mouths can't hurt. You can always stop us if we say anything you don't like."

Whether the guard would have responded they'd never know, because the teenage prisoner blurted out: "I'm bursting for a pee!"

Trying to smother a smile, the guard said: "Off you go then."

This was easier said than done, seeing that the prisoner was linked around the wrist to his escort. There was a toilet at the far end of the room, but how the two of them would tackle a urinary procedure was an interesting question. Who would pull down the prisoner's zip? Who would....? Let's not go into details.

As if reading Damian's mind, the guard said: "We allow them to unshackle in there. If I hear him trying anything funny I put a burst through the door. Killed with your pants down is not a good way to go. Probably drill holes in our guy as well, but that's an incentive for him to do his job properly."

So…. Prisoners were temporarily freed from their escorts when in the loo. Could this knowledge be turned to advantage? The youngest prisoner looked too immature and scared to be of much use, but his colleague who had received a fist in the face for making an uncalled for comment seemed to be made of sterner stuff. Could he be persuaded to play a part during the coming showdown?

Damian waited a while after the pair had returned from their toilet visit. Waited for the boredom factor to once more take effect. Then, during one of his circuits round the room, he stopped in front of one of the guards:

"We've been cooped up here all day and I still don't know your names. Can hardly be a state secret."

The guard said nothing.

Damian turned to his real targets: "At least let me know who my boys are. *Their names* can't be a state secret."

"Okay. But no funny stuff."

Damian stopped in front of the teenage prisoner, tied to his escort on the sofa: "You are?"

"Tony, sir."

"Don't worry, Tony. I'm working with the general to get you released."

Damian smiled to himself. 'Working with the general'. A nice touch. The guards would appreciate that.

Next was the older prisoner, also in a Siamese twin situation with his escort. Shorter, tougher, with a receding hairline, this man looked a more promising prospect.

"My name's Phil," he announced, unprompted.

The Prime Minister nodded at him, smiled. "Like I said to Tony, we're doing our best to solve this."

His words were *almost* the same, but not quite. Would Phil pick up the vibes? No mention this time of 'working with the general'. The 'we' might be referring to someone else.

As casual as he could, the Prime Minister announced to everyone in the room: "Courtesy of General Salah-ud-Din…" the ludicrous rank stuck in his throat as he said it, but keeping the guards on side was vital. "…I shall soon be leaving. When the polls close I'm told we can expect to hear a few celebrations, so a good opportunity for me to slip out unnoticed."

"Any chance of taking us with you?" asked Phil.

"Afraid not. You heard the general. I expect it'll be back to your cells, so…" as a throw-away comment: "Why not do like Tony and use the facilities here before they take you away."

If Phil took the hint, there might be one prisoner in the loo, unshackled, when Quilter's blitz started. Could hardly call it even a plan. But it was the best Damian could come up with.

62

As the time crept towards 10 pm Damian became increasingly nervous. Tried not to show it. Quilter's shock troops would need an acceptable level of noise before launching their attack. Then more time to scale the ramparts and come to grips with the inner fort. That might make zero hour for Damian 10.10? Maybe 10.15? Even as late as 10.20? Impossible to say.

Noises off started, as promised, on the dot of ten. But from their position inside the fort they were very muted. Barely audible.

Although expecting something, the guards shifted uneasily.

Damian forced a grin: "End of polling day. Like November the Fifth. Guy Fawkes."

The guards started waving their weapons around aimlessly, fingers uncomfortably close to the triggers.

"Jeez! Don't know what they put in that meal."

All heads turned towards Phil, who was writhing on the sofa. They had eaten a snack of fish and chips half an hour earlier.

"Sure was something powerful," he groaned.

The guards' attention was now on the prisoner, who was managing to look really bad. What an actor! Well, Damian hoped it was acting. No one else appeared to be stricken.

Phil struggled to his feet, pulling the escort with him. "If I don't get to that bog in thirty seconds...."

Although the guards were suspicious, they were in a quandary. What if the prisoner's symptoms were genuine?

Phil was now shakily upright, trying to undo his trouser belt, which was not easy with one arm still linked to his escort. Muttered: "Rather crap on the floor than in my pants."

The Prime Minister, two guards and the other prisoner pair looked on, enthralled.

Then Phil started retching. Paroxysm over, he gasped: "Soon be coming out both ends..."

"For Christ's sake!" Phil's manacled companion eyed the chief guard piteously.

By now the unhappy couple were halfway to the toilet, Phil's trousers down to knee level, an ensemble that made progress painfully slow.

"Cut him loose," snarled the guard.

To do this the escort had to fumble in his pocket for the handcuff key, a task so physically complex they came to a complete halt.

Damian was dimly aware of an increased noise level outside, but everyone in the room was so focussed on the performance in front of them they barely noticed.

When Phil's trousers were down to his ankles, it was time to get rid of his underpants. The escort was still desperately fishing around for the handcuff key. It was a macabre version of Strictly Come Dancing, the partners locked in an unwilling embrace that eventually saw them reduced to a writhing heap on the floor.

At last the escort found his handcuff key. Freed himself from the prisoner and thankfully scuttled clear. Phil, bare-bottomed, managed the last couple of yards to the loo on his hands and knees. Once inside, he locked the door with a bang.

With the drama over, everyone became aware of the outside world again. Which had turned very noisy. Surely far too noisy for a post-election celebration.

The number two guard opened the door to investigate. To the tune of a short salvo, he was propelled back into the room, dead before he hit the ground.

The other guard, now the only one with a weapon, had a choice of targets: a burst through the toilet door at Phil; Tony, the remaining prisoner, helpless in front of him; or the Prime Minister.

He was never granted an option, because Damian had spent the last moments of the preceding spectacle edging out of the guard's way and now hit him with a tackle that would have earned an immediate Red Card at West Ham.

As they crashed to the floor, the guard's rifle skidded across the room. In any decent movie the two protagonists would have spent the next few minutes grappling for the discarded weapon, but in this case they were denied any such drama.

A voice above them yelled: "Freeze!"

The Prime Minister found himself looking down the barrel of a gun. Holding it, finger poised on the trigger, was the Major.

"Good to see you, sir!" He might have saluted, had his hands been free.

Before Damian could react, his eardrums were numbed by another burst of gunfire.

Felt no pain. Must be still alive.

"Dear, dear, he really shouldn't have gone for his weapon!" The Major didn't appear at all sorry as he looked down on the last guard, twitching in his death throes.

The Prime Minister got shakily to his feet. Shook the Major's hand and said: "My little pill must have worked."

"Like a dream, sir. Heavy casualties amongst the enemy, but no blue-on-blue."

At that point Phil emerged from the toilet, hitching up his trousers and grinning broadly.

"That man deserves and Oscar," said the Prime Minister.

"And a m..m..medal," stammered Tony, the other prisoner.

"I'm sure that can be fixed," said the Major. "But first let's get you out of here. You'll need a full de-brief."

63

By the time Fort Brockhurst had been declared free of insurgents, thus allowing evacuation by helicopter, it was approaching midnight. Too late for any de-briefing, which had been scheduled instead for that afternoon in the Cobra room.

The chopper had made a stopover at the Fareham safe house to drop off the two ex prisoners and pick up Chloe, after which it was back to Damian's flat in Wheatley, which they reached at a quarter to one in the morning.

Damian had crashed out at once, no nightmares, and now they were apparently no different from the millions of other British couples that Monday morning, digesting their breakfast and morning papers

But there *was* a difference. Damian was a hero.

Chloe told him it had been a yoyo voyage to that pinnacle because for much of the previous day he had been closer to a zero. The news that their Prime Minister was engaged in talks with terrorists had not gone down well with the public. At midday the media had been critical, in the evening even more so. It was only when the Defence Chief, Admiral Horrocks, had been able to reveal the true course of events that Damian's reputation had recovered.

The press accounts were so detailed they made the

forthcoming Cobra meeting almost superfluous.

Using aerial photo imagery, General Quilter's team had located what appeared to be two blind spots for Hamid's lookouts on the ramparts. As these were also places where vegetation grew tight up against the moat, Special Forces had been able to get men across the water and up against the ramparts without being seen. The nearest lookouts had been quietly liquidated, then the central Museum complex stormed.

Surprise had been complete and once Quilter had control of the central buildings his men could winkle out opposition in the rooms under the ramparts at their leisure.

The whole operation had taken less than twenty minutes, the British losing two men killed and half a dozen injured, whereas the Islamic Army of Hattin had been, in the official wording, 'annihilated'. The communiqué did not specify how many had been killed and how many captured, merely that their leader, Hamid Khan, had been amongst those confirmed dead.

'An official source' - in fact the Major - described how Prime Minister Damian White, given the option by Hamid to leave, had instead chosen to stay in order to try and protect the two prisoners. Damian's tracer pill did not feature in this account: no point in giving away too much.

Another 'official source' - this time the Prime Minister himself - mentioned how one of the prisoners, Private Philip Pavitt, had played a crucial part in the successful outcome by diverting the attention of his captors. There were no specifics as to how this was done.

All this left the British public in an excellent mood. They had plenty of heroes: the prime Minister, Special Forces and Private Pavitt.

The fact that the nation's crematoria were still working

flat out was no longer cause for comment. Individuals would still grieve, but the flu epidemic had become so much a part of life it was almost forgotten.

The election, which under normal circumstances would have filled the first few pages, was not mentioned in the Daily Mail until page six. It was not only that Fort Brockhurst had grabbed the headlines, even more that the new Single Transferable Vote would take much longer to count, the result not being known for several days. Instead of a mad rush for constituencies to declare their results, this time the ballot boxes had been tucked away overnight for counting to begin at midday today.

This did not preclude the usual exit-poll guesswork, so when the phone rang shortly after 10.30, Damian had a good idea who it might be. He was correct.

After congratulating him on his Fort Brockhurst exploits, election agent Alec Warbeck continued: "I think you should prepare for the worst, Prime Minister."

"It's that bad?"

"Can't be sure until the fat lady sings, as they say, but your timing yesterday was exquisitely poor."

"What do you mean?"

"When the polls opened, the mood was good. You're a popular fellow, don't need to tell you that. Hardly like a politician at all. Then the news broke that you were colluding with terrorists…."

"Pretending to negotiate, not colluding."

"The pretending bit was not obvious. People only saw you waving and smiling as you went in to chat with someone they'd watched on TV beheading a fellow."

"I wanted to appear optimistic."

"Sometimes gravitas goes down better."

"I don't do gravitas."

"Maybe that's your problem."

"I can't be something I'm not, Alec. And I *did* deliver."

"You sure did, Damian. In spades. But I fear it may have been too late. Almost the entire time people were casting their votes they thought you were selling them out."

"You know what they call me: the Interim Prime Minister. The Night Watchman. Maybe this is how it's meant to be."

"Maybe. But if you don't make it, it'll be a damned shame."

"When will we know?"

"We'll have a good idea by tomorrow. For sure by Wednesday."

"A couple more days in Number Ten, then. See you when they finish the count."

64

MAY 1st.

The job of an election agent does not end when the polls close. There's then the count to monitor. Cheating by returning officers' staff is virtually unknown, maybe because it's difficult to get away with, but there's always human error: a pile of votes for candidate A somehow finding its way into the pile for candidate B. So agents and candidates like to keep a careful watch.

Under the old system counts rarely took more than a few hours, but with the Single Transferable Vote it was a painfully slow progression towards that magic 'quota'. Damian's agent, Alec Warbeck, was super conscientious and had spent every waking hour watching votes moving from pile to pile as no-hope candidates were eliminated and their later preferences duly transferred. Early on it became clear that it was a four horse race: Conservative Rupert Delahaye, Labour Janet Smith, Lib Dem Elwyn Evans and Conservative Damian White. A four horse race for three places.

Late the previous day Alec had phoned Damian to tell him that the County of Oxfordshire would declare its result the next morning. When they met up in Oxford Town hall shortly after nine, Alec's face said it all. And it wasn't just that he was exhausted after a punishing campaign.

So they stood there: at the back of the stage a small army of candidates: in front a plump and jolly looking returning officer about to enjoy his moment in the limelight.

"…..I declare that the first three candidates to attain the quota and thereby be elected to represent the County of Oxfordshire are: Rupert Quintin Louis Delahaye…."

Roars from the Tories.

"Janet Valerie Smith"…."

Roars from Labour.

"And Elwyn Arthur Evans."

Even bigger roars from the Lib Dems, who had not really expected their man to make it.

There followed the usual speeches of congratulations and thanks.

As they left, Alec said: "It's so unfair!" He was almost in tears. "You can't believe how close it was. If the poll had come a day earlier, you'd have walked it. A day later, when everyone knew what you'd *really* done for them, I reckon you'd even have beaten Rupert into the number one spot."

Damian couldn't decide how he felt. Disappointed, obviously. Also a touch of relief. He was a maverick, who only obeyed the party whip when he felt it was right. Not suited to the usual run of politics. He'd been lucky enough to hit Number Ten when normal rules had briefly ceased to apply. Nothing similar was ever likely to happen again.

"You could call my reign short but sweet," said Damian. "New voting system. House of Lords gone. NHS and Benefits reformed. Flu bug put in its place. Terrorist gang beaten. Not bad for a spell of just a few weeks."

"A taste of what you might have done given more time."

"I don't think so, Alec. This country hates change. It takes something out of the ordinary, like a plane crash onto parliament, to make any real difference. Now it's business as usual. Changes will again be measured in centuries rather than days."

"What will you do?"

"We'd half anticipated this result, so Chloe suggests a few weeks in Greece to work on her best seller. I shall hold her hand, chew the cud, do some sailing, visit the tavernas…."

Alec Warbeck managed a smile. "Lucky sod!"

65

MAY 19th.

SKIATHOS, GREECE

The apartment faced east, giving them the morning sun with breakfast. It lay three hundred and twenty four steps up from harbour level, excellent for their cardiovascular systems, but not so good after an evening in a taverna. Occasionally a plane would pass by *below* them on its approach to the airport over to the left.

It was early in the season, the island still fresh and green, accommodation easy to come by. A priority had been reliable wifi, because this would be a working holiday, communication with the outside world vital. Chloe had set aside four hours a day for her book, which she was calling 'The Night Watchman'. It was not so much 'her' book as a joint venture, but Damian was happy to let her have the by-line.

Having lost his last job rather abruptly, Damian's main task was to map out a future. A CV which included British Prime Minister did confer some advantages, but decisions still had to be taken. The Tony Blair route of becoming filthy rich did not appeal; neither did spending his life in boardrooms. What then? He assessed possibilities by surfing the net and sending out emails. They'd rented a small Fiat to get around the island, kept fit by walking and idled the time away in tavernas. A life they felt they could put up with for a few weeks.

"Prime Minister Adam Tichbold has managed to cobble together a minority government," announced Chloe, scrolling down on her laptop. Their routine was to take in the news online over breakfast. Although the Conservatives had emerged as the largest party at the last election, they had failed to get an overall majority.

"Good for him. So he's landed the top job again without having to unseat me. That might have been messy. What about Bessie?"

"Tory Chief Whip again."

"Excellent. Unlike me, she's an institutional sort of person. Would make a good nun."

"It says they're still meeting in Central Hall Westminster," continued Chloe. "Although plans for a new parliament are 'well advanced'. Doesn't say where."

"Wonder how Hermione is enjoying Number Ten," mused Damian. "Could ride Fidget in Hyde Park I suppose."

"Email Adam and find out," suggested Chloe. "And ask him if he really would have challenged you for the leadership had you got in."

Damian smiled. "Might do that. But after we've put in our regulation four hours with the Night Watchman. The book. Time is of the essence. People soon forget."

Chloe nodded. "Feels odd, doing it back to front. We both lived the part *after* the crash, but are only now discovering what led up to it."

Damian nodded. "If Captain McGregor had not been flying with a new first officer…"

Chloe: "And President Zumweski's mistress not found she was pregnant…

Damian: "…I'd still be nattering to people like Morgan in my Wheatley surgery…."

Chloe: "….And I'd be grappling with births, marriages and deaths for the Oxford Herald."

"Chaos theory," said the ex Prime Minister. "A butterfly flapping its wings in the Caribbean creates a storm in China."

THE END

NOTE: It's rare for an airliner to run out of fuel, but it can happen, most recently in 2016 in Colombia, when 71 people died. That same year there were over one hundred "low fuel" incidents and eleven fuel "Maydays", the call a pilot will only make in extremis. Running out of fuel over central London is unlikely but possible.

If you have enjoyed "Night Watchman" why not try Rolf Richardson's other e-books:

The Last Weiss

Coffin Corner

Bear Bugger Cruise

Printed in Great Britain
by Amazon